Towards New India

Towards New India

Editor

Sunil Vashisht

PRABHAT PRAKASHAN

Published by
PRABHAT PRAKASHAN PVT. LTD.
4/19 Asaf Ali Road,
New Delhi-110 002 (INDIA)
e-mail: prabhatbooks@gmail.com

ISBN 978-93-5322-069-3
TOWARDS NEW INDIA
Ed. Sunil Vashisht

Edition
2025

Price
₹ 600.00 (Rupees Six Hundred only)

Printed at
Shree Sai Printers, Sahibabad

A Concept of New India Vision & Mission

The main inspiration and guiding force for this book is the concept and movement of New India 2022 visualised by our worthy PM Narendra Bhai Modi and his untiring efforts in that direction.

This book is based on a unique concept, wherein we have amalgamated various thoughts, concepts, ideas and practical aspects, which have a direct bearing on the concept of New India 2022.

We have tried to address and analyse the critical problems faced by the country in various fields, like economical, financial, social, banking, political, judicial, governance, etc.

This book is dedicated to our worthy PM Narendra Bhai Modi with an optimistic thought of the transformation of New India into a reality by 2022.

डॉ. हर्ष वर्धन
Dr. Harsh Vardhan

मंत्री
विज्ञान और प्रौद्योगिकी एवं पृथ्वी विज्ञान;
पर्यावरण, वन और जलवायु परिवर्तन
भारत सरकार
नई दिल्ली-110001

MINISTER
SCIENCE & TECHNOLOGY AND
EACH SCIENCES; ENVIRONMENT,
FOREST AND CLIMATE CHANGE
GOVERNMENT OF INDIA
NEW DELHI-110001

Message

Shri Sunil Vashisht, a Chartered Accountant by profession, has varied interests towards current socio-economic issues in our country. '*Towards New India*' rightly captures the inclusive developments initiatives after the BJP Government assumed office under the dynamic leadership of Shri Narendra Modi. The saga of a far reaching reforms since 2014 makes an interesting reading of the book.

I find the collection of articles quite informative and well sourced, covering wide range of initiatives taken by Government like GST, RERA, Public Sector ad Banking reforms, the security scenario and economic reforms. I am sure the reader will find this compendium quite interesting.

(Dr. Harsh Vardhan)

209, अनुसंधान भवन, 2, रफी मार्ग, नई दिल्ली-110001 दूरभाष: +91-11-23316766, 23714230; फैक्स: +91-11-23316745
209, Anusandhan Bhawan, 2, Rafi Marg, New Delhi-110001 Ph: +91-11-23316766, 23714230; Fax: +91-11-23316745

चतुर्थ तल, आकाश विंग, पर्यावरण भवन, जोर बाग, नई दिल्ली-110003 दूरभाष: +91-11-24695136 फैक्स- +91-11-24695329
4th Floor, Aakash Wing, Paryavaran Bhawan, Jor Bagh, New Delhi-110003 Ph: +91-11-24695136; Fax: +91-11-24695329

प्रकाश जावडेकर
Prakash Javadekar

मंत्री
मानव संसाधन विकास
भारत सरकार
MINISTER
HUMAN RESOURCE DEVELOPMENT
GOVERNMENT OF INDIA

Message

Happy to know that noted Chartered Accountant and Prabhari of BJP Delhi Pradesh's Business Cell, Sunil Vashisht, has compiled and edited a book titled '*Towards New India*', is dedicated to the vision and mission of Honourable Prime Minister Shri Narendra Modi's relentless and passionate effort to take India to new heights, meet new aspirations and make it a NEW INDIA.

The 30-plus chapters in the book, written by subject specialists and experts, focus on diagnosing various development-related issues and spell out possible solutions to these issues to enables the country to move towards realizing the dream of a NEW INDIA.

The book covers diverse topics of national importance such as Economy, National Security, Bureaucracy, Judiciary, Social Media, etc. and advocates the desired changes and improvement for moving towards a NEW INDIA.

I would like to congratulate and extend my best wishes to the Editor, authors and publisher Prabhat Prakashan for their endeavor.

(Prakash Javadekar)

Room No. 3, 'C' Wing, 3rd Floor, Shastri Bhavan, New Delhi-110 115
Phone: 91-11-23782387, 23782698, Fax: 91-11-23382365,
E-mail: minister.hrd@gov.in

Dr. Mahesh Chandra Sharma
Chairman

एकात्म मानवदर्शन

एकात्म मानवदर्शन अनुसंधान एवं विकास प्रतिष्ठान
Research & Development Foundation for Integral Humanism

Dated: 21-08-2018

Message

I am glad to note that Shri Sunil Vashisht, a senior professional and noted Charted Accountant, have compiled and edited a book titled *'Towards New India'*. This is dedicated to the vision of Hon'ble Prime Minister Shri Narendra Bhai Modi, whose mission is to take India towards New India. The Editor is very much influenced by the thoughts, vision and action of Hon'ble PM Narendra Bhai Modi and dedicating the books to him.

The book contains topics of various issues concerning our nation such as woman upliftment, religion yuva bureaucracy, senior citizens, defense and other important issues directly effecting the health of the country. The topics relate to past, present and future ahead and a vision of make India a New India of Modiji.

Shri Sunil Vashisht who is a noted CA and is an expert in Banking and Finance, he is also associated with various religious, social, industrial and political organisations and his contribution to the society is commendable.

I would like to congratulate and extened my best wishes to the editor, author and publisher Prabhat Prakashan for their endeavor.

I hope this book shall leave an impact and a concrete direction towards the goal of a New India.

(Mahesh Chandra Sharma)

Ekatm Bhawan, 37, Deendayal Upadhyaya Marg, New Delhi-110002, INDIA
Ph: 011-23210074 E-mail: ekatmrdvf@yahoo.co.in

Foreword

Sunil Vashisht, a zealous nationalist, has been committed to the ideal of 'A New Age… A New Direction, and a Golden Era for India, since his youth. A Chartered Accountant by profession, he has been a committed worker of the Bharatiya Janata Party for many decades.

Sunilji is a man of many parts. Presently, Director of Syndicate Bank, Madras Fertilizers Ltd and an Ex-Director of the Bank of Maharashtra, he is also National President of the Rashtriya Vichaar Manch and Founder Trustee of the Sadbhavana Shanti and Jagrati Mission Foundation. He holds several other responsibilities and portfolios, but the most important of all is his spirit of dedication to the nation and its spiritual ethos.

As a child, he has participated in spiritual stage productions based on India's ancient Vedic texts and epics… such as 'Shabri'… the eternal legend of Sri Ram… as He embraced the 'low caste' Shabri, who was shunned by all. In doing so, He established the important message that one must eradicate the deep-rooted notions, which differentiate man and man and embrace all in a spirit of love and unity.

His participation in such stage presentations, probably moulded Sunilji's young mind, firing it with enthusiasm to serve the nation and participate in moulding the values of this nation. Therefore, although fully immersed in his profession of Chartered Accountancy, he found time to pursue and strengthen his nationalistic tendencies.

Mr. Narendra Modi, who epitomizes change in the basic fabric of inertia and corruption that had crept into the Indian ethos, is indeed a strong pillar of inspiration and motivation for the youth of India. Each one looks up to him to effect the much-needed change and to provide India with a corruption-free, strong and just governance.

Sunil Vashisht's upcoming saga '*Towards New India*' captures Mr. Narendra Modi's commitment to India, and gives substance to the hopes and aspirations of the youth and in fact all the citizens of this great land.

We all join to wish Sunilji all success in his endeavours. May God grant him the ability to encapture and encapsulate all the wonderful initiatives by Mr. Narendra Modi to truly make India the great land she is meant to be!

—Abha Bhandari
'ARPANA'

Preface

This book *'Towards New India'* is dedicated to our Prime Minister Narendra Bhai Modi, a great leader, who has a vision and mission to take India to new heights, achieve new aspirations and make it a NEW INDIA.

New India is targeted to be achieved by 2022 under his leadership, with a visionary and dedicated effort towards implementation of new policies and programmes for the upliftment of the common man and by proper utilization of the resources of country for achieving the great challenge and mission of a New India.

To take this mission forward the concept of Team India is of utmost importance. Team India stands for the collective effort of 125 million Indians together towards the fulfilment of common goals of progress and development of India. It also involved the synergy in the acts of the Central government, state governments, social organisations and the common man at large towards making a NEW INDIA.

India is a land of unity in diversity with various customs, castes, creeds, religions and languages in different parts of the country. With such great diversity, there arise different national issues, which have a direct impact on the growth and development of India. With the collective efforts of everyone in such a diverse system, the overall progress and harmony of our great country can be achieved.

In this book '*Towards New India*', we have tried to touch various national issues being faced by our country and we have compiled the expressions and views of experts on such issues that have a direct bearing on the national development. We have tried to cover diverse topics of national importance such as economy, national security, reservation, bureaucracy, judiciary, social media etc. and have tried to study what are the desired changes and improvement for moving towards a NEW INDIA.

The effect of external factors such as terrorism, relationship with neighbouring countries have also been elaborated as they also have a direct impact on national development and growth of economy as nowadays the whole world is a global economy and we are also impacted by economic slowdown in other countries.

Opinions and views of the experts on various topics are focussed on diagnosing the problems at hand and advising upon the solutions and the best possible way outs for moving towards a win-win situation for national development. Also views expressed in this book are the personal views of the experts and the editor or the publisher does not take responsibility of the statements and opinions of the experts/ writers of the articles.

I also express my sincere regards and gratitude towards the writers and contributors of the articles who have spared their valuable time and devoted their thoughts towards various national issues and ultimately national development as a whole. Their contribution towards this book has helped me in fulfilling one of my dreams to enlarge the concept of a NEW INDIA as imagined by our worthy Prime Minister Modiji.

At the end, I feel proud of my parents, my family, friends and well-wishers, who always believe in serving the society and have always given me an inspiration to serve the society and the nation.

I feel that the publication of this book shall be helpful and fruitful towards the path of national development and towards the formulation of a New India.

—C.A. Sunil Vashisht

Contents

1

Vision New India 2022 – Way Forward (Special focus on CPSE's)

New India 2022 is a dream of our visionary Prime Minister Sh. Narendra Bhai Modi. The vision is called New India 2022 but the mission is to take back India to the glory of olden days, where we used to be the world leader and there was prosperity all around. An India where people are happy and feel social responsibility as part of team India and join hands towards national development. Thus creating an environment where people, society, private sector and government all work together to shape a New India.

In my opinion, the Central Public Sector Enterprises (CPSE's) have a great role to play if the vision of New India 2022 is to be accomplished. CPSE's are critical to India's development as it has presence across many core sectors of the economy and have a sizeable contribution to the central exchequer. They are also a source of employment, and through participation in the stock market, they also lead to creation of wealth for citizens. CPSE's also contribute to the society by initiating various CSR activities and projects. Also CPSE's have been instrumental in driving several flagship government schemes such as Ujjawala Yojna, Swachh Bharat Abhiyan etc.

The CPSE's can lead to a major transformation change by inculcating corporate governance, as per the need of the hour, by reinventing its human resources, by better management of the financial resources and by adapting to future technologies, innovation and research and development.

Of late, a process of strategic disinvestment of the CPSE's has been adopted, wherein there has been a paradigm shift from disinvestment to efficient management. Also increased focus is being given to optimum development of business potential and growth. Some CPSE's have also been identified for closure so that the tied-up capital is unlocked and the funds freed could be used productively.

An important step towards transformation of CPSE's is effective corporate governance. For effective corporate governance, first of all, internal and external challenges being faced by the CPSE's need to be identified and improved upon. Next vision and goals for CPSE's need to be formulated to take them to the transformational growth path for New India 2022. The CPSE's need to be aligned with national priorities, on one hand, and need to be made globally competitive, on the other hand.

Performance of CPSE's needs to be periodically monitored by independent agencies. Also the tendering and procurement policies of the CPSE's need to be streamlined to improve their performance. The role and contribution of the government nominee directors should be given due importance as the nominee directors act as a channel between the government and the CPSE's. CPSE's should also promote flagship schemes of the government like Start-up India by providing support to start-ups by providing technology and training or like Skill India by employing skill certificate-holders.

Second aspect of transformation of CPSE's is reinventing the human resource management. The best practices and processes being followed should be shared between CPSE's. Also periodic benchmarking should be done by CPSE's against global and national best-in-class practices. HRM policies also need to be reviewed by CPSE's for transformational governance. Young minds need to be included at various levels and also start-up support to be provided for budding entrepreneurs.

Financial re-engineering also needs to be undertaken for the transformative change of CPSE's. Consolidation and merger of similar CPSE's is one such step wherein the benefit of economies of scale can be achieved and also our CPSE's can deal with the increased global competitiveness. Efficiency and better financial management must be promoted amongst CPSE's. Increased procurement from MSME units should be encouraged so as to promote the MSME ecosystem.

Another important aspect of transformative change of CPSE's is adopting the future technology, innovation and research and development. Exports should be promoted and import substitution should be encouraged. Existing technology should be upgraded by promoting innovation and research and development activities. Also R&D activities should be shared within various CPSE's. Various aspects of digital India should be promoted by the CPSE's such as paperless office, digital payments, e-tendering, e-procurement, online inventory, etc.

In short, the transformation of CPSE's is essential for the vision of New India 2022 and an effective vision statement with various long-term, medium-term and short-term goals should be formulated. Also each CPSE should identify quantifiable goals and should streamline governance mechanism and financial architecture, reinvent strategic human resource management and should contribute towards national priorities.

Vision New India 2022 is very much achievable if we all put in our synergy towards achieving the transformation of making India a global superpower once again.

—C.A. Varun Vashisht

2
A Good Tax System

I. Objectives of Taxation

Objectives of taxes have been developed when the functions of the Government are developed. In the primitive communities a member was to pay his share to the Head of the tribe, who in return provided them with administration, security from foreign aggression and other civic amenities. But today taxation besides being the main resource for supporting government has became a tool for economic growth, social welfare; attract foreigner investment, economic stability, and income distribution. The Objectives of taxation in brief are as under:

- **Revenue –** This objective is the oldest, uppermost and primary objective. Taxes are imposed so as to produce the necessary amount of revenue to meet the requirement of the government, as the public expenditures is increasing in scope and size day by day. Therefore, the main objective of taxes is to raise revenue to meet the Govt. expenditures adequately.
- **Social objectives –** Taxes became a main goal for some of social objectives.

(a) Redistribution of income and wealth: Income is differ from one person to another in the society, inequity in income leads to many evils, and the government aims to reduction of inequalities between members of the society to secure social justice. Tax is a means of ensuring the redistribution of income and wealth in order to reduce poverty and promote social welfare. For achieving these goals government adopts following:

(i) Imposition of high rate tax upon luxury commodities.

(ii) Applying progressive tax system when levying taxes from taxpayers.

(iii) Imposition of tax exemption to basic goods.

(b) *Social welfare:* Social welfare is the basic need of the society in the modern age. The government functions have become very important to the society, because the society needs saving, protection, education, health, and so on. All these functions are necessary to make social welfare, so the government receives revenue from tax, and expends it for those function. Therefore revenue from taxes is fuel to the government for social welfare. Social welfare is indicator for development of the countries, so almost all the countries have competition to introduce these services in the societies.

(c) *Safety of society from bad and injurious customs:* Fighting the bad customs in the society is the primary task of the government, so tax is a tool for fighting some of those customs. From this angle tax imposition of very high percentage on the goods like tobacco and alcohol is an effort to reduce these habits.

II. Economic Significance of Taxes

Taxes are used from economic point of view, so taxation helps to encourage some economic activities, and as a tool to solve some economics problems. Tax is also a means for directing of scarce economic activities. Taxation helps to accelerate economic growth, and taxation plays very important role in case of economic stability.

- **Economic growth:** Taxes are considered as a tool for economic growth and it helps to accelerate growth of economic development. Economic development has placed considerable emphasis on objectives of taxation policy. Economic development is the main objective in all the countries of the world. Economic development depends on mobilization of resources and efficient use of such resources between different sectors of the economy activities. Tax policy must be designed so as to mobilize the internal resources and use these resources in productive manner. Taxation policy helps to increase production through raising the rate of capital formation, so it helps improve the economic welfare through better distribution of income and it becomes an important instrument for removing regional inequalities. Tax policy may serve directly to mobilize resources for capital formation in the public sector and indirectly to promote private saving and investment.
- **Enforcing government policy:** Government policy can be easily enforced by adoption of suitable tax policy. The Government can encourage investment, saving, consumption, export, protection of home industry, employment, production, protection of society from harmful customs, and economic stability through suitable tax policy. Therefore, the government gives tax exemption to the investment and saving.

- **Directing limited scarce resources into effective and essential channels:** Tax policy plays crucial role for directing scarce resources into essential commodities. This is achieved by giving tax exemption to certain industries and imposition of heavy duties on other industries, so with the adoption of suitable tax policy, economic resources may be diverted to the production of necessary articles and investors will go to the exemption industries.
- **Economic stability:** Maintaining economic stability is one of the tax objectives. Economic stability is a very important factor for the sustained economic growth. Government can effectively use taxes in the case of inflation and depression. These may be increased in inflationary situations. Increase in the rates of existing taxes and the imposition of new taxes would check consumption, decrease the level of effective demand and therefore help in bringing up stability in prices. Heavy taxation transfer purchasing power from the hand of people to the government which if used for productive purpose will increase the level of economic activity and employment.
- **Regulatory Objective:** A second objective of taxation is that of regulation or control. This is 'sumptuary taxation'. Technically the term sumptuary refers to the regulation or control of private expenditures. In public finance it came to represent all extra revenue objective of taxation. There are some taxes where primary objective is to control and regulate consumption. For example, restrictions on the consumption of alcoholic liquors are effected by means of restrictive excise duties.

Taxation as a Means of Regulating the Level of National Income: Now a days taxation is advocated as a measure to regulate the flow of income. This is an extension of the regulative aspect of taxation. Taxes transfer income from individuals to government. This in turn will alter the pattern of private consumption and investment and thus influence the level of national income.

- **Incentive Objective:** In recent years a good deal of emphasis has been given on 'incentive taxation'. It includes a variety of proposals, designed to provide preferential treatment for income from business enterprises and establishing rewards and penalties to stimulate output. Its purpose is to stimulate the larger flow of investment activities in the desired channel and to prevent its flow into undesired channels. Several types of incentives are provided under incentive taxation to stimulate investment activity.
- **Reduction of Inequalities:** It is now generally accepted that taxation ought to be used as a means of regulating the socio-economic life of the community, it is an effective tool to reduce the glaring inequalities of income and wealth existing in the modern society. Democratic governments aim at securing social justice. Progressive tax system is designed to achieve this objective.

In the case of depression taxes play a different role. Purchasing power in the hand of people is reduced and they are able to spend less and the demand for commodities and services is reduced. All these lead to a shrinkage of business activity and employment. In this case government should increase the purchasing power in the hand of public through reducing the burden of taxation on the people and impose tax upon saving and hoarding so that people may be encouraged to spend more and thus help to create more demand for goods and more business activity and employment.

III. Canons of Taxes

Canons of taxation refer to the administrative aspect of a tax. They are related to the rate, amount, method of levy, and collection of a tax. Despite the modern development of economic sciences, Adam smith's canons of taxation, still continue to be widely accepted as providing a good basis by which to judge taxes and these principles still apply today. The fundamental canons of taxation are as follows:

1. **Canon of equity:** This canon implies that any tax system should be based on the principle of social justice. Equity refers to both horizontal and vertical equity. Horizontal equity describes the concept that, taxpayers with equal abilities to pay should pay the same amount of tax. Vertical equity means that taxpayers with a greater ability to pay should pay more tax.
2. **Canon of Certainty:** The tax rules should clearly specify when the tax is to be paid, how it is to be paid,and how the amount to be paid is to be determined. Objective of this canon is to create trust between two parties, first party taxpayer who is to pay the tax and second party the authority whom receipt tax. If taxpayers have difficulty measuring the tax base or determining the applicable tax rate or the tax consequences of a transaction, then certainty doesn't exist. Certainty might also be viewed as the level of confidence a person has that the tax is being calculated correctly.

3. **Canon of Convenience:** A tax should be due at a time or in a manner that is most likely to be convenient for the taxpayer. Convenience in paying a tax helps to ensure compliance. The appropriate payment mechanism depends on the amount of the liability and the how easy or difficult it is to collect. Discussion of this principle in designing a particular rule or tax system would focus on whether it is best to collect the tax from the manufacturer, wholesaler, retailer or customer, as well as the frequency of collection.
4. **Canon of Economy:** This canon implies that decreasing the administrative cost of collection of the tax at the lowest level. The costs to collect a tax should be kept to a minimum for both the government and taxpayers. This principle considers the number of revenue officers needed to administer a tax. Compliance costs for taxpayers should also be considered. This principle is closely related to the principle of simplicity.
5. **Canon of Productivity:** Productivity or physical adequacy means that, the tax system should sufficiently yield the revenue needed to meet the requirements of the state.
6. **Canon of Elasticity:** Elasticity is closely connected with fiscal adequacy. This canon implies that yield from taxation should grow along with increase in population and development of economy.
7. **Simplicity:** The tax system should be simple, plain and intelligible to the common man. As far as the underdeveloped countries are concerned, this is a very important characteristic of good tax system; since the common taxpayers are illiterate.

8. **Flexibility:** Flexibility means that there should be no rigidity in the tax system, so that it can be quickly adjusted to new conditions. Under a flexible system, a new tax can be imposed or an old tax can be withdrawn to adjust to the changed situation.
9. **Diversity:** There should be a variety of taxes properly coordinated, so as to form a united and consistent system. The tax system should be broad based. This canon requires that the tax system should not rely on a few taxes. There should be a large number and variety of taxes, so that it can touch all sections of the people in the society.
10. **Neutrality:** The tax system should not distort the working of the market mechanism. Taxes should not produce any adverse effect in the economy. This canon means that taxes should be able to avoid undesirable effect upon the economic system of the country.
11. **Canon of Co-Ordination:** In a federal system of government, taxes are imposed by the central, state and local governments. Hence there must be a well stitched coordination between the taxes imposed by different taxing authorities.
12. **Canon of Expediency:** This canon insists that taxes should not be covered in controversy. Taxpayers should have no doubt about its desirability.

The canons of taxation have a sound philosophy behind them and exhibit an insight into the practical experience of tax administration and its effects. Since the days of Adam Smith many other principles have been added.

Supplementing Smith's four canons, Bastable adds the maxims of productivity and elasticity and holds productivity to be the most important principle.

IV. Characteristic of Good Taxation System

(A) Equity

Should be based on ability to pay.

(B) Certainty

Know your tax liability

(C) Economy

Cost of collection must be low

(D) Automatic Stabiliser

Should have stabiling effect on national income level

(E) Convenience

Must be easy to collect tax

(F) Redistribution

Taxation should enable to redistribute wealth from rich to poor

(G) Flexibility

Changeable to suit economic conditions

(H) Not Discourage Work or Investment

To summarise, in India what is required is a tax system which is simple and stable. Frequent changes in the tax system, which we have experienced in the past make it complex and tax compliance becomes a victim. To move from a non-compliant to a tax compliant economy, a easy, simple and stable tax system is imperative.

—Dr. Girish Ahuja

3
Towards New India

It is rightly said in Hindi phrase *"Gudhri Ke Lal"*, fits on worthy PM NARENDRA BHAI MODI. Born in a very poor family, he has risen to such a level that shows his inherent strength by his thoughts, efforts, deeds, *junoon*, and untiring devotion to his mission of NEW INDIA.

It appears to observe Narendra Bhai Modi that destiny, luck, *kismat*, and *bhagya* always change by your good deeds, sincere efforts, dedication and faithfulness in framing your vision and its implementation.

It is very difficult to define him in words, his deeds reveal his fame internationally.

The present Prime Minister of India Shri Narendra Modi is one of the most influential leaders in the democratic history of the country. He was born in the state of Gujarat and he was the Chief Minister of Gujarat from 2001 to 2014. It won't be easy to express his journey from a village to be Prime Minister in a few words.

He was born to a Gujarati family in Vadnagar as Narendra Damodardas Modi. He helped his father sell tea as a child, and later ran his own stall to earn his living. He was introduced to the RSS (Rashtriya Swayamsevak Sangh) at the age of eight as a junior cadet, beginning a long association with the organisation. He travelled across India and visited a number of religious centres and various ashrams to seek spiritual knowledge and clarity. He returned to Gujarat and moved to Ahmedabad in 1969.

After schooling, there was a long gap in his education as he travelled across the country for his intellectual and spiritual pursuits. However, he earned a degree in Political Science from Delhi University in the year 1979 and later an MA in Political Science from Gujarat University in 1982.

While working with RSS, he came in contact with the members of Bharatiya Jana Sangh, which marked the beginning of his political career. His political style is strongly influenced by Santo Vallabhbhai Patel. It was during the Emergency period in 1975-77 that he got more active in politics. He was also a member of the ABVP, which is the student wing of the RSS.

Shri Modi joined the BJP (Bharatiya Janata Party) in the year 1985, and started working in the electoral unit in Gujarat. He was appointed the BJP national secretary in 1995 and later BJP general secretary in 1998. He was appointed Chief Minister of Gujarat in 2001 due to Keshubhai Patel's failing health. His policies as Chief Minister, credited with encouraging economic growth, have received praise. Under Modi's leadership, Gujarat witnessed great economic growth and promoted the use of technology and global investment to revamp the economy and industries of Gujarat.

Shri Modi led the BJP in the 2014 general election, which gave the party a majority in the Lok Sabha, the first time a single party had achieved this since 1984. He himself was elected to Parliament from Varanasi. Since taking charge, Modi's administration has tried to raise foreign direct investment in the Indian economy, increased spending on infrastructure, healthcare and social welfare programmes.

He has attempted to improve efficiency in the bureaucracy, and centralised power through the abolition of the planning commission.

Narendra Modi's Tenure as Chief Minister of Gujarat

In 2001, Keshubhai Patel's health was failing and the BJP lost a few state assembly seats in by-elections. The BJP national-leadership sought a new candidate for the chief ministership, and Modi, who had expressed misgivings about Patel's administration, was chosen as a replacement. Although BJP leader L.K. Advani did not want to ostracise Patel and was concerned about Modi's lack of experience in government, Modi declined an offer to be Patel's deputy chief minister, telling Advani and Atal Bihari Vajpayee that "he was going to be fully responsible for Gujarat or not at all". On 3rd October, 2001 he replaced Patel as Chief Minister of Gujarat, with the responsibility of preparing the BJP for the December 2002 elections.

As the Chief Minister of Gujarat, he had promoted the state as "Vibrant Gujarat", claiming that it had made rapid progress in terms of infrastructural development and economic growth. He became Chief Minister of Gujarat for consecutive four terms (2001 to 2002, 2002 to 2007, 2007 to 2012 and 2012 to 2014). He established financial and technology parks in Gujarat and during the 2007 Vibrant Gujarat summit, real-estate investment deals worth 6.6 trillion were signed. By December 2008, 500,000 structures had been built, of which 113,738 were check dams, which helped recharge the aquifers beneath them. Sixty of the 112 tehsils, which had depleted the water table in 2004, regained their normal groundwater levels by 2010 due only to his vision. As a result, the state's production of genetically modified cotton increased to become the largest in India. From 2001 to 2010, Gujarat recorded an agricultural growth rate of 10.97 percent. The GDP growth rate of Gujarat averaged 10 per cent during his tenure, a value above that of the country as a whole, and similar to other highly industrialised states.

Lok Sabha: 2014 Indian General Election and Ahead

In the 2014 Parliamentary elections, the Bharatiya Janata Party rode strongly on the wave of Modi's development agenda of Gujarat and of the inefficient administration of the incumbent Congress Party. This resulted in BJP's victory and more than doubled its tally in Lok Sabha to 282, becoming the first party to win a majority of seats on its own since 1984. The Congress was restricted to 44 seats, its lowest ever tally in the Parliament. The historic man made for the BJP affirmed Shri Modi as a leader of a huge stature and also marked the beginning of a new phase in the Indian politics.

Shri Modi took oath to serve as Prime Minister of India on 26th May, 2014, and called himself "*Pradhan Sevak*" (biggest servant to the nation). As a Prime Minister, Mr. Modi built his image as a tough decision-maker and a leader who does not shy away from taking bold decisions.

Shri Modi lives a very active and disciplined life and he served as a Chief Minister of Gujarat for a span of thirteen years and during his office, he did not take any leave. Also, in response to an RTI applicant, the PMO (Prime Minister Office) revealed that PM Narendra Modi has not taken a single leave since he came to power. He is a workaholic and is an early riser and determined to his duty. Shri Modi is a kind-heated man also and he used a new word "*Divya-aang*" (blessed with some God-gifted organ) to represent handicapped earlier said as "*Appang*". This is only an example of his valuable thoughts.

On the holy day of Gandhi Jayanti, i.e., on 2 October 2014, Shri Modi launched the Swachh Bharat Abhiyan ("Clean India") campaign. In this programme, Sh. Modi focussed on eliminating open defecation and manual scavenging. It was a five-year plan. As part of the programme, the Indian government began constructing millions of toilets in rural areas and encouraging people to use them. The government also announced plans to build new sewage treatment plants. The administration plans to construct 60 million toilets by 2019. The construction projects have faced allegations of corruption, and have faced severe difficultly in getting people to use the toilets constructed for them.

Shri Modi has raised his voice against terrorism at international platform and made collaboration with world's most powerful nations to fight against terrorism. It is the effort of Shri Modi that all world powers came at one platform to fight against terrorism. As a result, U.N. has stopped its grant to Pakistan's army and warned them to take strong actions to fight against terrorism. In addition, Shri Modi has sent out a strong message of hitting out hard at terrorism by having surgical strike across Pakistan border, The most recent and well-known addition in this list has to be the demonetisation, which is being considered a historic step to curb black money and control corruption in the country.

To make India grow faster from now Rajdhani Express to Bullet Train, he has started various schemes – "Start up India" and various other programmes. Then, Shri Modi realised that India has a lot of unutilised resources and if they would be utilised, then India's GDP can grow at double digit. For improving understanding and business relations,

Shri Modi visited various countries – U.S.A., Japan, U.K., Russia, U.A.E., etc. and met with various top industrialists to invest in India. Shri Modi has liberalised India's foreign direct investment policies, allowing more foreign investment in several industries, including defence and railway.

Shri Modi launched a programme intended to develop 100 smart cities on 25th June, 2015. The Smart City initiative isn't about Union government pumping in extra resources for urban development. The critical element is about citizens planning and interpreting smartness. The Smart City proposals of the "winning" cities offer insights into how citizens, states and ULBs have interpreted this smartness differently. The "Smart Cities" programme is expected to bring Information Technology companies an extra benefit of ₹ 20 billion (US $310 million). In June 2015, Modi launched the "Housing for All by 2022" project, which intends to eliminate slums in India by building about 20 million affordable homes for India's urban poor.

Shri Modi understands the feelings of his nation and his public. He noticed that there are a lot of households who are not capable to use LPG gas clyinder due to their poverty. Then, he appealed to the nation to give up their subsidy on LPG gas cylinder and this subsidy will go to the home of economically poor people to enlighten their stove and named it as "Giveitup". Around 11 million people have given up their subsidy so far and that means there is a collection of around ₹ 4,166 crores, which will be used for the poor and needy people.

To simplify taxation system and attract more foreign investors, Modi government put in place the Goods and Services Tax, the biggest tax reform in the country since Independence. It subsumed around 17 different taxes and became effective from 1st July, 2017. This is necessary to make taxation system more transparent. Before GST, India has various acts related to indirect taxation. Investors had not enough courage to invest, but now the things are changed. With GST, India became more capable to run fast and it is not so far when India will surpass China and become one of the developed countries.

Schemes Launched by Prime Minister Narendra Modi

- ✓ Pradhan Mantri Jan Dhan Yojana (for financial inclusion)
- ✓ Swachh Bharat Mission (for clean public places and better sanitation facilities)
- ✓ Pradhan Mantri Ujjwala Yojana (provision of LPG to families living under BPL)
- ✓ Pradhan Mantri Krishi Sinchai Yojana (efficiency in irrigation)
- ✓ Pradhan Mantri Fasal Bima Yojana (insurance against crop failure)
- ✓ Pahal (LPG subsidy)
- ✓ Mudra Bank Yojana (banking services for medium and Small Enterprises)
- ✓ Pradhan Mantri Kaushal Vikas Yojana (to provide skill training to the young workforce)
- ✓ Sansad Adarsh Gram Yojana (to strengthen rural infrastructure)
- ✓ Make in India (to boost the manufacturing sector)
- ✓ Garib Kalyan Yojana (address welfare needs of people)
- ✓ E-basta (online learning forum)
- ✓ Sukanya Samriddhi Yojana (financial empowerment of girl child)

- ✓ Padhe Bharat, Badhe Bharat (to enhance children's reading, writing and mathematical skills)
- ✓ DDU-Grameen Kaushalya Yojana (vocational training to the rural youth as part of 'Skill India' mission)
- ✓ Nayi Manzil Yojana (skills based to madrasa students)
- ✓ Start Up India (support to women and SC/ST entrepreneurs)
- ✓ Atal Pension Scheme (pension scheme for unorganised sector employees)
- ✓ Pradhan Mantri Suraksha Bima Yojana (insurance against accidents)
- ✓ Jeevan Jyoti Bima Yojana (life insurance)
- ✓ Sagar Mala Project (for developing port infrastructure)
- ✓ Smart Cities Project (building urban infrastructure)
- ✓ Rurban Mission (modem facilities in villages)
- ✓ Pradhan Mantri Awaas Yojana (affordable housing for all)
- ✓ Jan Aushadhi Scheme (provision for affordable medicines)
- ✓ Digital India (for a digitally equipped nation and economy)
- ✓ Digilocker (securing documents online)
- ✓ School Nursery Yojana (afforestation programme by and for young citizens)
- ✓ Gold Monetisation Scheme (involve gold stocks lying idle in households in the economy)
- ✓ Green Urban Transport Scheme (develop and improve climate-friendly transport system in urban areas)
- ✓ Pradhan Mantri Surakshit Sadak Yojana (make the road safer by eliminating the dangerous sport on highways)

- ✓ Pradhan Mantri Gram Parivahan Yojana (to create a better transporation system)
- ✓ National Health Protection Scheme (health insurance scheme for poor)
- ✓ Ek Bharat Shreshta Bharat Campaign (strengthen cultural relation of various parts of the country)
- ✓ Atal Bhujal Yojana (water conservation scheme)
- ✓ Deendayal Upadhyaya Gram Jyoti Yojana (provide continuous power supply to rural urban)

There are other social reforms and scheme that are effective and are being launched by him to make India a great India, a new India and towards a new India.

—C.A. Sunil Vashisht

❐

4

Refashioning Politics, Rebuilding India

The tally was changing very fast. The BJP was winning seats after seats and so were the allies. Gauging the mood of the nation from a busy newsroom of one of India's leading television channels, it was apparent that India had voted for a massive changc. Commentators in the studios were busy analysing the immediate political fallouts. By afternoon, the BJP had written history by becoming the first non-Congress party since Independence that was given absolute majority. The BJP and its NDA allies had won the elections with absolute majority, the first since 1984 when Rajiv Gandhi won riding a sympathy wave after Indira Gandhi's assassination.

As the results were announced, the media went ecstatic in pouring over Modi's win. Though some stereotyped political commentators did declare, "Corporate India and Hindu majoritarianism have won this particular round", largely media saw the victory as the one that "has lifted India out of the politics of the last century and liberated it from the feudal rule of the Congress Party's Gandhi dynasty".

A BJP win was not unexpected but a "tectonic shift" came as a major surprise. But, then, the script was written differently this time.

In September 2013, the BJP decided to project Narendra Modi as the Prime Ministerial candidate. This was a well-crafted political strategy. Coming from a poor Other Backward Class (OBC) background, Narendra Modi represented a development narrative successfully, build, in Gujarat and was well-echoed by other BJP-ruled states that challenged divisive and dynastic politics of 67 years of independent India. He also represented the staunch nationalist perspective that suited his ideological mentor — the Rashtriya Swayamsewak Sangh (RSS).

Soon after winning elections, Narendra Modi in his victory speech declared: "The age of divisive politics has ended. From today onwards, the politics of uniting people will begin. We want more strength for the well-being of the country. I see a glorious and prosperous India."

This was the kind of paradigm change India had been anxiously waiting for. And Prime Minister Modi lost no time in rolling out the agenda. Speaking at the Central Hall of Parliament, Modi said: A government is the one that thinks about the poor, listens to the poor and exists for the poor. Therefore, the new government is dedicated to the poor, millions of youth and mothers and daughters, who are striving for their respect and honour. Villagers, farmers, Dalits and the oppressed, this government is for them, for their aspirations and this is our responsibility.

And in the same breath, he thundered with optimism: Who says that such an aware democratic country — the largest in the world — cannot move forward? If 125 crore Indians resolve to take one step forward, the entire country will travel 125 crore steps forward.

An era of optimism and hope began in 2014. Three years later, Indians are busy laying foundation stones of a

New India, as envisioned by Prime Minister Narendra Modi. "A new India of the dreams of 65 per cent population of under-35 youth and of uniquely aware women groups. A new India in which the poor are looking for an opportunity to do something, instead of seeking something." It is a vision of a new India of 2022 when India completes 75 years of Independence. This new India "will be powered by the strength of each and every citizen of India, an India driven by innovation, hard work and creativity, an India characterised by peace, unity and brotherhood, an India free from corruption, terrorism, black money and dirt".

No wonder, this vision of a new India brings in most disruptive and transformative measures such as GST, bankruptcy code, law against *benami* properties, statutorily guaranteed autonomy for the RBI for inflation targeting, increasing use of the JAM (Jan Dhan Yojana, Aadhar and Mobile number) trinity to direct subsidy transfers, and demonetisation for rooting out systemic corruption.

Modi's politics rests on planks of governance and development beating the old maths of caste and community. It is a major departure from identity politics.

Modi has the capability of countering the false narrative that pits entrepreneurs against the poor. He makes "Ease of Doing Business" a priority and also tells India Inc. that he's not interested in corporate lobbying. He can convince the poor that he's for them and against the crooked rich and is also the leader who can persuade rich Indian professionals living abroad to come and build a new India.

India is "refashioning politics" under Prime Minister Modi, where performance and only performance counts. Good days are coming and the journey has started just yet.

—Anup Sinha

❐

5
Make in India

'Make in India' is an initiative launched by our Prime Minister Shri Narendra Modi on 25th September, 2014, to encourage multinational as well as national companies to manufacture their products in India.

The initiative is to ease and motivate the manufacturing concerns at domestic and international levels to produce their products in India. The major objective is the creation of jobs and enhancement of skills among the youngsters through easy and conducive environment for the manufacturing concerns to put capital and investment in 25 identified sectors of the economy.

1. Automobiles
2. Automobile components
3. Aviation
4. Biotechnology
5. Chemicals
6. Construction
7. Defence manufacturing
8. Electrical machinery
9. Electronic systems
10. Food processing
11. Information technology and business process management

12. Leather
13. Media and entertainment
14. Mining
15. Oil and gas
16. Pharmaceuticals
17. Ports and shipping
18. Railways
19. Renewable energy
20. Roads and highways
21. Space and astronomy
22. Textiles and garments
23. Thermal power
24. Tourism and hospitality
25. Wellness

are the 25 sectors judicially identified in the economy.

Indian industries have the potential to compete with the best in the world in these sectors. These sectors are listed on the 'Make in India' web portal and separate brochures for these sectors are released along with a general brochure to guide companies and provide them details of growth drivers, investment opportunities, FDI and other policies specific to that sector with details of relevant agencies.

The Modi government has also permitted 100 per cent FDI in the said sectors, except for space – 74 per cent, defence – 49 per cent and news media – 26 per cent. After the initiation of this programme, India emerged as the top destination globally for foreign direct investment, surpassing the United States of America and China.

Earlier, foreign companies used to target the Indian labour class to carry out the manufacturing process in foreign countries and earn huge profits due to low cost. Now, India is becoming the hub for manufacturing concerns all over the globe and investment is increasing many-fold due to availability of skilled and technical manpower at a low cost. The investment is being made in almost all the sectors — from electrical to electronics, from automobile to agriculture, from satellite to submarine, etc.

Earlier, rigid policies & regulations, labour law, political situation and other external factors were the hurdles in the minds of the investors to explore business in some other nation. Mr. Modi acknowledged this fact that India, being ranked low for doing business by World Bank, has to start actions to ease the environment in India to attract foreign investors to do business in India. Now, this initiative has invited top companies across the globe and top Indian companies who are doing quite well in their business ventures. They are investing and exploring their business ventures in the Indian soil, resulting in increased flow of foreign capital in India.

The Modi government has formulated a special cell in the Commerce Ministry named 'Invest India', which would guide foreign investors in terms of regulatory and policy issues and assists them to obtain the clearances and to complete the obligations in carrying business in Indian land.

The main key factors of this initiative are:

i. To increase and facilitate foreign direct investment in India and convincing Indian and foreign companies to produce their goods in India,
ii. To create new employment opportunities with better employment conditions,
iii. To attract the flow of foreign capital in the Indian economy,
iv. To create a demand for well-equipped, skilled and trained people,
v. To improve brand name of India in the international arena to facilitate flow of foreign capital in India.

The initiative seeks to attract domestic and foreign investors by promising a conducive business environment. In the PM's words: "India will offer red carpet to an investor instead of red tape that they faced." However, the Central government, various state governments, business chambers and overseas Indian Missions are all expected to play a key role in the successful operation of this initiative.

India is a country that is rich in natural resources. But the irony is that we as a nation could not extract those resources judiciously and failed to develop our manufacturing belt as did China, Germany and other western countries. The vision behind this initiative is to use India's own potential to develop its industrial sectors.

In India, labour is plenty and skilled labour is easily available due to high rates of unemployment in the educated class of the country. With Asia emerging as the manufacturing hub, India will soon become the preferred manufacturing destination of most investors across the globe.

'Invest India' is the country's official agency for investment promotion and facilitation. The agency guides foreign investors on all aspects of regulatory and policy issues and would also help them in obtaining regulatory clearances. A web portal "www.makeinindia.com" has also been created to answer investor's queries.

The portal has a comprehensive set of FAQs, which helps the investor find instant answers to their general queries. Additionally, the portal has a backend support team also, which answers specific queries within 72 hours.

Visitors can also register on the website to receive relevant information and updates with newsletters. An investor facilitation cell will provide assistance to the foreign investors from the time of their arrival in the country to the time of their departure. The initiative also seeks to actively target top companies across key sectors in identified countries to encourage them to invest in India.

Domestically, the 'Make in India' initiative aims at identifying domestic companies having leadership in innovation and new technology for turning them into global players. The focus is on promoting green and advanced manufacturing and helping these companies become an important part of the global value chain.

The 'Make in India' campaign has its origin in Hon'ble Prime Minister's Independence Day speech, in which he gave a clarion call for "Make in India" and "Zero Defect, Zero Effect" policies. It aims at facilitating investment, encourage innovation, enhance skill development, shield intellectual property, and build best-in-class manufacturing infrastructure in India.

In his open invitation to overseas investors that "Come, Make in India", Mr. Modi urged the global investor community. Sell anywhere but make them in India. He pointed out: "We have got skill, talent, discipline and determination to do something." Second, he sought to sell the 'Made in India' idea to youth. With these twin calls—one to investors from abroad and the other to young Indians—Mr. Modi has, in a way, set in motion the policy course of his government.

However, for achieving the objectives of 'Make in India', many more fronts need to be addressed, viz., policy/law, land, labour, taxation, cost of logistics, etc. Manufacturing sector and locations of manufacturing units are highly dependent on the cost of logistics.

Land

Land issue affects both current and new manufacturing units. "Right to Fair Compensation and Transparency in Land

Acquisition, Rehabilitation and Resettlement Bill 2015" is a stepping stone to address the land issues. Land Acquisition Act 2013 (LAA 2013) was containing thirteen special categories, whereas this bill creates five special categories of land use. Those are:

1. Defence,
2. Rural infrastructure,
3. Affordable housing,
4. Industrial corridors, and
5. Infrastructure projects including Public Private Partnership (PPP) projects, where the Central government owns the land.

This bill exempts these five categories of land from obtaining consent of land owners, which was mandatory in LAA 2013 for thirteen categories. This bill changes acquisition of land for private companies to acquisition for 'private entities, which could include companies, corporations and non-profit organisations. The government is aware that development cannot be done by government alone.

Human Resource

Cities dependent on manufacturing are no longer attracting the best employees, as they are located in places, where it is not appealing an ambitious youth to live. Smart cities concept will address this issue, wherein cities will be combined with manufacturing clusters in a manner that creates liveable places for a workforce. Manufacturing does not exist in vacuum. It needs an ecosystem of labour markets, liveable spaces, and access to markets.

We know that after law and land, labour is an important element. In an increasingly globalised economy, jobs tend to move where the labour is cheap. Being a democratic nation, India is differently positioned than other countries vis-à-vis the labour. Outdated labour laws have spawned inefficiency in the economy and have proved a strong deterrent for any overseas company to set shop in India. A smooth and friendly human resource is needed for Indian or multinational industry to come up and sustain.

In Indian context, the subject of labour has often acquired political underpinnings with varied stakeholders taking a narrow stand. The Congress-affiliated 'Indian National Trade Union Congress' (INTUC) controlled more than 33 million workers. The BJP-friendly 'Bharatiya Mazdoor Sangh' (BMS) controlled 17 million. Communist party-run unions had 20 million on their rolls. Replacing the existing labour laws with a new set is the need of the hour to provide momentum to the process.

We need to learn from the past, there were common issues involved in Maruti, Nokia, Ford and Hyundai cases. All have had strikes and protests in India at their manufacturing plants in the recent years. Non-democratic countries can keep workers in control and wage costs in check. India has labour laws and organised unions that can hinder smooth expansion.

Skill Development

With increasing globalisation, knowledge and competition, there is a need for a highly skilled workforce in both developing and developed nations. Prime Minister Shri Narendra Modi came up with the Skill India Programme to make India the skill capital of the world and to provide the youth of the country with better means of livelihood.

It has been identified that 104.62 million fresh entrants to the workforce, over the next seven years (by 2022), will need to be skilled. Additionally, 298.25 million of existing farm and non-farm sector workforce will also need to be

India was far behind other nations in imparting skill training to its workers. A major effort is underway under the 'National Skill Development Corporation' (NSDC). NSDC estimated a need for 120 million skilled people, i.e., 10 per cent of the population against mere 2 per cent as of now, to ensure a robust ecosystem with outcome-based skill courses that will certainly contribute to the country's economic growth.

The main goal is to create opportunities, space and scope for the development of the talents of the Indian youth. The new programme aims at providing training and skill development to 500 million youth of our country by 2020, covering each and every village. Also, there is a requirement for multi-skill talent. Today, a security guard doubles up as a receptionist as well.

NSDC's most important and conscious effort is towards making everyone respect and aspire for skills so that they aren't considered just another added course to one's resume. People must realise that the value is in the work one does and not just in what one learns.

Regulations

Trading in imported goods for mass consumption, especially in the food, consumer goods, electrical and light engineering goods needs to be controlled. Control should not be physical barriers but smart barriers. Processed imported food is flooding the markets. There should be strong regulations on quality clearances. Foreign chocolates and candies flood the Indian markets since importers presently do not have to take Food and Drugs Administration's (FDA's) permission. Smart barriers should check dumping of 'Made for India' goods, having technology, which was outdated years ago in advanced world.

Procurement process needs to be more efficient, time-bound and predictable. Traditional policy and practice of awarding contract to L1 needs relook. This often discriminates against companies with latest technology and advanced equipment. Our thought about purchase or procurement is more or less 'cost centric' than value addition.

Logistics

The government has speeded up the pace of infrastructure development in roads, ports, high-speed rails and air transport with 'Regional Connectivity Scheme', improving logistics and connectivity. This is the need of the hour.

India is lagging about a decade behind the western countries from technological point of view. But we can turn this situation in our advantage by learning from the mistakes of the advanced world and trying to adopt the best-ever technology in the years to come.

Taxation

Another confidence booster from the government is required by reduction in the corporate tax. Currently, India's tax rate for companies compared to most other emerging economies is distracting industries. Tax rate should be brought down in sync with world standards.

'Make in India' initiative also aims at transforming India from the highly potential market to the powerhouse of manufacturing, thereby creating millions of job opportunities. In short, the campaign is conceived and designed to achieve multiple objectives and far-reaching impact on the economy.

This is an initiative taken by the Modi government to boost the Indian economy and the long-term vision is to make India an industrially developed nation. In fact, 'Make in India' is not a brand, nor is it a slogan. It is a new national movement, which covers the whole spectrum of our government, society and business. India has already emerged as one of the fastest growing economies of the world and has become the top attractive destination for foreign investment.

When we talk about 'Make in India', we inevitably think 'Made in India' to be synonymous with it. For many decades, we have been striving to get recognition to 'Made in India' products or brand India. We need to understand that 'Made in India is a pride, whereas 'Make in India' is the process.

You invite outsiders to 'Make in India' but insiders go out to 'make world-class companies'. Mr. Modi would do well to ensure that home-grown talent stays in India as well.

During the Modi government, FDI inflow has jumped to \$60 billion in 2016-17 from \$36 billion in 2013-14. 'Make in India' is the most visionary economy boosting plan of India to uplift the manufacturing sector with the ultimate objective to increase the GDP of India.

—Dheeraj K. Upadhyaya

❐

6
Indian Banking System & Reforms

Indian banking system is passing through a turbulent phase. Profitability of PSBs is expected to remain weak. Provisioning cost of PSBs is declining with the passage of time, but it is still high. Banks play a very crucial role in the Indian financial system. On one hand, major part of household saving is channelised through banking system, on the other hand, major chunk of commercial credit is provided by banks. Further, the government-owned or PSU banks are in predominant position having 70 per cent share of banking system. PSU banks are facing problems related to profitability, asset quality, capital position and governance. There is sluggish demand for credit and simultaneously high growth in deposit leading to high liquidity in banking system. These features have necessitated resolving the problem of banking system at the earliest. The RBI as well as the government under the leadership of Honourable Prime Minister Shri Narendra Modi has initiated reform steps to handle the problem faced by banking sector.

Steps of RBI

The RBI introduced several restructuring schemes (such as Strategic Debt Restructuring, Corporate Debt

Restructuring, 5/25 scheme and Joint Lenders Forum) to handle NPA problem. These restructuring schemes provided better repayment terms to corporates and have relieved banks from mounting NPAs.

Indradhanush

On 14th August, 2016, the Modi government introduced Indradhanush programme, a seven-pronged strategy to revamp PSU banks.

1. **Appointments:**
   The post of Chairman & Managing Director in PSBs was split into two, i.e., one MD & CEO and another Non-Executive Chairman. This policy is brought in by the government to align the Indian banking policy with global best practices and introduced better checks and balances.
2. **Bank Board Bureau (BBB):**
   This is a body of eminent professionals and officials to replace the Appointments Board. BBB is responsible for appointments of whole-time directors and non-executive chairman.
3. **Capitalisation:**
   The government has planned to adequately capitalise all PSU banks to keep a safe buffer over and above the minimum norms of Basel III. The capital requirement is not only for meeting growth, but also to remain solvent. The government is left with two options – either to go for re-capitalisation or force large banks to acquire small banks. But both the scenarios require fresh additional capital. In view of this, the government has already proposed to make available ₹ 70,000 crores of budgetary allocation for four years. Further, PSBs are required to raise another ₹ 1,10,000 crore from the market.

4. De-stressing:

The major recipients of PSB funding are infrastructure projects and core sector. So, these sectors are also major contributors to NPAs. The government has planned following steps to address this issue:

i. Project Monitoring Groups formed to address issues of pending approvals/permits.

ii. Make available long-term source of fuel for projects.

iii. Reform in discoms.

iv. Promoters to be encouraged to bring additional equity in order to improve leverage ratios.

v. Flexibility in restructuring of existing loans wherever banks find viability in projects. The flexible restructuring of the existing loans not only provides breather to companies, but also saves banks from mounting NPAs.

Strengthening Risk Control Measures and NPA Disclosure

In addition to provisions of DRT & SARFAESI, the government has come with other solutions such as early recognition of financial distress, creation of Central Repository of Information on Large Credits (CRILC), formation of Joint Lender Forum (JLF), flexible structuring of Long-Term Project Loans to Infrastructure and Core Industries, Assets Reconstruction Companies; and establishment of six new DRTs.

5. Empowerment:

The government has mandated strict non-interference in banks' decision-making process. The government has further asked banks to establish grievance redressal mechanisms for customers as well as staff. A policy to provide greater flexibility in hiring manpower is put in place.

6. **Framework of Accountability:**
   PSBs are to be assessed on the basis of new Key Performance Indicators (KPIs). KPI includes quantitative (NPAs, return on capital, growth and diversification of business and financial inclusion) as well as qualitative parameters (human resource initiative and strategic steps to improve asset quality).
7. **Governance Reforms:**
   The process of governance reforms started with "Gyan Sangam" – a conclave of PSBs and other stakeholders in 2015. Gyan Sangam recommendations included optimising capital, digitising process, strengthening risk management, improving managerial process and financial inclusion.

In addition to the above-mentioned direct measures to reform banking system, the government has taken some other steps that will positively impact banks.

Demonetisation: The government announced demonetisation of ₹ 500 and ₹ 1000 currency notes from mid-night of 8th November, 2016. This decision was a major jolt to the black economy. The informal economy is shrinking rapidly as the government cracks down on black money, making it difficult for any business to operate without paying taxes. Thus, the grey economy will either perish or move to transact through the banking system. This step will increase GDP and revenue realisation in the long run.

The Parliament passed the Wages Act on 8th February, 2017 with a mandate to business units to pay their workers only through the banking system.

The Sick Industrial Companies (Special Provisions) Act (SICA), 1985 was enacted for identification of sickness and revival of potentially viable units/companies. Under SICA, the Board of Industrial & Financial Reconstruction (BIFR) was set up with a mandate to access the viability of units and refer non-viable companies to the High Court for liquidation. These provisions were ineffective in handling the issue of NPAs and were misused by promoters to delay the process and for siphoning off assets. The Modi government enacted the Insolvency and Bankruptcy Code, 2016 (IBC) to consolidate the existing bankruptcy framework. Under the provisions of IBC Act and Companies Act, 2013, the government has set up National Company Law Tribunal (NCLT) and National Company Law Appellate Tribunal (NCLAT). All matters pending under Companies Act, 1956 and SICA have been transferred to these tribunals. Further, to facilitate the Insolvency and Bankruptcy Code, the government has also notified the repeal of the Sick Industrial Companies (Special Provisions) Act, 1958.

Consolidation: Merger/consolidation is considered to be one solution to various problems being faced by banks. The Modi government is actually considering merging the existing banks to create few large banks of global size. The government has already merged associate banks of State Bank Group with the parent State Bank of India. Now the government is in the process of consolidation of other PSU banks. The merger of two or more banks is expected to result in substantial value addition for the combined entity. The merger is expected to have the following benefits:

a. The merger of weak bank with strong bank will reduce the requirement of additional capital.
b. PSBs are facing talent crunch and persons with right skill set to handle critical issues. Merger is expected to address this problem to some extent.

c. The merged entity will be in a position to utilise its physical infrastructure more efficiently.

There was problem of higher lending rate and sluggish growth of credit for banks. To address this problem, the RBI and the government migrated from Base Rate (BR) regime to Marginal Cost of Lending Rate (MCLR) with effect from 1st April, 2016 to reduce the lending rates. The government has also enhanced public expenditure to increase money supply in the system. Further, the government has implemented recommendations of 7th Pay Commission, thereby increasing the disposable income of the central government employees.

Indian banking system is at a turning point. PSBs are burdened with heavy NPAs, lower profitability, higher provisioning requirement and lower credit demand. The changing environment and advent of technology and new-age banks have provided market with a lot of options. Future of banks will primarily depend on the direction in which customer will move and how banking players react to the situation.

Policies of the Modi government have provided freedom to bank managements along with adequate capital and talent. Consolidation will result in robust global-sized banks. The combined entity will be capable of facing competition in the market and delivering social schemes. In the near future, we may see five to six PSU banks with global or national presence. These banks will be better positioned to handle any crisis in the financial market.

While concluding, I would add that these positive steps to strengthen the banking industry and do away with crony capitalism practised by earstwhile governments have been possible only due to the visionary leadership and political will show by our Prime Minister Shri Narendra Modi. The banking foundation of new India has been laid.

—Basant Seth

7
The Great Transformation

It is now more than four years after Shri Narendra Modi stormed to power uprooting the Congress government, which had been ruling Delhi for the previous ten years. The people of India were fed up with the high level of corruption and the total lack of leadership of the Congress and saw in Modi a strong person with a proven track record of development and good governance in Gujarat.

Modi inherited an economy in shambles. High inflation and high interest rates had killed investment. Corruption in key sectors like telecom and coal had led to huge diversion of taxpayers' money into private hands. This had led to a depressing feeling about India and many of us were ashamed to call ourselves Indians when we went to foreign shores. Populist schemes like NREGA and Food Security – though laudable as schemes – became new avenues for corruption as leakages took away taxpayers' money reaching the deserving. No wonder, business confidence was low and people were eager for a change.

We can evaluate the Modi government's performance from some key areas. First and foremost is the management of the macro economy. Today, no one can deny that the Indian economy is on a sound footing. Foreign exchange reserves are at an all-time high of close to USD 400 bn because of huge inflows from foreign investors who have imposed faith and confidence in the Modi leadership. This is in spite of falling remittances from the Middle-East, where terrible business conditions are forcing many Indians out of jobs. The rupee continues its strength and has given the government the power to resort to imports to keep prices under control for the common man. This has also enabled India to modernise its defence forces, which were being starved of funds under the previous regime.

Subsidies have been brought down dramatically. Historically, Indian economy has been plagued by subsidies for petro-products and food. Over a period, the Modi government has removed petro-product subsidies by introducing a dual-pricing mechanism for LPG gas so that the subsidy has got reduced drastically. Diesel subsidies have been gradually eliminated without the users feeling any pinch. The last subsidy that needs to be dismantled is kerosene. For that, a very imaginative approach has been used. A massive programme for providing gas to rural households was first launched and now a majority of Indian kitchens have gas supply. With this in place, efforts have started to slowly dismantle kersosene subsidies. In the next two years, India may have said good-bye to all petro-product subsidies – something undreamt off. The other tough subsidy has been food subsidy. Every democratic government has the responsibility to ensure that no citizen goes hungry and the Modi government, while reducing subsidies, has ensured that there is no dilution in the quality or quantity of food delivered. But what it has managed to do is to automate the whole payment process through cash transfers using the Aadhaar identification cards. Today almost every Indian has an Aadhaar card. But this was not enough. The recipients needed to have bank accounts. So, through the Jan Dhan programme banks were pushed to open bank accounts for as many citizens as possible so that direct transfers to bank accounts could be done. The results have been startling. The government has managed to save more than ₹ 35,000 crore in the last two years.

So, better management of the macro-economy has meant low inflation, high reserves, record foreign inflows, strong fiscal position – a creditable performance by any hardstick.

Another major initiative of the Modi government, which has been tough but necessary, is the ferocious war launched against black money. During the UPA government, lip service was being paid to ending the scourge of black money. Black money had totally distorted economic activity in the country. Firstly, the government was denied its rightful share of Income Tax, Stamp Duty, etc. Secondly, it distorted asset prices. Housing became out of reach because black-moneyed persons could buy property with cash while salaried people could not afford it. Also businessmen and politicians took money overseas and parked them overseas. In fact, many businessmen became NRIs to evade paying taxes and avoid detection!

So, the first task was to handle the black money stashed away abroad. For this purpose, the Modi government got into a dialogue with tax havens such as Switzerland, Mauritius, Cyprus, Jersey, Singapore, and Dubai so that they would provide information on black money held by Indians. This unclogging of information flow was most critical and that has now been achieved. The heat is being applied through tough money-laundering laws. Result has been that the amount of money held by Indians overseas has come down significantly and action has been initiated against thousands of tax-evaders.

Efforts within India have been more dramatic. One quiet November evening, Prime Minister Modi went on air and announced that ₹ 1000 and ₹ 500 notes have been demonetised. In one swoop, black money stashed away in bank lockers, home almirahs was made worthless. The pain was felt for two months but the people rose to the occasion and backed Modi to the hilt. This resulted in an enormous increase in tax collections and the number of persons filing tax returns. Property prices have fallen significantly making houses affordable for all. All this has meant that the government has been able to push through an ambitious programme of public investment for building top class infrastructure. In the last Budget alone more than ₹ one lakh crore has been set apart for key infrastructure sectors. Realising that Railways are the biggest public asset, a three-pronged attack has been initiated for creation of freight corridors, improving the quality of travel for passengers through faster trains, better stations, etc. and last but not least, improving safety through modern technology.

The spectre of coal imports and power shortages has been eliminated. Today, India produces enough power and huge coal imports have practically disappeared. Health of electricity boards has been improved through the Uday Programme. Investments are being made in transmission so that the common man and industry do not have any problems in this key area.

Many more initiatives have been taken but space does not permit to discuss all of them. The Smart City programme is totally changing the face of Indian cities and towns. The Digital India push is ensuring that broadband reaches every Indian, and the potential of Intent is ensuring faster payments, education, etc. Skill India is making millions of Indians job-ready. Real Estate Act is, at last, giving a voice to home buyers, who have been left high and dry by greedy builders. Education is being revamped and a clampdown on prices is ensuring that health care is available at low costs.

Last but not least is the initiative of introducing the Goods and Services Tax (GST). This step has been in the making of more than 10 years, but it needed the locomotive effect of the Prime Minister to make it happen. It will eventually lead to a more efficient and inclusive economy and less tax leakages.

India is a nation on the move. Not that every mountain has been climbed or every hurdle crossed. Banks have mounting bad debts; demand in the economy has slackened as black money has substantially been taken out. But these are all issues that the government will tackle, given its determination. Most importantly, the people of India are totally behind the Prime Minister as they realise he is honest, hard working and capable of delivering the goods.

—P.N. Vijay

❒

8
Acharya Chanakya's Arthashastra and Modinomics

People ask me why it is relevant to discuss Chanakya after 2500 years? They say we were a backward country and the British developed us and helped us stand on our feet and it is because of them and the systems designed by them that we are able to run the country.

Has anybody thought that today we are contributing only 6 per cent of the global GDP, whereas at the end of the 17th century, our contribution was about 24 percent! And at the start of the 1st century, we were 1/3rd of the world economy!! Mind it, these figures were not calculated by us but by a British economic historian Angus Madisson. How were we such a great economy at that time? The answer will be found in Acharya Chanakya's *Arthashastra*, because he was the man who built strong foundation of economic administration and development of ancient India.

Acharya Chanakya's *Arthashastra* is the world's oldest book on economic administration of a state. According to him, the economy comprises three components:

1. Agriculture and cattle rearing;
2. Manufacturing;
3. Services and trade;

Using these, the king obtained a treasury and an army, which were then used to bring under his control both his own people and the people of the enemy. Vitality and stability of a country, according to him, were dependent on a strong treasury.

The wealth of the state was totality of the surplus stored in the king's treasury; the king was advised to devote his best attention to it because all the activities of the state depend on it. In the order of importance, the treasury was placed immediately below the king and the ministers. The treasury was ranked above the army since the army is dependent on finance. The best treasury was the one that was large enough to enable the country to withstand even a long period of calamities when there would have been no income.

The state gathered the surplus by means of revenue from state enterprises, state-controlled activities, taxes, trading, fees and other service charges, and the entire activity is well documented in *Arthashastra*. In Chanakya's economic model, a king who found himself in financial difficulties could collect additional revenue by special methods. Further, the aim of the elaborate structure of punishment was not merely to maintain order but also to collect revenue.

The main guiding principle of the administration of the economy was that the state should run diversified economic activities efficiently, prudently and profitably. The king is advised to be active in the management of the economy because the root of wealth is economic activity; inactivity brings material distress, without an active policy, both current property and future gains are destroyed.

Arthashastra contains several verses relating to efficient financial administration of the state including the responsibilities of the Chief Comptroller of Accounts and

Audits; the proper maintenance and timely submission of accounts; inspection and audit collecting the right amount of revenue (neither more nor less) controlling erring officials and the many ways of controlling dishonest officials who could cheat the government, the public or both.

The king was advised to maintain a diversified economy within the limits of the technology available at that time; keep in good repair existing productive forests, reservoirs or mines; start new mines, factories, forests and cattle herds; promote trade and commerce by setting up market towns, port and trade routes; build storage reservoirs; and organise new settlements. Efficient management was encouraged. Any official who did not generate adequate profits in a state-owned undertaking was punished for 'swallowing the labour of workers'.

Acharya said, "Power comes from the countryside, which is the source of all activities because most of the productive economic activities took place in the Janapada (city comprising adjacent rural area). Janapada should be rich enough to support taxation and a large army. Its people should be predominantly agriculturists, artisans and craftsmen, devoted to work, honest, loyal and intelligent.

The controller was expected to keep precise yields and detailed records of land use and anticipated revenue, helped by magistrates and secret agents.

Availability of water was important. It was necessary to build storage reservoirs because the water stored after a good rainfall could be made available continuously for irrigation. A dam built to impound water of a flowing river was better than a reservoir to which water had to be brought by man-made canal.

Manufacturing activity was in the state sector as well as in the private sector and was controlled through various controllers appointed for the purpose.

The *Arthashastra* treats in detail every aspect of trade, the third pillar of economic activity. Apart from promoting trade by improving the infrastructure, the state was required to keep trade routes free of harassment by courtiers, state officials, thieves and frontier guards.

It was better to have a large number of trade routes even if those all were not built to high standards. Acharya Chanakya's order of preference for establishing trade routes was – inland route, preferably to the south; a water route on the coast; and an inland waterway.

The state and private merchants, both local and foreign, were involved in trade. The Chief Controller of the State Trading was responsible for equitable distribution of local and foreign goods, buffer stocking, sale of state commodities and public distribution. A crucial duty regarding trade with foreign countries given to the Chief Controller of State Trading was – 'Generate profits; avoid losses'.

The Chief Controller of Private Trading kept a watch over merchants, by inspecting periodically their weights and measures and ensuring that they did not hoard, adulterate or add excessive mark-ups.

King: The Protector and Promoter of Welfare

Since the king is synonymous with the Acharya Chanakya's state, the kind of attitude and behaviour that Acharya Chanakya recommends for him is very important. The verse 'in happiness of his subjects lies his own happiness…' summarises it. According to him, a king should be well trained and should be able to practise self-control. An ideal king is the one who has the highest qualities of leadership, intellect, energy and personal attributes and who behaves like a sage monarch, a *rajarishi*. Among other things, a *rajarishi* is the one who is ever-active in promoting the *yogakshema* of the people and 'who endears himself to his people by enriching them and doing good to them'. The word '*yogakshema*' is a compound made up of *yoga*, the successful accomplishment of an objective, and *kshema*, its peaceful enjoyment. Thus, peaceful enjoyment of prosperity, i.e., the welfare of the people was given as much importance as knowledge, self-control and observance of *dharma*. The king's own *dharma* is to be just, impartial and lenient in protecting his people.

A king should not only follow *rajadharma* but should also ensure that his subjects followed their respective *dharma*, for, 'when *adharma* overwhelms *dharma*, the king himself will be destroyed'. The king's attitude to his people should be like that of a father to his children, particularly when any danger threatened the population. He should treat leniently, like a father, with those in new settlements, whose tax exemptions had ceased to be effective.

The king should not tax the people unjustly because 'that will make the people angry and will spoil the very sources of revenue'. A king who needed to recoup his depleted strength should try to promote the welfare of his people so that he might have the support of countryside.

Protection of life and livelihood constituted, in that order, the elements of securing welfare of the people. Protection of livelihood extended to protecting major areas of economic activity. Agriculture was protected from being oppressed by onerous taxes, fines and demands from labour; herds of cattle from thieves, wild animals, poisons, crocodiles and diseases; and trade routes from harassment by countries, state officials, thieves and frontier officers (customs officers).

Principles of fair trading, as enunciated in the text, were designed to promote welfare of the people. The phrase 'to be sold for the benefit of the public' occurs in several places. When state commodities were sold, no artificial scarcity was to be created and even a large profit should be foregone if it was likely to cause harm to the public. Special favours were shown to those who did things that benefited the people, such as building embankments and road bridges, beautifying villages or protecting them. **(PS: If we see from above, the inflation and exploitation, which are cause of concern today, were very well addressed by Acharya Chanakya.)**

Social security was both a private and a state matter. The primary responsibility for maintaining the family – wife, children, parents, minor brother and unmarried or widowed sisters – lay with head of the family; however, the state had the obligation to provide a safety net and maintain children, the aged, childless women and the helpless. But, when the state had to maintain the young with no family of their own, these could be recruited into the secret service. (Very important lesson from Acharya Chanakya).

From the above account of Acharya Chanakya's *Arthashastra*, we can very well visualise and understand that India was a thriving developed economy some 2,500 years back when most of the world was struggling to understand the basics. We can also understand from the above that economic model of today's developed economies of the world has lot of similarities with Acharya Chanakya's real operative economy.

Now, from the above brief on Chanakya's economic model emanates Modinomics, the economic model of Modiji. Our well read and knowledgeable prime minister, it seems, has gone through *Arthashastra* and studied it in great detail.

The three components of economy, i.e., agriculture and cattle-rearing; manufacturing; services and trade, make up the GDP, an important economic parameter, based on which the economic progress of any country is measured and Chanakya placed great emphasis for strengthening the treasury. Modiji like Chanakya is putting great emphasis on balancing these three since he knows and understands that only through balanced growth, the overall development and higher GDP can be achieved.

His efforts to double the farm income, giving protection to cow, developing markets to sell the farm produce and fixing realistic procurement prices for various agriculture products are efforts in the right direction to strengthen the first component: agriculture and cattle-rearing. Here emphasis on cattle-rearing is unique to our country and has the potential to increase the GDP multifold.

'Make in India', 'Stand up India', 'Start up India', and many more such efforts to develop manufacturing base of and in India are his dedicated efforts in mission mode to increase GDP in the manufacturing sector.

The third and most important component of GDP from our perspective is services and trade since we have the highest young population in the world which if efficiently utilised has the potential to increase the GDP of our country to the level from where we can say that we are at the top of the world. Our honourable Prime Minister realised this potential early on and on the day of taking over the charge of the central government, he declared 'Skill India Mission' to develop all-round skills of international standards for our youth and to give push to trade, he is travelling across the globe tirelessly and negotiating bilateral trade agreements with various countries.

His policies on infrastructure development are bound to bring this country to the forefront in the world economic map because of steps being taken in this direction, such as regional connectivity by air, development of roads, ports, bridges, inland waterways and sea beaches.

The Digital India and other technology measures are revolutionising agriculture and other aspects of economy and we are confident that the suicides as well as loan waivers to farmers can become a thing of the past.

GST, demonetisation, consolidation of banks and other structural changes in the financial sector are to improve the financial administration of the country and make it robust as was in Mauryan era under Acharya Chanakya and Chandragupta Maurya.

The Acharya's Janapada is very much a part of Modinomics as he is making all-out efforts to develop smart cities and smart villages.

His crusade against corruption and corrupt practices along with putting strong vigilance mechanism reminds us of Acharya Chanakya and his strong measures to protect the country and strict policies to check leakage of finances.

The Jan Dhan Yojana and push for digital transfer of funds to bring the last man into the main financial stream as well as transfer the benefits to him directly draw similarities with Chanakya's resolve for overall economic development of India, which was almost as big as it is today.

When Acharya Chanakya defines the qualities of a king, his resolve and his dedication for his people, we can instantly draw the similarities between Chandragupta Maurya and Modiji. Both are compared with great Indian Lion, the king of kings.

—Dr. Rajeev Lochan Bishnoi

❒

9
NAMO – Visionary of Digitisation at Grassroots Level

Over the last decade, India has made a remarkable progress in the field of computerisation. The widespread use of computers started a process, which enabled the Indian companies like Infosys and Wipro to become global players. It also showcased to the world the capabilities of Indian engineers, particularly those of the prestigious IITs. While this established the firm foothold of the top technology companies as well as the engineering graduates in the US and Europe, the social impact of this digital revolution was restricted largely to the educated upper-middle class and well-to-do Indians and a few large industrial houses.

Since the time Modiji took oath as Prime Minister of India, a tectonic shift has taken place as the impact of digital revolution has swept across the nation. While earlier, the fruits of this digital transformation were largely limited to the elite groups mentioned above, Shri Narendra Modi's personal connect with the grassroots of Indian society has ensured that the impact of digital revolution has been inclusive and all-encompassing – sweeping across every segment of our country's diverse population.

Many recent commentaries have focussed on the impact of demonetisation in ensuring that the digital economy reached across every strata of society. Undoubtedly, the magnitude of impact of digitisation has been more visible post-demonetisation. This is because there is virtually no sector or segment of society that can meaningfully operate or survive without the facilitation provided by money or currency. Therefore, when that tap of easy flow of cash was turned off, naturally, everyone – the rich or the poor, the educated or the uneducated, the male or the female, the employed or in the business – all had to take notice and make adjustments in their lifestyle and way of operation.

But, mind you, this was only the sudden visible impact that no one could miss! But a more careful analysis will reveal that the whole thrust towards 'inclusive digitalisation' was neither sudden or headline-grabbing. The move in the direction of digitalisation was part of a well thought-out, well-planned and carefully crafted larger economic strategy – put in motion in the first few months of the Modi government. The basic foundation having been laid in 2014, the structure was built brick-by-brick to suit a master plan that Modiji had conceived much earlier. One can truly compare the method of the digital reform process to the conceptualisation of the master plan of the Kailasa temple at Ellora. The entire structure was conceived in the mind of the master architect, and then a huge rock was carved from top-downwards to create the wonder of what we know as the temple of Kailasa today. The master plan for a digital economy is comparable in terms of being grand, intricate and planned to the last detail. Let us consider the master plan that is even today unfolding. I do not believe that 'demonetisation' is or was ever intended to be a culmination of the process. At most, it is a part of the master plan that NAMO has for the nation.

With the typical vision that only a 'pracharak', who has worked in every strata of society, can have, Modiji's vision for digitisation was intended to cover every region in the country, every community, every economic strata of society and every type of citizen, the rich, the poor, the educated, the uneducated, the salaried, the small trader, the businessman or the industrialist. Modiji was acutely aware that for the nation to truly move ahead, the entire nation and not just certain classes or segments of society must share in the fruits of digitalisation. The benefit must pass to all these stakeholders in order to really reap the benefits of technology.

To see how this master plan was systematically given effect to, let us quickly review the major milestones of the road already travelled on this digital highway.

(a) Aadhaar: Though launched by the previous governments, the visionary and statesman in Modiji recognised that it was in the larger national interest. Not only did he continue the project, he even invited its chief architect to continue and, in fact, significantly enhanced the budgetary allocation for the scheme. Thus, the concept, initialed by the Vajpayee government, carried forward during the Congress tenure, finally got legislative backing by Act passed in March 2016. Today, thanks to the continuing efforts of the government, direct transfers of subsidies on the basis of Aadhaar cards is a reality, saving crores of rupees and eliminating waste and corruption.

(b) Jan Dhan Yojana: It was initiated within six months of Modiji forming his government. The fact is that this scheme has benefited nearly 300 million people, who were outside the banking system. Besides, this has brought into circulation a whopping ₹ 650 billion

– leading to significant inputs into the economy. The decline in inflation and corresponding fall in RBI repo rates and prime lending rates is a direct consequence. More importantly, the social cause has also been served as the poorer classes of society have been covered by an accident insurance scheme and also been provided a Rupay card.

(c) Digital banking and use of Rupay cards across all classes of society have familiarised all people with the concept of digital services. More importantly, use of these cards (especially post-demonetisation) has shown the poor and the uneducated that they too can use services like ATM and debit cards. The elimination of the fear factor has been a big step in moving towards a class-less society, where all are equal in sharing the fruits of the efforts of the government.

In fact, it would be an error to consider only the initiatives taken by Modiji after becoming the Prime Minister. As mentioned earlier, in his long years in public life, he has learnt lessons in matters that are not taught in the highest institutions such as IIM and IIT. Thus, ensuring that digital technology is available to the common man, is of course, an important factor. This is the simpler part as can be seen from the extensive use of 3G & 4G technology for mobile phone connectivity, which is now available across the country. What is more important, and often more difficult, is to harness the available technology to innovative uses that would provide the maximum benefit to the maximum people. This is where innovative use, such as the BHIM app, facilitation of e-transfers, mobile banking, etc. plays a significant role in reaching the available technology to the last mile. Therefore, the use of digital technology and the achievement in this regard under Modiji's leadership should not be judged only on the basis of economic impact.

To illustrate this point, I may point to a few other features of the use of electronics and digitisation. As the Chief Minister of Gujarat, Modiji was known to use the telecom network to conduct teleconferences with the district collectors, secretaries and other administrators with a view to addressing grievances of the common man. Over the years, Indian administrators (or *babus*) had become immune to the various letters sent by secretaries and even ministers as they attended to the same according to their own individual convenience, whims and fancies, knowing fully well that no person at the top government level could keep exchanging correspondence over issues relating to the common citizen, which in a macro perspective appear trivial. Modiji revolutionised this process by institutionalising a conference call based on a regular interaction with the officials concerned such as district collectors and department heads. The impact of personally answering a question to the Chief Minister (with the aggrieved citizen often sitting before the CM) shook up the establishment in a way nothing else could. This was truly harnessing the power of digitisation. Modiji often gave instantaneous instructions after listening to clarifications provided by the official and, more importantly, got the assent of the secretary or collector concerned to acting within a specified time line. This was not a question of simply giving instructions but a matter of harnessing the digital medium to ensure that the message of "action to be taken" goes across a firm and practical manner. In similar ways, the various initiatives taken for establishment of smart cities, spreading the Internet and broadband capabilities across the country, provision of wi-fi on trains and other such initiatives are still continually revolutionising the way India operates.

Apart from making the masses fully familiar with the potential that a digital economy provides, it also showcases to the world the power, that is India. It is very evident that Modiji is looking at targets not just for the next year, not just for the next election, but rather for the next generation where Indians will occupy leadership positions across the world. Thus, India, harnessing the power of its people and its digital infrastructure will truly become a powerhouse to the world economy. That is the foundation for growth that the visionary leadership of Shri Narendra Modi has been able to provide in the short span of three years that his government has held office. We can now truly dream of much greater achievements in the coming years under Modiji's inspirational leadership.

—Jayant Gokhale

❐

10

Transformational Governance

Governance reform is a complex process. It is much easier to reform policies, planning, operations, financial management, but when it comes to reforming governance, it is ridden with resistance from deeply entrenched silos and vested interests. Unfortunately, unless governance is reformed, all other reforms can fetch only incremental benefits. Without reform of governance, systems can always recoil to older patterns. The present government knows this only too well, and started focussing on governance reform, which only can usher in critical changes in public system and public administration.

Governance reforms can manifest in several forms. It can just target cosmetic governance, incremental governance and even effective governance. This government seeks beyond all these, and it truly seeks transformational governance (TG). The government looks for transformational governance with high leverage and high impact. Cosmetic governance is like a bypass surgery and looks for superfluous changes. Incremental governance looks for small wins but without seeking to disturb status quo. Effective governance goes a step further and does seek beyond small wins and looks for large gains in terms of performance. It still tries not to upset the apple cart-vested interests and silos are left untouched.

The governance core remained the same. The public system reform in India is tired of these reforms, which left the institutions intact and outcomes notional. It is TG that seeks not only complete overhaul but also to uproot the deeply entrenched stakeholders. It is this that this government seeks. TG asks for hard options from which does not deter this government.

Easier Choices

There is a plethora of examples for cosmetic governance. For example, we have attempted several reforms in making tax laws simplified, which is welcome but left the core problem of evasion and compliance untouched. On the contrary, this government put to good use the tenets of double taxation agreements and succeeded in plugging loopholes. The previous governments made laws to widen tax base, but this government exploited Information Technology to not only widen tax base, but achieve deeper mining of tax base through nationwide surveillance. The gains are significant and permanent, and not just ad hoc.

One can cite several reforms of effective governance interventions of past governments but these were incomplete with gaps, which left scope for rent-seekers. Gas subsidy is a classic case. The entire process was mapped and all gaps plugged. The benefits directly reach beneficiaries. The middlemen were brought in line and they lost the scope for making money through diversion and non-existing connections. The icing on cake of all these is that it came with huge savings in expenditure. The effective governance interventions were such that they targeted change but remained half-hearted. It lacked will to target vested interests.

Aspects of Transformational Governance

TG, as we mentioned, seeks critical changes and not just significant changes. Reforms, as mentioned earlier, can be in the areas of policies, planning, execution, technology, institutions, financing, performance evaluation, etc. These are easily attained because very soon organisations and actors learn to game the system and the system recoils fast. The actors will soon be back in their games, maybe in some other form. These failed interventions, in fact, act as immunisation against any future reform. These become the precedents and bad ones, and deter any future reforms. We have a macro excuse for this. We invariably say the policy-making and planning are good but it is execution that fails. Faulty execution is nothing but a manifestation of faulty governance design. It is the failure to address governance issues that leaves many interventions in despair. This requires government to take governance reforms head-on and in a radical way. It should leave no leeway for vested interest to bounce back. If we look at some of the reforms ushered in by the present government, we can infer some key aspects of TG. These are discussed below.

Radical Interventions

TG requires radical interventions as anything short leaves scope for revival of old ways. The governments may not be lacking in intention but definitely lack risk appetite for reforms. The complexity of the interventions and fear of failure deterred reforms in many critical areas. Various governments have toyed with various interventions for curbing black money, tax evasion, *hawala*, etc. This government took the drastic decision of banning notes of higher denomination and substituting these with new currencies. This one step alone struck at the root of black money. There were criticisms, grievances and skeptics but in the end, people welcomed it and they put up with the inconveniences without any protest. Their acceptance of the problems of transitions showed strong sense of aversion to black money and ill-gotten money of hoarders. It also showed, if need be, people are willing to bear some pain and willing to pay some price, if it can help clean up the system. This is a major departure from previous interventions, in which the people doubted the intentions of the prevailing governments. Here they trusted the government.

Accountability at the Highest Level

The accountability for performance is now located at the highest level of government, that is at Secretary, Additional Secretary and Joint Secretary levels as they are the key policy-making and execution personnel. The previous governments did introduce MoUs at Ministry level but it had no consequences. There were no consequences of poor performance. It stopped at measuring and did not follow it through. On the other hand, this government introduced a system to identify poor performers. This itself has shaken the bureaucracy out of the comfort zone. This has sent strong signals across bureaucracy. It also showed up on appointments to high offices and higher positions. Building up a team to deliver is the first challenge any leader would face. This government tries to fit personnel with positions. Meritocracy prevailed predominantly and fair processes were followed in empaneling and selection. This is key to delivering on governance.

Trust-Based System

The present government is making serious attempt to change the relationship provider – beneficiary relationship. It is making the system trust-driven rather than distrust-driven.

The classic example of this is the issue of gas subsidy. It was a fact that substantial number of users of gas subsidy are those, who can afford to pay for it. The Prime Minister made an appeal to such users to voluntarily surrender their subsidy as this can go towards subsidising poor households and rural households. Lakhs of consumers surrendered their subsidy voluntarily and this led to thousands of crores of benefit to the government. This is in contrast to the previous policy of identifying leakages and penalising the misuse, which never worked in practice. Many declarations today are based on trust and self-declarations rather than authentication and notarisation. This has changed the agency relationship and has placed the onus on the citizen rather than the providers. The main highlight of this policy is that the citizen responded overwhelmingly just on the basis of an appeal. This was heart-warming. These are paradigmic changes and require contrary thinking.

Transparency

Transparency in public system has always been talked about but was always elusive. Information Technology has been a key driver of transparency and has been tried in several ways in many ministries. Still the opaqueness remained and transparency eluded. This government tried in different ways. Auctioning of natural resources is a good example of transparent system. The process was entirely transparent and helped extract maximum value. Even in the implementation of development programmes, transparency has improved through direct communication with the beneficiaries. It also seeks 360-degree cycle of process and information. For example, in the direct benefit transfers, the beneficiaries get the information as well. In the gas subsidy case, as soon as a beneficiary is credited, he gets the information. This ensures complete reconciliation of accounts. This completes the feedback loop.

Citizen Engagement

The thrust of the government has been engaging the citizens in matters of administration and civic interests. A good example of this is the smart city initiative. The smart city initiative expects the municipal administration to seek citizens opinions and this was one of the criteria for selecting smart cities. It was highly encouraging that in cities like Pune and Visakhapatnam, thousands of citizens participate through mobiles and internet. The projects were also tuned in alignment with the citizens' wishes. The encouraging aspect of this step was not that it was sought but that there was overwhelming participation in the process. This is in contrast to the lukewarm responses that elections to local government attract. These are simple but still high-risk ventures as the responses may be lukewarm and draw ridicule. However, by linking, funding and incentivising feedback as a mechanism, it is ensured the feedbacks are looked into, rather leaving it to actors concerned to act or not upon the feedback.

Conclusion

A New India has to become a reality. It has to adopt paradigmic changes, which can lead to transformational changes. Incremental efforts and results cannot fulfill the aspirations of the citizens. If a New India has to deliver, it cannot just remain a potential. It has to seek ways to become reality.

—Prof. G. Ramesh

❐

11
The Role of Bureaucracy in New India

Views about the bureaucracy in India have swung between two extremes. Lauded as the "Steel frame of India," by Sardar Vallabhbhai Patel, the bureaucracy has been credited with holding the nation together, by providing continuity in administration. On the other hand the bureaucracy has been criticized for being isolated from the masses and has often been perceived as being rule-bound and slothful. The bureaucracy, comprising All India Services and Central Services, is a merit based generalist civil service, and is the successor of the Indian Civil Service, envisioned by the Macaulay Committee in 1864.

After Independence, the focus of the bureaucracy has shifted from 'regulatory' to 'responsive' administration. However the vision of a New India articulated by Honorable Prime Minister Shri Narendra Modi to make India a global power and the pace of its implementation means that the bureaucracy, the implementing arm of the government, has to work with renewed vigour and energy in order to deliver. The Government is committed to providing a corruption free, pro-active administration and has sought changes at the policy level, in the functioning of government departments, and in the launching of programmes.

Each new step undertaken by the Government would be a step towards the vision of a new India. The seven key focus areas, which will be the overarching theme of the future initiatives, include India's Culture, Agriculture, Women, Natural Resources, Youth Power, Democracy and Knowledge. The 8 Point Development Model enunciated by the Honorable Prime Minister includes Education and Job Opportunities for Youth, Children and Women's Empowerment, Urban Development/Infrastructure, Inflation/Price Control, Agriculture Reforms, Health For All, Federal Structure and Anti-corruption measures. Niti Aayog has worked on a 15-year vision — "India 2031-32: Vision, Strategy and Action Agenda," which is a three-tier action plan comprising of a seven-year medium-term strategy and a three-year action agenda.

The bureaucracy, particularly the Indian Administrative Service, is concerned primarily with rolling out the reforms which will transform India. It has also to ensure that it adheres to the prescribed time frame. The time-lines for the reforms are fairly stringent. For instance, on the housing front the 'Pradhan Mantri Awas Yojna (Urban)' aims to provide 'Housing For All' by 2022 by constructing 2 crore houses for beneficiaries belonging to the economically weaker sections. The Deendayal Upadhyaya Gram Jyoti Yojana, which was launched to ensure continuous electricity supply to farmers and rural households aims to electrify the country's villages in 1,000 days and ensure that by 2018, all Indian citizens would have access to electricity. The goal of Swachh Bharat has to be accomplished by 2019, the 150th birth centenary of Mahatma Gandhi. The bureaucracy has to work in a time-bound manner in order to accomplish these goals.

The bureaucracy must work in collaboration and not in silos, as all the major reforms are multi-sectoral and involve a large number of departments and the state governments. This collaboration starts with designing the reforms and continues with their implementation. The collaboration is not informal but is incorporated in the schemes themselves.

Work on achieving the Vision of New India has already begun. The demonetization exercise, under which old Rs. 500 and Rs. 1,000 notes were scrapped to root out black money and fake currency in the system, has helped flush black money out of the system, deterred the circulation of fake currency and ensured that income tax defaulters be brought under scrutiny. The demonetization exercise involved not just the Reserve Bank of India and other banks but also the Ministry of Finance, particularly the Department of Financial Services and the Income Tax Department.

Arguably the most important tax reform after independence, the Goods and Services Tax (GST), a comprehensive indirect tax on manufacture, sale and consumption of goods and services throughout India to replace taxes levied by the central and state governments, became effective from 1st July 2017. It is a remarkable exercise in co-operative federalism. It has taken a great deal of bureaucratic effort to roll out the reforms and lay down the guidelines for an effective GST regime.

The Pradhan Mantri Jan-Dhan Yojana, a financial inclusion scheme of the Department of Financial Services, was launched on 28 August 2014, to provide access to formal banking services to the unbanked population in the country. The success of this scheme is unprecedented. By August 2017, the beneficiaries under the scheme are estimated to be 29.42 crore, of which 23.72 crore are from public sector banks alone.

To achieve the vision of 'Skilled India' the National Skill Development Mission was launched on 15.07.2015. The

Mission has been developed to create convergence across sectors and states in terms of skill training activities. The newly set up

Ministry of Skill Development and Entrepreneurship Development aims to provide employment opportunities to the youth, by bridging the gap between the need and the availability of skilled manpower, while harnessing the youth potential in order to reap the demographic dividend.

Addressing the issue of declining sex ratios, a matter of grave concern for the country, the "Beti Bachao Beti Padhao, "Andolan has been launched. This is being implemented through a national campaign and a multi sector action in 100 selected districts low in child sex ratio, covering all States and UTs. The objectives of the campaign are-prevention of sex selective elimination; ensuring survival and protection of the girl child, ensuring education and participation of the girl child. This is a joint initiative of the Ministry of Women and Child Development, Ministry of Health and Family Welfare and the Ministry of Human Resource Development. The bureaucracy is learning to consult, collaborate and deliver.

The purpose of the Smart Cities Mission is to improve the quality of life of people by enabling local area development and harnessing technology, especially technology that leads to Smart outcomes. The deliverables under the SMART CITIES include among others, adequate water supply, assured electricity supply, sanitation, including solid waste management, efficient urban mobility and public transport, affordable housing, especially for the poor, robust IT connectivity and digitalization, good governance, especially e-Governance, citizen participation and sustainable environment. In the spirit of cooperative federalism, the Mission provides flexibility to the States for choosing the best options amongst four verticals of the Mission to meet the demand of housing in their states. Rolling out a reform of this magnitude requires detailed planning, systematic convergence, expertise, and robust funding.

Infrastructure development is one of the key priorities for India and the development of roads and highways is a major concern for the government. An ambitious target has been set to increase the length of national highways to 200,000 km. The government aims to build at least 90,000 km of highway network in its 5-year tenure. The vision to build an exceptional road infrastructure for the nation is already bearing fruit with a record 22 km of highway constructed per day in 2016-17.

The Make in India Initiative was launched globally in September, 2014 as a part of the Government of India's renewed focus on invigorating the country's manufacturing sector.

It aims to focus on job creation and skill enhancement in 25 key sectors of the economy, including automobiles, aviation, biotechnology, Defence manufacturing, electrical machinery, food processing, oil & gas, and pharmaceuticals, among others.

The program has been built on layers of collaborative effort. A National Workshop on sector specific industries was held in December 2014 in which Secretaries to the Government of India, State Governments and industry leaders came together to debate and formulate an action plan for the next three years, aimed at raising the contribution of the manufacturing sector to 25% of the GDP by 2020. The Ease of Doing Business, concomitant to the success of Make in India, involved a gigantic bureaucratic exercise involving many departments in which rules and formats were simplified and obsolete and redundant rules were discarded. The achievements were overwhelming. During 2015 itself, India recorded its highest FDI flows. During the first two years, 127 Ease of Doing Business Reforms were completed, including simplifying the registration process for manufacturing units, single page application forms and buyer seller sessions.

On the technology front, to ensure that the digital revolution does not by-pass the country, Digital India has been launched which addresses the needs of the state, the society and the people. Digital India aims to provide a much needed thrust to the nine pillars of growth areas, which include Broadband, Highways, Universal Access to Mobile Connectivity, Public Internet Access Programme, E-Governance-Reforming Government through Technology, e-Kranti, Electronic Delivery of Services, Information for All; IT for Jobs, Electronics Manufacturing and Early Harvest Programme. Digital India is being implemented by the entire Government and the overall coordination is being done by the Department of Electronics and Information Technology (DeitY).

In order to boost agriculture and ensure "More Crop Per Drop," the Pradhan Mantri Krishi Sinchayee Yojana (PMKSY) has been launched which dwells upon the need to conserve water and ensure its efficient use to boost agricultural productivity, enhance groundwater resources, withstand drought and adverse impact of climate change, and bring about behavioural changes regarding the impact of water. It is an initiative involving three ministries, the Ministry of Agriculture and Farmer's Welfare, the Ministry of Water Resources, River Development and Ganga Rejuvenation and the Ministry of Rural Development including the

Department of Land Resources, as approximately 40% of the land is irrigated, 60% of the land is rain-fed and the mandate concerns all the three Ministries.

The vision of Swachh Bharat, a gigantic exercise which aims to Clean India, end open defecation by construction of rural toilets, and clean the Ganga cannot be achieved in a time bound manner by 2019, the 150th birth anniversary of Mahatma Gandhi, unless multi- pronged efforts are undertaken by the Ministry of Drinking Water and Sanitation, Ministry of Housing and Urban Affairs, Ministry of Water Resources, River Development and Ganga Rejuvenation, to name just a few. The achievements of Swachh Bharat are heartening. By August 2017, 100% villages along the banks of the river Ganga in Uttarakhand, Uttar Pradesh, Bihar, Jharkhand and West Bengal have become open defecation free, as have 193 districts and 5 states. The mission is set to achieve its target by October 2019.

The vision of a New India cannot be implemented except in partnership with the state governments. Keeping in view the principles of Cooperative Federalism the government reduced the number of centrally-sponsored schemes from 66 to 28. With 42% of the tax collected going to states, Cooperative Federalism is being strengthened.

To ensure that the bureaucracy, particularly the Indian Administrative Service, remains geared to the pace of the reforms, civil service reforms are under implementation. The Department of Personnel and Training(DoPT) has launched the 'Online Probity Management System' in association with other ministries so that assessing the integrity and performance levels of officers can be made easier. The SPARROW (Smart Performance Appraisal Report Recording Online Window) system of the DoPT is being used to make the entire appraisal system online and accessible for review by the ministries concerned.

A major step in this regard has been the dismissal or compulsory of officers including Indian Administrative Service (IAS) officers who were either non-performers or persons with doubtful integrity. The message, "Perform or Perish," has been conveyed to the bureaucrats. A reform measure on the anvil is the induction of lateral entrants into the echelons of the higher civil service, which aims to draw fresh blood from the market for induction at the highest levels of the government, in an attempt to garner their expertise.

The bureaucracy in India will have to learn to share its turf, collaborate amicably, work tirelessly, monitor vigorously and deliver rapidly in order to create a New India.

—Vandana Kumari Jena

❑

12

GST – One Nation, One Tax, One Market

Introduction

'Nothing in this world is permanent' is an ancient adage. In the context of indirect taxes, the aforesaid maxim held true on 01.07.2017 when one of the most eagerly-awaited tax reforms in the history of independent India, namely Goods and Services Tax (GST in short), came into effect. Before discussing GST, it shall be worthwhile to outline that in the earlier regime of indirect taxes, the Central government used to levy many indirect taxes such as Central Excise Duty, Service Tax, Central Sales Tax (CST), etc. Similarly, State governments used to levy many Indirect Taxes such as Value Added Tax (VAT), Entry Tax, Luxury Tax, Purchase Tax, etc. Consequently, multiple taxes were being levied in the same supply chain.

Further, in the pre-GST regime, taxable event used to be 'manufacture' 'sale', and 'services provided or agreed to be provided' under erstwhile Central Excise Act, Central Sales Tax Act/ Local VAT Act and Service Tax Law, respectively. Similarly, in other Indirect Taxes, different prescribed events used to be taxable events. In general, the earlier regime was broadly suffering from the following drawbacks:

1. Lack of uniformity in taxation laws, rules and rates
2. Lack of automation in many acts

3. Different taxable events
4. Different exemption levels
5. Lack of uniformity in the same form under different acts
6. Lack of cross-verification with other tax administration

New Features of GST

GST, as the name suggests, is a tax on goods and services. It is an activity-based tax. The new features of GST are as under:

(A) Taxable Event

In the pre-GST regime, taxable event used to be 'manufacture' 'sale', and 'services provided or agreed to be provided' under erstwhile Central Excise Act, Central Sales Tax Act/Local VAT Act and Service Tax Law, respectively. Similarly, in other Indirect Taxes, different prescribed events used to be taxable events. However, in the GST, taxable event shall be supply of goods or services or both.

(B) Change in the Scope of Goods or Services

Meaning of goods and services is not to be taken in conventional sense. The subject matter of earlier indirect taxes and GST shall continue to be goods and services but in GST, the meaning of Goods and Services has to be derived with reference to Schedule II of CGST Act, 2017. For instance, execution of works contract, as defined in Section 2(119) of CGST Act, is deemed to be supply of service, even though in such contract transfer of property in goods, either as goods or in any other form, is also involved. Similarly, supply of goods without transfer of ownership for specified period for a consideration shall also be considered supply of service irrespective of the fact, whether effective control or possession is parted to the lessee or not. In the earlier law, where effective control and possession was transferred, it was considered to be deeming sale in terms of Article 369A of the constitution. However, in GST, deeming sales of this kind is also considered to be service as provided in Schedule II to the CGST Act, 2017.

(C) Destination-Based Consumption Tax

GST is based on destination-based consumption tax principle. On the contrary, erstwhile Central Sales Tax is origin-based tax. Destination-based taxation, as the name suggests, is the taxation based on destination or consumption of the goods or services. This principle seeks to tax the goods and services on simple theory that the goods or services should be taxed at the place where their consumption takes place, rather than the point where their origin takes place. The entire revenue relating to the goods or services shall accrue in the jurisdiction, where they are being ultimately consumed. For example, if Mr. A in Delhi produces the goods and sells the goods to Mr. B in Haryana, then, in such cases, the tax shall accrue to the State of Haryana and not to the State of Delhi. On the other hand, origin-based taxation, as the name suggests, is the taxation system where the tax accrues to the state from where the transaction originates. Therefore, in case of origin-based taxation, the revenue accrues to the jurisdiction from where the transaction originates. Continuing the above example, under original-based taxation, the Central Sales Tax would be levied and collected in the State of Delhi and not in the State of Haryana.

(D) Self-supply of Goods or Services or Both shall Become Taxable

Under former indirect taxes, two separate legal entities were required to complete the transaction, whereas in GST, in specified situations, self-supply shall also be subject to tax.

Transfer of goods from one office of a person located in one state (say Punjab) to another office located in another state (say Andhra Pradesh) shall also be subject to tax under the GST Regime.

(E) Supply of Goods or Services or Both without Consideration shall be Subject to Tax in GST

The activities specified in Schedule I to the CGST Act shall be treated as supply even if made without consideration. For example, permanent transfer or disposal of business assets where input tax credit has been availed on such assets.

(F) No Centralised Registration Under GST in the Case of Supplier of Services

Keeping in view the destination-based principle, the concept of centralised registration has been dispensed with in GST regime, which can work satisfactorily when tax revenue goes to one government only, irrespective of the place of supply. In GST, it has been specifically provided that every supplier has to seek registration in all those states, from where they are supplying goods or services or both.

(G) Anti-Profiteering Measure

Anti-profiteering measure has been introduced vide Section 171 of the CGST Act in GST to ensure that any reduction in rate of tax on any supply of goods or services or the benefit of input tax credit shall be passed on the recipient by way of commensurate reduction in prices. Though the aforesaid provisions are likely to be litigated between revenue and registered persons, there is no doubt that it is a new feature and has been introduced in the interest of public at large though prone to litigation.

Advantages of GST

The broad advantages of GST have been outlined below:

(A) For Business

- Less number of laws to be complied with
- Uniformity in the application of provisions
- Removal of cascading effect
- Availability of greater Input Tax Credit
- Least physical interaction with tax administrators

(B) For Government

- Simple and easy administration
- Stricter control on revenue leakages
- Higher revenues
- Broad tax base

(C) For Consumers

- Reduction in overall tax burden, particularly in case of goods in the long run

GST – One Tax

Consequent upon subsuming of following indirect taxes in GST with effect from 01.07.2017, GST has become one big Indirect Tax:

CGST

- Central Excise Duty
- Additional Excise Duties (Goods of Special Importance)
- Additional Excise Duties (Textiles and Textile Products)
- The Excise Duty levied under the Medical and Toiletries Preparations (E.D.) Act, 1955
- Service Tax
- Special Additional Duty of customs – 4% (SAD)
- Central Sales Tax
- Central Cesses and Surcharges so far as they relate to supply of goods and services

SGST

- State VAT
- Entertainment and Amusement Tax (unless it is levied by the local bodies)
- Luxury Tax
- Taxes on Advertisement
- Taxes on Lottery, Betting and Gambling
- Octroi and Entry Tax
- Purchase Tax
- State Cesses and Surcharges so far as they relate to supply of goods and services

How GST shall Make Our Country as One Nation

India is one vast nation, having 29 States and 7 Union Territories. Ideally, the entire nation should be one at least on the economic and taxation fronts. However, practically there were many economic and taxation disparities amongst different States or Union Territories. The aforesaid disparities were causing a major hurdle in inviting adequate Foreign Direct Investments [FDIs], which are urgently required by our country for its rapid economic development, particularly in the infrastructure sector, which requires huge long-term investments. Besides, there was a long-time demand from various international financial institutions and other big stakeholders that taxation disparities amongst the various States/Union Territories must be removed at the earliest. In GST regime, there shall be indirect taxation uniformity amongst various States/Union Territories. The foregoing uniformity shall go a long way in projecting the image of our country as one nation not only geographically but from the standpoint of indirect taxation also.

How GST shall Help in Creating One Market

The pre-GST indirect taxation system created borders within borders and tax laws, tax rates differed from one State/Union Territory to another State/Union Territory. The erstwhile system did not provide tax credits for certain types of indirect taxes. For example, while discharging VAT liability, no credit was allowed either of Central Excise Duty or Central Sales Tax. This led to distortions in the allocation of resources and indirect taxes, which was a major concern while taking business decisions.

However, GST shall integrate India's economy into one market, which, in turn, shall avoid tax-cascading scenarios. It is also worthwhile adding here that GST shall be neutral to various factors of production, business processes, business models, organisational structures and geographical locations. Resultantly, decisions in GST regime shall be taken purely on business terms. Thus, taxation impact on the business decisions will not play a decisive role. In simple words, quantum of GST [indirect tax] on any particular goods or services or both shall remain the same throughout the country unlike pre-GST regime when indirect taxes used to vary from place to place. For example, VAT on cars in Haryana used to be lower than the corresponding VAT in Delhi. Thus, people preferred to purchase the cars from Haryana.

In addition, GST is expected to increase India's Gross Domestic Product [GDP] as well as its tax revenue collections. In the long run, GST shall also boost export of goods and services. Besides, GST by attracting FDIs shall increase employment opportunities in our country. Further, GST shall help the government in realising its dream project of "Make in India", which, in turn, will benefit smaller businesses in India.

Conclusion

At present, "GST – One Nation, One Tax and One Market" may appear to be an attractive slogan to some short-sighted and pessimistic people. However, in the long run, the aforesaid slogan can unquestionably become a pleasing and satisfactory reality if all stakeholders, namely Central government, state governments, suppliers of goods or services or both, tax administrators, consumers play their respective roles with full honesty and keeping the interest of our motherland uppermost in their minds. There shall be certain difficulties, obstacles and setbacks in the realisation of aforementioned slogan which can be undoubtedly surmounted with strong will power, honest endeavours and rising above paltry political gains. Finally, GST is not a "Gabbar Singh Tax" as alleged by some politicians. On the contrary, it shall eventually prove to be a "Good and Simple Tax" and surely create a win-win situation for everyone.

—C.A. Ashok Batra

❐

13

Recent Trends in Banking and Desired Reforms – A Practical Approach

The financial sector in any country is the catalyst that ensures the mobilisation and effective distribution of resources within the economy to attain and sustain higher rates of growth.

Within the financial sector, banks are the backbone of any financial ecosystem. It is, thus, very important that banks remain financially healthy. Otherwise, a financial crisis can hit a country, leading to recession. This is especially true for developing countries like India. "The banks are the lifelines of the economy and play a catalytic role in activating and sustaining economic growth, especially in the developing countries, and India is no exception. However, India's banks face different kinds of problems, which have affected their profitability and financial stability," said S.S. Mundra, Deputy Governor of the Reserve Bank of India, in a speech recently.

The Indian banking system consists of 21 public sector banks, 26 private sector banks, 43 foreign banks, 56 regional rural banks, 1,557 urban cooperative banks, 33 state cooperative banks, 366 district central cooperative banks, six small finance banks and two payments banks in addition to rural cooperative banks and cooperative credit institutions.

Public sector banks control more than 70 per cent of the banking system assets, thereby leaving a comparatively smaller share for its private peers.

The first major development in the banking sector was the nationalisation of 14 major banks on 19th July, 1969. The statement of objectives and reasons of the Banking Companies (Acquisition and Transfer of Undertakings) Act says: "The banking system touches the lives of millions and has to be inspired by a large social purpose and has to subserve national priorities and objectives, such as rapid growth of agriculture, small industries, exports, raising employment levels, encouragement of new entrepreneurs and development of backward areas."

The 'Mass Banking' philosophy led to swift branch expansion, massive recruitment, increased lending at concessional interest rates, declining quality of assets, etc. All these have added costs to the banks, eroded profitability and weakened control, thus lowering competitive efficiency of Indian Banks.

Considering that during the 20 years since nationalisation, the health of the banking industry deteriorated and the necessity for reforms of the financial sector was recognised, economic reforms were initiated in 1991.

This was the time when the country was facing two serious crises involving the financial sector:

- The balance of payments almost brought the country to default grade, putting its credibility at peril amongst the international community.
- The grave threat that the banking system would collapse mainly because of concealment of impaired assets and faulty balance sheet management.

Furthermore, the financial sector was burdened with some deep-rooted problems of the Indian economy in the early nineties, such as seizure of resources from the banking system by the government to finance its fiscal deficit through policy prescriptions. "Excessive structural and micro-regulation that inhibited financial innovation and increased transaction costs. Relatively inadequate level of prudential regulation in the financial sector. Poorly developed debt and money markets. And outdated (often primitive) technological and institutional structures that made the capital markets and the rest of the financial system highly inefficient" (Mathieu, 1998).

The financial sector reforms since 1991 had improved the situation somewhat. However, over the next 20 years, the issue of large-scale impaired assets surfaced, imperilling the banking system all over again.

It was also clear that the objectives of nationalisation were not even substantially met and inclusive growth still remained a perplexity.

This posed major challenges for the economy and the banking sector.

According to the Governor of RBI, "Our banking system, at the present juncture is, however, facing significant challenges from several quarters. These challenges, if not addressed quickly and adequately, may result in loss of opportunities as and when the economic growth starts picking up momentum. In a sense, it has implications for both the banks as well as for the economy as a whole, because a strong banking system is one of the essential prerequisites in the quest for growth."

The greatest risk to Indian banks is the rise in impaired assets. The slowdown in the economy in the last few years led to a rise in stressed assets. 36.9 per cent of the total debts in India are at risk, according to an IMF report. If these debts turn bad too, banks will face major losses.

In the last few years, CRAR or Capital-to-Risk Assets Ratio has declined steadily for Indian banks, especially for public-sector banks. Moreover, banks are not able to raise funds easily, especially public sector banks, which have higher impaired assets. If banks do not augment their capital soon, they would fail to meet the minimum capital requirements prescribed by the RBI.

Liquidity Coverage Ratio (LCR) has set a minimum requirement of 60 per cent to be gradually increased to 100 per cent by January 1, 2019 in a phased manner. The LCR is a ratio of High Quality Liquid Assets (HQLA) to the Total Net Cash Outflows. This has been prescribed to address the short-term liquidity risk of banks, which the banks would be required to maintain on an ongoing basis equal to the Total Net Cash Outflows.

"The wild gyrations in the forex market have the potential to inflict significant stress in the books of Indian companies who have heavily borrowed abroad," Mr. S.S. Mundra, DG, RBI, said in his speech. As a result, the RBI wants banks to ensure companies they lend to not to expose themselves to unnecessary debt in dollars.

A very large number of PSB employees are retiring. With young employees replacing them, there will be a vacuum at the senior levels, which would impact the decision-making process.

In the past few years, banks have tried to delay making provisions for future stressed assets. One reason for this is that a bank's chief executives have a short tenure, during which time they want to show improved net profits to keep stakeholders happy. "It must be appreciated that CEOs/ CMDs would come and go but the institutions are perpetual entities. The only thing which can perpetuate their existence is a stronger and healthier balance sheet," S.S. Mundra, DG, RBI.

Deferring provisioning reduces the ability of the banking sector to weather financial storms. This is even more unsettling, given the poor capital adequacy in Indian banks.

Technology has pervaded all areas of the lives of our population. Turnover times for all kinds of financial transactions have incredibly reduced. Banks have to constantly upgrade their technology offerings in order to be able to face the emerging competition and improve customer experience.

The banking space is now open as entry barriers have been lowered. Due to this, many new players have entered the market, such as private banks, foreign banks, and banking finance companies, etc. These entities bring with them hi-tech offerings.

For survival and growth in this highly competitive environment, banks must formulate customer-centric policies which ensure prompt and efficient customer service.

Globalisation throws up many challenges for domestic players as they have to compete with global players and to adopt to global best practices. A look at the Indian banking industry will show that there are 43 foreign banks operating in India, which pose a major challenge for nationalised and private sector banks.

Financial inclusion is a necessity in today's business ecosystem. Under the PMJDY scheme announced in August

2014, more than 14.5 crore accounts have been opened. The major challenge is to channelise the flow of individual savings, howsoever small, combined with funds from direct benefit transfer by ensuring that these accounts remain active and then to extend need-based credit so that the hitherto excluded population continues to contribute in the economic mainstream.

Another major challenge is that banks will be required to efficiently manage the banking correspondent system. The problems relating to their viability, cash management and control from a base branch will require attention. The entire financial inclusion ecosystem has to be very carefully developed if the thrust received from the whole exercise of the Prime Minister Jan Dhan Yojana is to provide sustained all-round benefit to all those who have been financially excluded.

The MUDRA and the Stand Up India schemes announced by the present government are designed to ensure that those who have the capacity but are financially deprived can be brought under the productive mainstream. The challenge is to change the mindset of the banking community, which has traditionally been apathetic towards schemes launched by the Government.

Customer education, protection and rights have gained prominence in recent times. The RBI has issued a Charter of Customer Rights based on the global best practices. The Charter comprises the following five rights:

- Right to Fair Treatment
- Right to Transparency, Fair and Honest Dealing
- Right to Suitability
- Right to Privacy
- Right to Grievance Redressal and Compensation

- Banks have to endeavour that these rights are constantly protected.

Strict compliance with the KYC/AML norms has to be ensured diligently in order that the financial system and banks are insulated from loss of credibility, reputational risk and financial loss.

In the background of legacy issues and the challenges faced by the financial system, especially banks, the present government along with the RBI has taken various steps to improve the desolate landscape.

This includes issuance of guidelines on:

- Early Recognition of Financial Distress,
- Prompt Steps for Resolution and Fair Recovery for Lenders,
- Framework for Revitalising Distressed Assets in the Economy,
- Detailed guidelines on the formation of Joint Lenders' Forum (JLF),
- Corrective Action Plan (CAP),
- Refinancing of Project Loans.

Sale of NPAs by banks and other regulatory measures, which emphasised the need for early recognition of financial distress and for taking prompt steps for rectification, restructuring or recovery, thereby ensuring that interests of lenders and investors are protected.

The first two years of the present government also saw the passage of the Insolvency and Bankruptcy Act in early 2016 in order to increase banking access and resolve stressed loans by speeding up the legal process.

UDAY, the scheme to revive state power distribution companies, came into operation.

Measures have been taken to speed up the transition of the economy to a cashless system, such as a ban on cash transactions over ₹ 2,00,000/- (US$ 3,100), promoting greater usage of non-cash modes of payments, making Aadhaar-based payments more widespread.

Amendment of Section 35 A of the Banking Regulation Act will allow the Reserve Bank of India to direct banks for the recovery of non-performing assets.

The indigenous payments application, BHIM (Bharat Interface for Money), has recorded 18 million downloads since its launch on December 30, 2016, according to Chief Executive Officer, NITI Aayog.

Launching of Mission Indradhanush which is a seven-pronged plan to address the challenges faced by public sector banks (PSBs).

The seven parts, which have now become the famous ABCDEFG, comprise:

- **Appointments** – Separation of posts of CEO and MD to check excess concentration of power and smoothen the functioning of banks as also induction of talent from private sector.
- **Bank Boards Bureau** – Will replace the Appointments Board of PSBs, advise the banks on how to raise funds and how to go ahead with mergers and acquisitions, hold bad assets of public sector banks, separate the functioning of the banks from the government by acting as a middle link.
- **Capitalisation** – Of the banks by inducting ₹ 70,000 crores into the banks in the next four years as banks are in need of capitalisation due to high NPAs and the need to meet the new BASEL-III norms.

- **De-stressing** – Solve issues in the infrastructure sector to check the problem of stressed assets in banks.
- **Empowerment** – Greater autonomy for banks and more flexibility for hiring manpower.
- **Framework of accountability** – The banks will be assessed on the basis of new key performance indicators, such as NPA management, return on capital, growth and diversification of business and financial inclusion as well as qualitative parameters, such as human resource initiatives and strategic steps to improve asset quality.
- **Governance Reforms** – Holding Gyan Sangam conferences between government officials and bankers for resolving issues in banking sector and chalking out future policy.

Going forward, in order to mitigate challenges, the mentioned Indian banks must cut their cost of services.

Apart from traditional banking services, Indian banks must adopt some product innovation so that they can compete with the ever-increasing competition.

Technology upgradation is an inevitable compulsion. The level of consumer awareness is significantly higher as compared to previous times. Thus, technology-based offerings have to be introduced and constantly improved.

Mr. Bill Gates, co-founder of Microsoft Corp, has stated that India will move quite rapidly to a digital payments economy in as little as seven years, based on the introduction of digital payment banks combined with other things, such as direct benefit transfers, universal payments interface and Aadhaar. Thus, our banks must be there in the centrestage of this transformation.

- Cut administrative overheads and improve response times.
- Improve their risk assessment and monitoring systems so that they can use the wealth of information they have gathered over the years to make sound lending decisions.
- Transformation will require more liberal hires in wages, for skilled loan officers, risk managers, forensic accountants, IT professionals, lawyers and human resource professionals.

While PSBs can undertake contractual hiring at market wages, it remains to be seen whether they can attract professionals without promising them the means for career advancement within the bank.

Public sector banks will also require more professional boards that can strategise and control effectively.

More decisions need to be decentralised from the government to the PSB boards once they have been fully professionalised.

Board members of PSBs have to be given market-related compensation if decent talent is to be attracted.

Enhanced spending on infrastructure, speedy implementation of projects and continuation of reforms will provide further strength to the industry exploring the option to launch contactless credit and debit cards.

Banks should not be treated as ordinary creditors, but must be given a special status to be able to resolve their impaired assets.

Wage revisions of banks should not be done on an industry level, but left to individual banks so that employees of the more efficient banks can be incentivised.

Bank boards should be given the freedom to set compensation structures and performance measures for their senior executives, including long-term stock options.

Banks should engage in conducting small business, which is their core competence as it has been proved that they are not competent to engage in large business.

Even though development banks have fallen into distress in the past, development finance should be conducted by them.

In order to ensure continuity of policies and strategic plans, the Chief Executives should have longer tenures.

Above all, the banking industry, especially the PSBs, will have to change their mindset at the operating level to improve customer satisfaction and have a positive approach towards the development schemes launched by the present government.

—Ajay Banerjee

❐

14
Reforms in Banking and Finance – A Practical Approach

Financial sector is the mainstay of any economy and it contributes immensely in the mobilisation and distribution of resources. Financial sector reforms have long been viewed as significant part of the programme for policy reform in the developing nations. Earlier, it was thought that they were expected to increase the efficiency of resource mobilisation and allocation in the real economy to generate higher rates of growth. Recently, they are also seen to be critical for macroeconomic stability.

The elements of the financial sector are banks, financial institutions, instruments and markets that mobilise the resources from the surplus sector and channelise the same to the different needy sectors in the economy. The process of accumulative capital growth through institutionalisation of savings and investment fosters economic growth. Reform of the financial sector was recognised, from the very beginning, as an integral part of the economic reforms initiated in 1991.

The economic reform process in India occurred amidst two serious crises involving the financial sector – the balance of payments crisis that endangered the international credibility of the country and pushed it to the edge of default, and the grave threat of insolvency confronting the banking system which had for years concealed its problems with the help of faulty accounting strategies.

In 1990, the tip of the iceberg was reached with a bloated current account deficit triggered by the Gulf war crisis and the fall of Soviet Union that created a situation for the Indian economy to nosedive owing to an increase in the prices of crude and virtual halt of our exports accompanied with a recession in the US. Since the insulated environment of the economy did not permit private foreign investment, Indian reserves were abysmally low and in mid-1991, India's exchange rate was subjected to a severe adjustment. This event began with a slide in the value of the rupee leading up to mid-1991. The authorities at the Reserve Bank of India slowed the decline in value by expending international reserves. With so much at stake emanating from reserves only left for three weeks of essential imports and refusal for assistance by the RBI, the Indian Government had no option but to resort to settle 67 tonnes of gold as collateral against $ 2.2 billion from the International Monetary Fund.

Immediate response to this crisis was the ushering of the monumental reforms that were short-term fiscal correction strategies aiming to evade the spillover of the economic breakdown by implementing macroeconomic stabilisations. The reform process in India was initiated with the aim of accelerating the pace of economic growth and eradication of poverty. It was only in 1991 that the Government signalled a systemic shift to a more open economy with greater reliance upon market forces, a larger role for the private sector including foreign investment, and a restructuring of the role of the Government.

The reforms of the last decade-and-a-half have gone a long way in freeing the domestic economy from the control regime. An important feature of India's reform programme is that it has emphasised gradualism and evolutionary transition rather than rapid restructuring or "shock therapy". This approach was adopted since the reforms were introduced in June 1991.

Furthermore, some deep-rooted problems of the Indian economy in the early nineties were also strongly related to the financial sector such as large-scale pre-emption of resources from the banking system by the government to finance its fiscal deficit. Excessive structural and microregulation that inhibited financial innovation and increased transaction costs, relatively inadequate level of prudential regulation in the financial sector, poorly developed debt and money markets and outdated (often primitive) technological and institutional structures that made the capital markets and the rest of the financial system highly inefficient.

Immediately after 1991 crisis, certain structural reforms were introduced. These were devaluation of the Indian rupee, introduction of liberalised new EXIM Policy and new Industrial Policy, which were the critical elements in structural reforms. Following these reforms, the Indian economy became more free and competitive. Successful implementation of trade and industrial policies demanded that the resource allocation needed to be market-driven.

Immediately after the BoP crisis of 1990, the Finance Ministry of Government of India set up the Narsimhan Committee to provide a blueprint for the reformation of the banking sector in India.

The following are the primary suggestions by the 1991 committee:

- Reduction of CRR and SLR
- Removal of Direct Credit Program

- Deregulation of Interest Rate regime
- Structural Reorganisation of Banks
- Removal of Dual Control by making RBI the sole agency for banking regulation
- Autonomy of Banks

Measures taken so far:

1. **Lowering CRR and SLR:**
   In the pre-liberalisation era, the banks' ability to lend was constrained by pre-emption of substantial resources by way of Cash Reserve Ratio and Statutory Liquidity Ratio which were ruling at as high a level as 15 per cent and 38.5 per cent, respectively. As of now, the CRR stands at 4 per cent and the SLR at 20 per cent. The reduction in CRR and SLR proved to be a game changer by putting more money in the hands of banks for lending.
2. **Prudential Norms for Income Recognition and Asset Classification (IRAC):**
   Prior to the introduction of this measure, banks were booking interest income on their credit portfolio on accrual basis without any reference to the recovery or otherwise of the interest applied in the borrower's account. With the result, the banks showed inflated profits and the quality of credit in terms of its recoverability was not realistically reflected in the bank balance sheet. With the introduction of IRAC norms, banks were required not only to derecognise interest not recovered in the borrowal accounts as income but also to make prudential provisions against profit for the non-performing assets (NPAs) on the basis of default history. This one measure has resulted in a great improvement in the operational

efficiency of the banks through better credit discipline and improved credit monitoring.

3. **Introduction of Capital Adequacy Norms:** The ability of the banks to lend was determined by the amount of deposit mobilised by them and it was not linked to any minimum capital requirements. This had the effect of building assets beyond the sustainable level jeopardising depositors' interests in the event of a major default in lending portfolio. In line with the global best banking practices, Capital Adequacy Norms (as suggested by the Basel Committee on Banking Supervision) were introduced for Indian banks also, thereby linking their ability to expand credit/build up assets to the amount of individual Bank's capital. Further, for the purpose of determining the capital required for carrying a certain level of assets, the assets on the balance sheet were subjected to assignment risk weights and the capital requirement was linked to risk-weighted assets.

   In calculating the capital requirements for meeting the adequacy ratio, the banks were required to factor the market risks also faced in the balance sheet portfolio.

   Taking this initiative forward, the capital adequacy norms were further tightened on the basis of recommendations of 1999 Narasimham Committee by applying the Basel II requirements and with effect from the year 2013, banks in India were required to move to capital requirements under Basel III in a phased manner over a specified time frame and Capital Provisioning for Operational Risks has also been mandated.

4. Deregulation of Interest Rates:

Though business of banking essentially consists of accepting deposits and lending, in the pre-reform era, the banks did not have the power to decide on the interest rates for both deposits and advances as they operated in an administered interest rate regime. Thus, there was no incentive for being professional and efficient since margin in any case was assured. Today, some of the banks offer as much as 6 per cent to 7 per cent interest on savings bank accounts as against 4 per cent offered by many banks. SBI has recently reduced savings bank interest rate to 3.5 per cent. Subsequent to that, many other banks are also reducing the rates on savings deposits.

Similarly, on the lending front, the various interest rate prescriptions of RBI for priority sector advances, etc. have been withdrawn and the banks are free to determine the rates on their own for all advances of the value in excess of ₹ 2,00,000. The initiative to deregulate interest rates led to the emergence of various concepts, such as Prime Lending Rate, Base Rate, Marginal Cost Based Lending Rate, etc. to ensure transparency in pricing of loan by banks. The Marginal Cost of Funds Based Lending Rate [MCLR] system introduced in April 2016 for improving the monetary transmission has not been entirely satisfactory, even though it has been an advance over the Base Rate system. An internal Study Group has been constituted by the Reserve Bank of India (RBI) to study the various aspects of the MCLR system from the perspective of improving the monetary transmission and exploring linking of the bank lending rates directly to the market-determined benchmarks. This group is tasked to submit its report by September 24, 2017.

5. **Strengthening Legal and Institutional Framework for Speeding the Process of Recovery of Debts:**

   Many initiatives were put in place in this regard, chief among them being establishment of Debt Recovery Tribunals for speedy disposal of recovery suits filed by the banks, enactment of SARFESIA, setting up of Asset Reconstruction Companies, etc. Also notable among the other initiatives were the introduction of Corporate Debt Recovery Scheme (CDR) to deal with high value problem loans to the Corporate Sector in the year 2001 and, based on the review of its working, the recent announcement of a new scheme of Strategic Debt Restructuring (SDR) empowering banks to effect change in management of defaulting and non-cooperative corporate borrowers. The other notable scheme is 5/25. The process is a continuous one and the latest is Insolvency and Bankruptcy Code, which is expected to help in speedier resolution of problem loans.

6. **Fostering Competition by Giving Licenses to New Banks in the Private Sector:**

   From the year 1969, when the banks were nationalised and till 1994, no new players in the private sector were licensed to set up a bank. Banking was almost the monopoly of Public Sector Banks barring a few banks in the Private Sector that were already in existence (whom we now call old-generation private sector banks). Thanks to the banking sector reforms, in the year 1994 alone, six banks in the private sector were given license to operate, which included, among others, ICICI Bank, HDFC Bank and UTI Bank (which took a new name later as Axis Bank) and IDBI Bank. The rules for entry of foreign banks in India were also relaxed substantially resulting in competition from foreign banks too forcing the PSBs to pull up their socks and improve the way of working to survive and protect their turf against onslaught by the competitors. In fact, PSBs have lost considerable market share to their new-generation competitors in the private sector.

In the year 2003, two more banks, namely Yes Bank and Kotak Mahindra Bank, were given banking license to operate followed by two more banking licenses for Bandhan Bank and IDFC Bank in 2014. Taking the reform measures further in this space, the RBI has promoted differentiated banking by granting licenses to 11 players for setting up payment banks and 10 players for setting up small finance banks in the year 2015. Today, the bank customer has a wide range of banks to choose from on the basis of their specific banking requirements, efficiency of operations of the banks and the quality of customer service.

7. **Access to Capital Markets for Banks:**

With the change in the rules of the game towards capital adequacy and given the constraints of the government to continuously provide additional capital to banks due to its implications on the fiscal front, the banks have been given freedom to access capital markets to support their capital requirements for business growth. This has been facilitated through suitable legislative changes providing for dilution in government stake in PSBs from 100 per cent upto 51 per cent so that the management control could still vest with the government. Today, there is practically no bank in the public sector whose shares have not been listed in any of the stock exchanges. The status of a listed entity has exposed the banks to the rigours of market discipline. Efficiency parameters like Return on Assets and Return on Equity, Net Interest Margin, CRAR, Coverage Ratios, have all become the new yardsticks for measuring the operational efficiency and financial health of the banks and these parameters determine the bank's ability to get additional capital for business expansion.

8. **Phasing of Directed Credit:**
   Though the Narasimham Committee recommended for phased withdrawal of guidelines on mandatory lending to priority sector, keeping in view the importance of bank credit to this sector towards the socio-economic development objectives, the government on the lines of recommendations by Nair Committee on Priority Sector Lending (Chairman: Mr. M.V. Nair) revised and broad-based the definition of priority sector to include newer activities which require credit support and to facilitate active participation of the banks in achieving the lending target under this sector.
9. **Structural Reorganisation in the Banking Sector:**
   It was proposed to bring about a consolidation in the banking sector to have a three-tier structure with (i) three-to-four large banks to develop as international

banks; (ii) eight-to-ten banks with national presence and offering universal banking; and (iii) local area banks for primarily region-specific banking.

In pursuance of this objective, many banks have merged. The industry witnessed many consolidations in the market, recent being merger of SBI and its associates.

The post-reform era saw the removing of the dividing line between development banking and commercial banking and the commercial banks have increasingly started engaging in long gestation term loan projects and infrastructure lending. The RBI has also come out with a helping hand to enable the banks to tide over the asset-liability mismatch because of longer repayment schedules, by announcing a 5/25 scheme for infrastructure finance by banks in the year 2014.

The liberalisation process emboldened some of the strong banks to specialise in activities such as loan syndication, wealth management services, etc. This brought to the fore the importance of and the need for sound risk management and asset-liability management practices the guidelines on which are being given by RBI from time to time helped by Basel Committee Recommendations.

The banks were also permitted to foray into newer areas of financial services like mutual fund and insurance by either acting as Corporate Agents for selling specific insurance/mutual fund products of other insurance and mutual fund companies or by floating mutual fund and insurance subsidiaries by forging alliance with global players of repute in the respective fields.

These initiatives enable the banks to have different streams of income to supplement to the income from the regular banking business.

10. **Strengthening Banking Supervision and Regulatory Oversight of Banks:**
    In the wake of extensive bank liberalisation and more emphasis on self-regulation by banks, the responsibility of RBI as the controller of banks has become more onerous. In recognition of this fact, a number of steps have been initiated, chief among them being establishment of an exclusive department for banking supervision and implementing many of the recommendations of successive Basel Committee Reports on banking supervision and issuing exhaustive guidelines on risk management policies and practices, asset-liability management, capital provisioning, compliance, etc., which are aimed at strengthening the banking system to withstand the challenges of any future economic/financial sector crisis. The detailed guidelines given by the RBI in its communications on Basel III compliance covers all the three pillars, namely minimum capital requirement, supervisory review process and market discipline.

Conclusion

The implementation of various reform measures in the banking sector coupled with path-breaking reform initiatives taken in other financial sectors like capital and debt markets and the slew of economic reform measures have enabled the country to rapidly come out of the deep economic crisis of 1991 and emerge as the third largest global economy by 2011.

In recent times, the public sector banks have come under a lot of criticism on the mounting NPAs and many of the banks have reported huge losses on the back of substantial provisions made for bad loans. In this context, the following observations made by a panel of banking experts in a public discussion forum organised by Centre for Policy Research, Delhi recently merit a mention: *"The sudden rise in NPA in PSBs is due to excessive lending to the infrastructure projects in 2010-11 which helped in boosting growth. So, if banks are attacked now for bad loans, they should also be given credit for helping growth at that time..."* . The spurt in NPA is due to the attempts by banks to clean up their books by March 2017 as directed by RBI.

The "Indradhanush" plan announced by the government addresses the issues currently faced by the PSBs and promises to correct the anomalies by recapitalising banks, revamping bank boards and giving operational freedom, governance reform and inducting professionals in management positions selected through recently constituted Bank Board Bureau, etc. Consolidation of banks is being pursued to strengthen the PSBs. Similarly, to resolve the issue of high NPAs in banks, many initiatives have been taken including the recent Insolvency and Bankruptcy Code. These initiatives coupled with the expected pick-up in the economic growth, it is hoped, would enable the PSBs to come out of the present crisis and bounce back to great strength. The banks have shown resilience in the past and there is no reason why they will not do it again.

India continues its journey towards a financially inclusive regime through innovative policies involving a multi-pronged approach. India has come a long way from a financially repressive regime to a modern financial sector, where public sector financial institutions tend to compete with the private sector financial institutions. The Indian authorities, while reforming the financial sector, had to constantly keep the issues of equity and efficiency in mind.

—Dr. Rashmi Tripathi

❐

15

National Security: Changing Contours Under Shri Narendra Modi for Building a Strong and Secure India

The Concept and Evolution of National Security

The Indian concept of national security was closely linked with the people and economy. Kautilya, the great Indian seer and philosopher, warned that before undertaking military operations, the king must know the resultant inevitable financial hardship, which the country will face. He summed it up as the people's loss and the public loss. Further reading of the *Arthashastra* elaborates that the king must first make the country economically strong and indulge in military operations only when it is inevitable and when there is very high probability of success. Kautilya also underlined the types of threats and declared that the most dangerous threat is internal threat abetted by external support or direct aggressions by external enemy. The Chinese philosopher Sun Tzu opined that warfare is the greatest affair of the state. Sun Tzu also suggested that victory must be achieved with minimal sacrifice in men and material. According to the French military thinker, Clausewitz, national security is an affair of people, government and the military.

All the military thinkers till the beginning of twentieth century underlined the basic components of national security:

- Economic might is very important for successful outcome from military operations.
- Losses to the national infrastructure and lives of ordinary citizens must be minimised.
- Kautilya was very specific in highlighting the threat from internal turmoil.

Nevertheless, two basic issues remain vague in the earlier concept of security. Security for 'whom' and security from 'what'? A UN Human Development report in 1994 observed: "Concept of security has been too long interpreted narrowly.... It has been more related to nation states than people... Forgotten are the legitimate concerns of the ordinary people who sought security in their daily lives." The second aspect of security is expressed in terms of territorial integrity, cultural identity, value system, political entity and sovereignty. Most definitions of national security indicate external military threats against the territory and the people as also threats of political nature aimed at undermining the internal stability of the state.

Against this backdrop, it will be interesting to scan the entire conflict spectrum from peace to no war, no peace to proxy war through terrorism followed by full-scale war (below the nuclear threshold) followed by negotiation and conflict termination.

National Security in Information-Driven Knowledge Era

In the modern knowledge era dependent on information infrastructure and contextual knowledge, many nations engage in undeclared war. This can be in the form of economic competitions, trade wars, political maneuvering and perception management. In the most intense form, this conflict can be in the form of proxy war like the one waged by Pakistan (intimately supported by China) against us. These operations exploit the insecurities of the society/target audience via broad access provided by the Global Information Infrastructure and National Information Infrastructure, hostile foreign media and compromised national media. It is an ongoing process and forms of conflict are sequential and overlapping when mapped on conventional conflict time line. It escalates from peace to war before de-escalating to peace. Please see schematic figure herewith:

Information Operations
Conducted throughout all phases
Infrastructure attack
Command and control attack

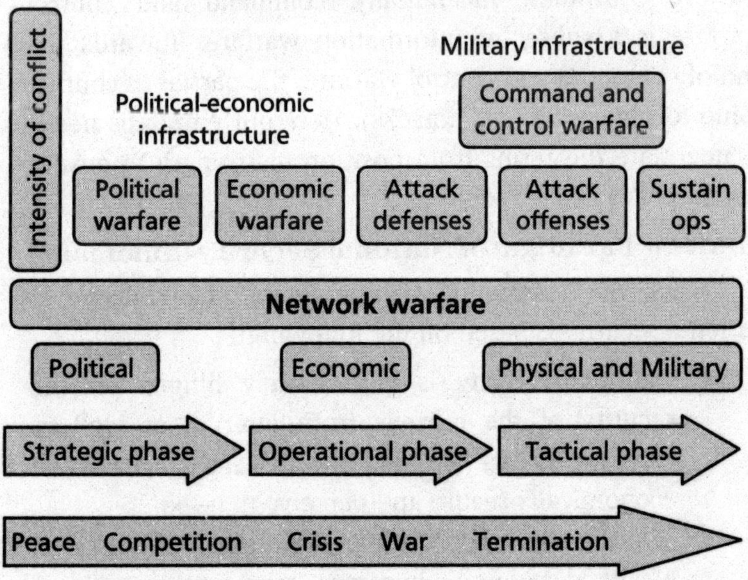

In the beginning (left extreme of the figure), nations exist in peace and harmony with mutually beneficial trade and other transactions. The first signs of conflict may emerge in the form of competition of any kind – trade, economic, regional leadership, ideological, and so on. During this part of the conflict spectrum, political systems, economy and even physical/information infrastructure will become the targets. As the conflict intensifies, the military gets involved in what is known as command and control warfare. This form of warfare (command and control warfare) is defined as synergistic application of operation security, deception, psychological operations, physical destruction supported by timely and contextual actionable intelligence in real time. The primary objective of this form of warfare, undertaken overtly by the military, is to deny information and influence/degrade/destroy the command and control capabilities of the adversary. At the apex level, the political and economic warfare continues. Incidentally, command and control warfare is a subset of information warfare. Towards the end of command and control warfare, the parties in conflict come to the conflict termination. Here our emphasis needs to negotiate the terms from position of strength to ensure lasting peace in the region.

The New Paradigm of National Security (Summary)

Thus, in information age societies, the concept of national security is based on the following:

- National security is very closely hinged on the security of the citizens from internal as well as external threats. Besides, the citizens must also be economically secure and perceive to be so.
- Hence, economic growth and reduction in equality in wealth distribution becomes important ingredients of national security.

- There is also a need for strong and stable political leadership. The political leadership needs to be bold when it comes to taking important decisions in the interest of national security, at the same time, the political leadership needs to maintain strong international relations to ensure requisite support in case of open hostilities.
- We need to defend our information infrastructure against cyber attack. Also there is a need to defend our citizens from the enemy design of perception management through propaganda by hostile national and international media.
- In the event of declaration of open hostilities in the form of a conventional war, the defense forces need to be fully prepared and have enough liberty to take professionally sound military decisions.
- The political leadership must ensure that the conflict termination is done in a manner that the gains of conflict are optimised.
- The political leadership must also endeavour to maintain a favourable international opinion in consonance with our national interests. It is here that the foreign policy merges with the strategic defense posture.

Our Approach on National Security form 1947 to 2014

It may be prudent to list out the major strategic events during the period first and then summarise the approach taken by the political leadership during the period.

- **J&K Operations, 1948:** The political leadership stopped the winning Indian Army in its tracks and handed the issue over to UN without any plausible strategic reasons to do so. The unresolved Kashmir problem has been bleeding the Indian economy and the defence forces since then.

- **Accepting Chinese Suzerainty over Tibet:** The Chinese Communist Party came to power in China in 1950. In 1954, the then political leadership in India accepted Chinese suzerainty over Tibet. Dalai Lama fled from Tibet. An impregnable buffer between China and India was removed by this political blunder. All military issues with China emanate from this strategic blunder. It needs to be noted that the British always kept Tibet as a protectorate due to its strategic military importance. Tibet is a high-altitude plateau with average height of 15,000 feet, surrounded by high mountains all around ranging from 19,000 to 25,000 feet high. It is connected to mainland China by three highways – Central, Eastern and Western highways. These highways negotiate difficult mountain passes. If these passes are secured, it is very difficult for any invading forces to attack India from the North. However, once Tibet is in Chinese hands, the Indian defences in the Northern and the Eastern states are compromised.
- **Strategically Disastrous Conflict Termination in 1971 War:** After a resounding victory in 1971 war with Pakistan (liberation of Bangladesh, 90,000 Pakistani Prisoners of War), what we gained in Shimla agreement was a very poor reward to the nation. The Kashmir problem remained unresolved. Pakistan enhanced her military strength. It became a nuclear weapon state. Today, the proxy war, waged by Pakistan with open support from China, has become a major security threat to India.

- **Compromising National Security in Addressing Kashmir Issue:** The ruling dispensation at the Centre till 2014 had been placating the Hurriyat leaders to the extent that these pro-Pakistan leaders were always part of the Kashmir dialogue. This trend was extremely dangerous and did compromise the security of the country.

Thus, our approach to national security has been very inconsistent with our national interests. In fact, almost all the problems that we are facing in the realm of national security emanate from inapt handling of security concerns of the nation. We have projected ourselves as a meek and unreliable nation.

Threat to National Security in the Light of the New Security Paradigm and the Way We Addressed the National Security till 2014

- **Security of the People, Extreme Poverty Abetted by Increasing Corruption, Vote Bank Politics:** As per the evaluation by World Economic Forum, we, as a nation, have been consistently rated very low on Human Development Index. Corruption, institutional credibility, judiciary, macro-economic fundamentals, ease of doing business, infrastructure, vote-bank politics resulted in rampant support to criminal activities, absence of law and order. In fact, we went to the extent of tarnishing the image of honest army officers and other nationalistic organisation, in order to please the fringe elements of vocal minority community. This policy suited the military operations of hostile neighbour and undermined the morale of own people and the defense forces.

- **Very Weak Political Leadership at the Centre (Leadership by Proxy):** For almost ten years, the constitutional authority of the highest office of the executive in India (the PMO) had been undermined by non-constitutional political entities. This weakened our international position and eroded the public confidence in governance. This also led to unbridled corruption, massive loss to the exchequer and continued inefficiency in all departments of governance. In the context of national security, this is a very dangerous situation. Our adversaries and internal enemies exploited the situation to the fullest.
- **Low Morale of Armed Forces Due to Inept and Weak Handling of Cross-Border Terrorism:** The armed forces were saddled with stringent control by the political bosses in taking operational decisions to neutralise cross-border terrorism. Hence, our operational and tactical superiority at the LoC was neutralised by lack of political will.
- **Acute Shortage of War-Fighting Material with the Defence Forces:** In May 2014, when Prime Minister Narendra Modi took over the reigns of the nation, the three services were facing acute shortage of major and minor arms, ammunition and related defence equipment. Besides, the procurement policy was too cumbersome. Babudom was at its best in undermining the stature and legitimate demands of the services.

Threats from Pakistan: Perception Management by Pakistan; Formation of Pakistan; her World View, Specifics of J & K Macro Strategy. Since Independence of India and Pakistan, the two nations fought four conventional wars –

1948, 1965, 1971 and 1999 in Kargil. 1971 was a decisive victory, which created Bangladesh. War in Kargil also exposed Pakistan's ill-designs on India. However, Pakistan has always been and will remain inimical to India. In order to understand the goals, objectives and the compulsions of Pakistan, which forced her to create a virtual world, it is important to understand the reality of Pakistan. Pakistani authorities target their operations at three levels – insurgency, terrorism and ideological subversion. They have been getting sustained support from China even now. Earlier, the Pakistani establishment gained military and economic support from the US and the Western European countries. However, 9/11 and subsequent happening in Afghanistan along with Prime Minister Modi's active intervention have changed that situation. It is only China in her support now. At present, threat from Pakistan is largely in terms of proxy war, which is unfortunately being supported by some parts of the compromised media and ill-informed intelligentsia including some of the mainstream political parties. With the arrest of Hurriyat leaders and no nonsense approach to national security, the situation is likely to improve in the near future.

An Ill-informed and Hostile Intelligentsia in the Country: Our policies related to military matters have been strategically incorrect for the last 70-odd years. The governments at the Centre had been more interested in promoting their narrow political, and, at times, dynastic agenda. True nationalism has generally been scoffed at. Very vague and woolly ideas have been pedalled intellectual excellence. This has created a very vociferous group of people, who have harmed the nation. Recent happenings in JNU, Jadhavpur, Hyderabad, misleading the investigation in Samjhauta blast case, coining of the saffron terror bogey, implicating an honest Army officer (Col. Purohit) as a terrorist have been just a few prominent cases of anti-national ideas germinating in the heart of our political system. This has serious implications for national security

- **Threat from China:** The way we handled China since 1950 itself is a case study depicting our exceptionally poor, unrealistic foreign and national security policy, which has paved the way for the current mess that we are in – particularly on our Eastern and North-Eastern borders. When we gained our Independence in 1947, Tibet was an autonomous region. In fact, it was a British protectorate. Indian troops were stationed in Tibet. Geographically, Tibet is a plateau with vast flat plain at an average height of 15,000 feet. As discussed earlier in this article, accepting Tibet as a part of China was a strategic blunder. However, the bigger folly has been ignoring very clear signals from China with regard to her military design and strategic intent. To start with, China fought the Korean war against the US forces way back in 1951 – just one year after the formation of the People Liberation Army (PLA). Thus, China was instrumental in creating North Korea. We know what North Korea is in terms of major reason for disturbing peace in the region. Secondly, the Chinese presence in Aksai Chin was noticed as early as 1954. Aksai Chin is North-Western tip of Ladakh and is an Indian territory. Chinese were seen building road in this high-altitude area across the Karakoram pass. The then Prime Minister dismissed this event – saying that in Aksai Chin not a blade of grass can grow. Today, the One

Belt One Road (OBOR) initiative is through this area. In 1957, Chinese were spotted in Barahoti region of the then Uttar Pradesh (now Uttarakhand). In 1959, there were skirmishes between our security forces and Chinese troops in the Barahoti and Thagla Ridge areas. In spite of these clear indicators, we did not prepare our defences against China. Consequently, in October 1962, when the late Jawaharlal Nehru, the then Prime Minister, declared that he had ordered the Indian Army to throw the Chinese out – it was an act of utmost military naivety and down-right foolishness. The Chinese were well-prepared, battle-hardened and much larger in number. Indian troops were ill-equipped, much less in number and had no logistic back-up to withstand Chinese counter-action. The 1962 war was a disaster, invited by an utterly inefficient, ill-informed, ignorant and arrogant political system. In fact, China has been consistently inimical to Indian interests.

How Prime Minister Narendra Modi is Building a Secure and Strong India

- **Fastest Growing Economy:** With the advent of Shri Narendra Modi government at the Centre, a series of macro-economic steps were taken, which placed the economy on very firm footing. While the economies of all emerging nations (Brazil, Russia, China and South Africa) slowed down, the Indian economy has been the only economy in the world that registered the fastest growth at 7.5 per cent per year. The political scams disappeared, the governance ushered in an era of honesty and transparency. BSNL, and coal sector started registering profits. Power sector bloomed; infrastructure started growing at the fastest pace in the history of independent India. As discussed earlier, this was the first step in enhancing long-term national security. Demonetisation further encouraged digital transactions, the implementation of GST ensured that business environment became transparent, user- and business-friendly. It is encouraging to note that the additional 24 per cent of population has come under the Income Tax regime. Incidentally, the tax-to-GDP ratio in India has been the poorest in the developing region. This state is going to change very fast. Additional revenue in the hands of an honest government will definitely boost the national security.

- **Empowerment of the Citizens:** Secure, safe and empowered citizens ensure secure nations. The present government, under Shri Narendra Modi, took some path-breaking and innovative steps. First and most critical step has been the launching of Jan Dhan Yojna, followed by zero balance account, free minimum insurance to the poor, allotting money for the farmers and girls from the poor families for marriage – all through 'direct to bank transfer' to the beneficiary. This empowered the ordinary poor citizens, removed leakage in the financial pipeline. More than 10 million poor women were given free LPG connections, subsidies to the rich and middle-class citizens were removed, mostly voluntarily.
- **International Support:** The most important transformation Shri Narendra Modi has brought about single-handedly is in complete turnaround of international opinion in favour of India. He not

only developed personal bonds of friendship with the global leaders, but also endeared himself to the Indian settled in the countries he visited. His visit to Israel has been the most important international visit. No one other than the stature of Shri Narendra Modi could have taken this bold step. This proves the point that for the current Prime Minister, nothing is above national interest. Compare this with the late Jawaharlal, who refused to recognise Israel in 1948 due to fear of Muslim nations and communities going against him. Thanks to Shri Narendra Modi's foreign overtures, bulk of the international community is firmly in support of Indian stand against the current Chinese threat in Doka la/Doklam. FDI is at record high. We are ahead of China in this respect.

- **Fighting Corruption, Communalism, Inefficiency and Unclean Surroundings:** As per World Economic Forum before Shri Narendra Modi took over, India was ranked much below China in corruption. In fact, India was one of the most corrupt nations (ranked at 122 or so). Recent publication by World Economic Forum has placed India much ahead of China. We are now in 70s. The PM has openly declared to throw out communalism on the eve of commemoration of Quit India celebration. For the first time in the history of independent India, a PM has got after inefficient and corrupt IAS and other public service officers. Without making much fuss about the whole issues, a large number of these officers have been removed, their appraisal system has been made 360 degrees and completely transparent. An efficient bureaucracy adds to the national security.

- **Developing Infrastructure in the North-East:** It is another first in the history of independent India that the government has taken an exceptionally bold initiative in developing the road and related infrastructure in the North-East – especially in Arunachal Pradesh – a state along the India-China border. Since China lays claims on Arunachal Pradesh and declares this a disputed area, no other previous government had the courage of building major infrastructure in this state. Arunachal Pradesh not only has major roads, advanced landing ground, but also has major defence logistic bases to support major military operations should the need arise. India had to wait for a Prime Minister like Shri Narendra Modi to restore the Indian pride in the far East Indian state. It may be pertinent to note here that the late Jawaharlal Nehru was ready to write off Arunachal Pradesh at the height of 1962 war!
- **Equipping and Empowering the Defence Forces:** India under the late Jawaharlal Nehru, the first Prime Minister of independent India (ruled from 1947 to 1964 – for seventeen years), adopted a policy of massive public sector undertaking for making defense equipment. The Ordnance Factory, DRDO and other public sector companies were entrusted with the task of modernising Indian defense equipment and war material. These establishments became epitome of inefficiency, corruption and bled the Indian exchequer, while the defence forces suffered outdated equipment and continued deficiencies. The bureaucrats and politicians established a nexus, which kept the arms import bill and related

kickbacks very high and increasing every year. Thus, while the defence forces suffered critical deficiencies (even during war), the political leaders including one of the late Prime Ministers and his relatives made huge amount of money through kickbacks. The private sector was kept away from defense production. The service chiefs had very inadequate financial powers. Prime Minister Narendra Modi changed all these. First, the Services (Vice Chiefs) have been given unlimited financial powers to make up deficiencies. Private sector is now involved in manufacturing missiles, guns, armoured fighting vehicles, battleships, and so on. It must be noted here that almost all the developed countries depend very heavily on the private sector for all defense needs. It is very realistic to expect that during the next five to ten years, the defense forces will get most modern weapon systems and support produced in India.

- **Conducting Massive Surgical Strike in PoK: A Game-Changer:** Pakistan had been aiding and abetting cross-border infiltration and terrorism with impunity for the last two-and a-half decades. The Indian response till as late as 2014 had been of containment and taking all defensive action inside its own territory. Post-May 2014, when Shri Narendra Modi became the PM, things started to change. Forces deployed along the LoC got a free hand to take operational decisions. The PM extended the hand of friendship to Pakistan like no other Indian PM had done so far (unscheduled visit to Pakistan when the Pakistani PM extended a surprise invitation). However, when the Pakistani design became more sinister (terrorist attack in Uri on the Army camp), Prime Minister Modi took the most daring strategic military action in allowing a surgical strike on the terrorist camps inside PoK. The attack was meticulously planned, aided by real-time intelligence through own satellite, conducted by elite para-commando troops. The enemy was taken by complete surprise. Casualty on terrorists and the Pak Army was very heavy. All Indian troops returned safe. Most importantly, the Indian leadership owned up the strike and did not hide from their responsibility. Pakistan was so shell-shocked that the political and military leadership was unable to accept that the strike was actually conducted. In one stroke, Prime Minister of India conveyed to Pakistan and the international community that the political establishment in India was not what it used to be for the last 70 years. The resolve of political leadership, when it comes to national security, will like a sledge hammer hitting deep inside the enemy psyche. Pakistan has not recovered from the effect of surgical strike so far.

- **Standing up to Chinese Hegemony:** The Indian response to Chinese hegemony in Doka La/Doklam also depicts Shri Narendra Modi's unique personality and clarity of mind. To start with, he hosted the Chinese President in India with his trademark warmth and friendship. He also endeavoured to engage China in bilateral trade and openly praised Chinese economic and industrial growth. At the same time, the infrastructure projects in Arunachal Pradesh were being implemented with an exceptional speed and clarity. This included roads, ALGs, logistic bases, information infrastructure, etc. The mountain strike corps was raised in addition to the three existing corps in the East (3, 4, and 33). Brahmos missiles and multi-role fighter aircraft were deployed. Artillery was strengthened. When Chinese tried to extend the Indo-Bhutan-China tri-junction to the South, closer to the Silliguri corridor, the Indian Army acted quickly and resolutely in pushing the Chinese back and holding position to thwart any future adventure. Since then, India has not blinked. The Malabar Naval exercise in the Bay of Bengal by the mighty Navies of the US, Japan and India checked the Chinese Navy in the region. Operationally, India is in a much stronger position in East and North Sikkim to foil any ingress by the PLA. It is not like 1962. The troops are sufficient, well-equipped and armed. Their logistic bases are well-connected and well-supplied. All the three Services are infused with high morale. There is no political interference by the political leadership in military matters. The Army, the Navy and the Air Force have full support from the political leadership.

- **Implementation of 'One Rank-One Pension-Removing' the Dichotomy in Seventh Pay Commission for the Defense Forces:** It is a time-tested fact that victory in war depends on the 'man behind the gun'. Shri Narendra Modi has taken a number of epoch-making initiatives in this field. First, the long outstanding demand of 'One Rank-One Pay' was met. No other Prime Minister could have done this, given the resistance imposed by the bureaucracy. Second, the anomalies in the seventh pay commission were also removed with active intervention of the PMO.

Conclusion

It is quite evident that since Independence, the political leadership had not addressed national security issue with sincerity and firm resolve. Most of the top leadership was driven by narrow, personal and political agenda. At times, they were downright corrupt. Owing to this the national security apparatus and the environment suffered a lot.

This has changed with Prime Minister Modi occupying the centre stage. He has commenced a process, which will pave the way for a strong India, full of happy and proud people. At the same time, our traditional and future enemies will be kept at bay by the Indian military and economic strength coupled with international reputation. India is on her way to the golden age under Shri Narendra Modi.

—Brig Dr. Ashok Pathak

16
Role of Judiciary in Good Governance

Democracy runs on the set rules of governance. Indian system of democracy stands on the three definite pillars of administration, i.e., the judiciary, the executive and the legislature. When the Constitution of India was enacted, the principle of separation of powers was impliedly incorporated so that all the organs may work freely as the master of its own sphere but check and balances were also provided in it to avoid any encroachments in the realm of others. Amongst three organs, judiciary has been given onerous task not only of adjudication but also of acting as the interpreter and guardian of the Constitution and to keep all the organs within its legitimate bounds and precincts judiciary has to put a lot of efforts. It has been nearly six decades that we inherited a well-entrenched system of judicial administration besides elaborate and codified, substantive and procedural laws from Britishers. These laws had generally stood the test of time. Therefore, we adopted them with suitable corrections, wherever required. Over the years, we have finetuned the judicial administration so as to meet the needs of changing times and aspirations of the modern India. The concept of governance is as old as human civilisation. What is "governance"? It simply means the process of decision-making and the process, by which decisions are implemented. The quality of governance depends, on a large measure, upon the indulgence shown by subjects. Speaking on the basis of experiences of medieval period and the times of colonial rule, in particular in the continents of Africa and Asia, some political scientists would use sarcasm in describing the system of governance. One such scientist said: "The marvel of all history is the patience with which men and women submit to burdens unnecessarily laid upon them by their governments." Yet others would not mince words in describing the business of governance thus: "So they (the government) go on in strange paradox, decided only to be undecided, resolved to be irresolute, adamant for drift, solid for fluidity, all powerful to be impotent." The world has come a long way since the times of such skepticism. The majority of the member States of the comity of nations today are founded on the principle of "Welfare State", run with full participation of their respective inhabitants, striving to achieve the common good and in the process, affording optimum opportunity and involvement for growth of the individual so as to subserve the societal interests. This has led to evolution of "good governance", as opposed to mere governance, as the umbrella concept encompassing within it a system of governance that is able to unequivocally discover the basic values of the society where standards concern economic, political and William H. Borah, Sir Winston Churchill, former Prime Minister of England, in an Address on 12th November, 1936 socio-cultural issues including those involving human rights, and follows the same through an accountable and upright administration.

Good governance signifies the way an administration improves the standard of living of the members of its society by creating and making available the basic amenities of life; providing its people security and the opportunity to better their lot; instill hope in their heart for a promising future; providing, on an equal and equitable basis, access to opportunities for personal growth; affording participation and capacity to influence in decision-making in public affairs; sustaining a responsive judicial system which dispenses justice on merits in a fair, unbiased and meaningful manner; and maintaining accountability and honesty in each wing or functionary of the government. As per the United Nation's Commission on Human Rights, the key attributes of good governance include transparency, responsibility, accountability, participation and responsiveness to the needs of the people. Good governance is thus linked to an enabling environment conducive to the enjoyment of human rights and promoting growth and sustainable human development. The expectation of every civil society of its government is that it would fulfill its commitments and provide an equitable atmosphere contributing to individual's growth. A government is expected to be fully accountable to its people and transparent in the use of public resources. It enforces the human rights including economic, social and cultural rights and has no place for corruption of any kind since dishonesty is anathema to economic well being as it transmits public money allocated for development unjustly into private coffers depriving the citizenry of its use for their welfare. In a nutshell, good governance entails effective participation in public policy-making, the prevalence of the rule of law and an independent judiciary, besides a system of institutional checks and balances through horizontal and vertical separation of powers, and effective oversight agencies. The views evolved in UN Economic and Social Commission for Asia & the Pacific are almost identical. It holds: "Good governance has eight major characteristics. It is participatory, consensus-oriented, accountable, transparent, responsive, effective and efficient, equitable and inclusive and follows the rule of law. It assures that corruption is minimised, the views of minorities are taken into account and that the voices of the most vulnerable in society are heard in decision-making. It is also responsive to the present and future needs of society." All these expressions convey theories pregnant with time-tested concepts. The "participation", in order to be effective, needs to be informed and organised and, therefore, depends upon the availability to the subjects "freedom of association and expression", on one hand, and existence of "an organised civil society", on the other. This necessarily is a pointer to "representative democracy". The attribute of "rule of law" inheres as prerequisite "fair legal frameworks" that are enforced impartially and particularly "full protection of human rights", especially of the vulnerable sections of the society. The factor of "transparency" requires that information is freely available and the decisions are taken or enforced in a manner that adheres to the rules and regulations. The attribute of "responsiveness" necessitates that all public institutions and their processes strive "to serve all stake-holders within a reasonable time frame". Democracy, liberty and the rule of law together represent the troika that is universally accepted now as the index of a civil society. Democracy signifies a government of, by and for the people. The protection of individual liberties follows the notion of democracy as a natural corollary. This entails the espousal of a methodical configuration of laws by which society might be regulated and different conflicting interests can be harmonised to the fullest extent. This is why "the rule of law" is indispensable. It envisages the pre-eminence of law as opposed to anarchy or capricious dictates. It involves equal accountability of all before the law, irrespective of high or low status. Democracy has been evolved through centuries of experience amongst the people, who care for human person, dignity and rights as the best and most acceptable form of good governance. It is a concept that occasions the idea that all citizens have a right to participate in the decision-making processes that lead to adoption of policies that are applicable to the societies. It also means that there are some limits on majority of decision-making and, hence, the inevitability of certain basic 3 See Article 25 of the International Covenant on Civil and Political Rights; Article 3 of Protocol I to the European Convention on Human Rights; and Article 23 of the International American Convention on Human Rights 6 rights being protected. It rests on maintaining a necessary equilibrium between the numerous competing interests, demands, constraints and compulsions that exist in any civic society eager for development. India was founded as a democratic welfare State, which would allow equal opportunity to one and all, irrespective of caste, creed, colour, sex or any other form of discrimination; a State where everyone would have equal opportunity for personal growth and for contributing to the cause of nation. Democracy has been defined as "a government by the people, of the people and for the people". The founding fathers of modern India took this theory further by reading the expression "for the people" as indicative of the desirability to set up a governance that works "for the welfare of the people". The members of the Constituent Assembly were not only great visionaries but also architects of consummate skill and fidelity. They created a document that reflected an acute awareness on their part that it was incumbent to entrench the concept of rule of law into the Indian polity, given the possibility of conflicts of interests arising amongst various sections in a free developing society. In order for Abraham Lincoln to further the solemn resolve to constitute India into a sovereign, socialist, secular, republic that assured "the dignity of the individual" and secured for one and all not only liberty of thought, expression, belief, faith and worship and equality of status and opportunity but also justice in all its hues, parliamentary democracy was chosen as the form of government, in which the State power is divided amongst the three chief organs, namely the legislature, the executive and the judiciary. India incorporated a number of basic human rights as guaranteed fundamental rights, elaborated in every possible manner, in Part III of the Constitution. These fundamental rights go much beyond the American Bill of Rights. They did draw upon the Universal Declaration of Human Rights issued by the United Nations in 1948 but went ahead of them by incorporating alongside, in Part IV of the Constitution, certain 'Directive Principles of State Policy', which are principles that would be fundamental for "good governance" of this country. The Directive Principles have been used as fundamental principles of governance tempered by the Fundamental Rights. From Article 37, time to time, adjustments have been made in the Fundamental Rights – through legislative measures, executive action or judicial pronouncements – so as to further the object sought to be achieved by the Directive Principles. After all, the purpose of the Fundamental Rights, on the one hand, and the Directive Principles, on the other, is common, viz., to provide for an environment that can ensure dignified growth and development of each individual as a useful human being. In order to guarantee that the role of law would inure to, and for, everyone and the promises made by the Constitution would not remain merely on paper, the Constitution-makers made provisions for independence of the judiciary. The judiciary in India enjoys a very significant position since it has been made the guardian and custodian of the Constitution. It is not only a watchdog against violation of fundamental rights guaranteed under the Constitution and, thus, insulates all persons, Indians and aliens alike, against discrimination, abuse of State power, arbitrariness, etc. but borrowing the words of one of the founding fathers of the American Constitution, James Medison, I would say that the judiciary in India is "truly the only defensive armour of the country and its constitution and laws". If this armour were to be stripped of its onerous functions, it would mean, "the door is wide open for nullification, anarchy and convulsion". Liberty and equality have well survived and thrived in India due to the proactive role played by the Indian judiciary. The rule of law, one of the most significant characteristics of good governance, prevails because India has an independent judiciary that has been sustained, amongst others, because of support and assistance from an independent bar, which has been fearless in advocating the cause of the underprivileged, the cause of deprived, the cause of such sections of society as are ignorant or unable to secure their rights owing to various handicaps, an enlightened public opinion and vibrant media that keeps all the agencies of the State on their respective toes. One of the most important principles of just democratic governance is the presence of constitutional limits on the extent of government power. Such limits include periodic elections, guarantees of civil rights, and an independent judiciary, which allows citizens to seek protection of their rights and redress against government actions. These limits help make branches of government accountable to each other and to the people. An independent judiciary is important for preserving the rule of law and is, therefore, most important facet of good governance. The judicial system has an important role to play ultimately in ensuring better public governance. There may be a plethora of regulations, rules and procedures but when disputes arise, they have to be settled in a court of law. There is no area where the judgements of Supreme Court have not played a significant contribution in the governance – good governance – whether it be environment, human rights, gender justice, education, minorities, police reforms, elections or limits on constituent powers of Parliament to amend the Constitution. This is only illustrative. Indian Judiciary has been proactive and has scrupulously and over zealously guarded the rights fundamental for human existence. The scope of right to life has been enlarged so as to read within its compass the right to live with dignity, right to healthy environment, right to humane conditions of work, right to education, right to shelter and social security, right to know, right to adequate nutrition and clothing, and so on. This has been achieved by filling the vacuum in municipal law by applying, wherever necessary, international instruments governing human rights. The Supreme Court has, over the years, elaborated the scope of Fundamental Rights consistently, strenuously opposing intrusions into them by agents of the State, thereby upholding the rights and dignity of individual, in true spirit of good governance. In case after case, the Court has issued a range of commands for law enforcement, dealing with an array of aspects of executive action in general, and of police at the cutting-edge level in particular.

Some instances: (i) Reiterating the view taken in Moti Ram, the Supreme Court in Hussainara Khatoon case expressed anguish at the "travesty of justice" on account of under-trial prisoners spending extended time in custody due to unrealistic. If any illustration is required of this approach of Indian judiciary, reference can be readily made to the cases of Apparel Export Promotion Council vs. A.K. Chopra [(1999) 1 SCC 759]; Vishaka vs. State of Rajasthan [(1997) 6 SCC 241] and T.N. Godavarman Thirumalpad vs. Union of India & Ors. [(2002) 10 SCC 606]. Motiram and others vs. State of M.P. AIR 1978 SC 1594 Hussainara Khatoon and others vs. Home Secretary State of Bihar AIR 1979 SC 1360 excessive conditions of bail imposed by the magistracy or the police and issued requisite corrective guidelines, holding that "the procedure established by law" for depriving a person of life or personal liberty (Article 21) also should be "reasonable, fair and just". (ii) In Prem Shankar Shukla case, the Supreme Court found the practice of using handcuffs and fetters on prisoners violating the guarantee of basic human dignity, which is part of the constitutional culture in India and, thus, not standing the test of equality before law (Article 14), fundamental freedoms (Article 19) and the right to life and personal liberty (Article 21). It observed: "To bind a man hand and foot, fetter his limbs with hoops of steel, shuffle him along in the streets, and to stand him for hours in the courts is to torture him, defile his dignity, vulgarise society, and foul the soul of our constitutional culture." Strongly denouncing handcuffing of prisoners as a matter of routine, the Supreme Court said that to "manacle a man 9 Prem Shankar Shukla vs. Delhi Administration 1980 SCC 526 is more than to mortify him, it is to dehumanise him, and, therefore, to violate his personhood...." The rule thus laid down was reiterated in the case of Citizens for Democracy. (iii) In Icchu Devi Choraria, the Court declared that personal liberty is a most precious possession and that life without it would not be worth living. Terming it its duty to uphold the right to personal liberty, the court condemned detention of suspects without trial observing that "the power of preventive detention is a draconian power, justified only in the interest of public security and order and it is tolerated in a free society only as a necessary evil".

(iv) In Nilabati Behera case, the Supreme Court asserted the jurisdiction of the judiciary as "protector of civil liberties" under the obligation "to repair damage caused by officers of the State to fundamental rights of the citizens", holding the State responsible to pay compensation to the near and Citizens for Democracy vs. State of Assam 1995 SCC 743Icchu Devi Choraria vs. Union of India 1980 SCC 531 Nilabati Behera vs. State of Orissa 1993 SCC 746 dear ones of a person who has been deprived of life by their wrongful action, reading into Article 21 the "duty of care", which could not be denied to anyone. For this purpose, the Court referred to Article 9 (5) of the International Covenant on Civil and Political Rights, 1966, which lays down: "Anyone who has been the victim of unlawful arrest or detention shall have an enforceable right to compensation."

(v) In Joginder Kumar case, the Court ruled: "The law of arrest is one of balancing individual rights, liberties and privileges on the one hand and individual duties, obligations and responsibilities on the other, of weighing and balancing the rights, liberties of the single individual and those of individuals collectively..."

(vi) In Delhi Domestic Working Women's Forum case, the Court asserted that "speedy trial is one of the essential requisites of law" and that expeditious investigations and trial only could give meaning to the guarantee of "equal protection of law" under Article 21 of the Constitution. Joginder Kumar vs. State of UP and Others 1994 SCC 260 14 Delhi Domestic Working Women's Forum vs. Union of India and Others 1995 SCC 14.

(vii) In PUCL, the dicta in Article 17 of the International Covenant on Civil and Political Rights, 1966 was treated as part of the domestic law prohibiting "arbitrary interference with privacy, family, home or correspondence" and stipulating that everyone has the right to protection of the law against such intrusions.

(viii) In D.K. Basu case, the Court found custodial torture "a naked violation of human dignity" and ruled that law does not permit the use of third degree methods or torture on an accused person since "actions of the State must be right, just and fair, torture for extracting any kind of confession would neither be right nor just nor fair".

(ix) In Vishaka case, the Supreme Court said: "Gender equality includes protection from sexual harassment and right to work with dignity, which is a universally recognised basic human right. The common minimum requirement of this right has received global acceptance. In the absence of People's Union for Civil Liberties [PUCL] vs. Union of India and another AIR 1997 SC 568 D.K. Basu vs. State of West Bengal, AIR 1997 SC 610 Vishaka and Ors. vs. State of Rajasthan and Ors., (1997) 6 SCC 241 domestic law occupying the field, to formulate effective measures to check the evil of sexual harassment of working women at all workplaces, the contents of international conventions and norms are significant for the purpose of interpretation of the guarantee of gender equality, right to work with human dignity in Articles 14, 15, 19(1)(g) and 21 of the Constitution and the safeguards against sexual harassment implicit therein and for the formulation of guidelines to achieve this purpose.... in the absence of enacted law to provide for the effective enforcement of the basic human right of gender equality and guarantee against sexual harassment and abuse, more particularly against sexual harassment at all workplaces, guidelines and norms are hereby laid down for strict observance at all workplaces or other institutions, until a legislation is enacted for the purpose. This is done in exercise of the powers available under Article 32 for enforcement of the Fundamental Rights and it is further emphasised that this would be treated as the law declared by the Supreme Court under Article 141 of the Constitution." The aforesaid cases are only few examples from numerous judgements concerning human rights. Playing a proactive role in the matters involving environment, the judiciary in India has read the right to life enshrined in Article 21 as inclusive of right to clean environment. It has mandated to protect and improve the environment as found in a series of legislative enactments and held the State duty-bound to ensure sustainable development, where common natural resources were properties held by the government in trusteeship for the free and unimpeded use of the general public as also for the future generation. The Court has consistently expressed concern about impact of pollution on ecology in present and in future and the obligation of the State to anticipate, prevent and attach the causes of environmental degradation and the responsibility of the State to secure the health of the people, improve public health and protect and improve the environment. See M.C. Mehta vs. Union of India [(1986) 2 SCC 176]; Indian Council for Enviro-Legal Action vs. Union of India [(1996) 3 SCC 212]; Vellore Citizens' Welfare Forum vs. Union of India [(1996) 5 SCC 647]; M.C. Mehta vs. Kamal Nath, [(1997) 1 SCC 388]; S. Jagannath vs. Union of India, [(1997) 2 SCC 87]; M.C. Mehta (Taj Trapezium Matter) vs. Union of India, [(1997) 2 SCC 353]; M.C. Mehta (Calcutta Tanneries' Matter) vs. Union of India, [(1997) 2 SCC 411]; M.C. Mehta (Badkhal and Surajkund Lakes Matter) vs. Union of India [(1997) 3 SCC 715]; Bittu Sehgal vs. Union of India, [(2001) 9 SCC 181] and M.C. Mehta vs. Union of India, [(2002) 4 SCC 356]. Eighteen democratic forms of the government of the kind adopted by India depends in its success of a system of free and fair elections regulated, monitored and controlled by an independent agency. We have in position a high-powered Election Commission as an autonomous body to oversee the electoral process. The judiciary has made significant contributions through various pronouncements to plug loopholes and preclude the possibility of abuse by the candidates. I would illustrate this by just one instance. Criminalisation of politics has been one smoldering issue since it has an immediate bearing on the choice of candidates in an election and goes to the root of expectation of good governance through the elected representatives. Treating the right to vote as akin to freedom of speech and expression under Article 19(1)(a) of the Constitution and enforcing the "right to get information" as "a natural right" flowing from the concept of democracy, in the case of Association for Democratic Reforms 19, the judiciary brought about a major electoral reform by holding that a proper disclosure of the antecedents by candidates in election in a democratic society might influence intelligently the Union of India vs. Association for Democratic Reforms and Anr. (2002) 5 SCC 294. decisions made by the voters while casting their votes. Observing that casting of a vote by a misinformed and non-informed voter, or a voter having a one-sided information only, is bound to affect the democracy seriously, the Court gave various directions making it obligatory on the part of candidates at the election to furnish information about their personal profile, background, qualifications and antecedents. In the field of education and the rights of minority, there are various judgements in the last about 50 years, which have contributed immensely in both these fields. Instead of going back 50 years to the cases of Kerala Education Bill, St. Xavier College, St. Stephen College, let me only make a mention of few decisions in the last about 15 years [Mohini Jain, Unni Krishnan (leading to insertion of Article 21-A), TMA Pai, Islamic Acadamy and P.A. Inamdar (leading to insertion of Article 15(5)]. Discussion on this subject would be incomplete without a brief reference to certain decisions that led to the formation of the doctrine of 20 in Re. Kerala Education Bill, 1957. 1959 SCR 995; The Ahmedabad St. Xavier's Society & Anr. vs. State of Gujarat & Anr. (1974) 1 SCC 717; St. Stephen's College etc. etc. vs. University of Delhi etc. (1992) 1 SCC 558.21 Mohini Jain vs. State of Karnataka & Ors. (1992) 3

SCC 666; Unni Krishnan & Ors. vs. State of Andhra Pradesh & Ors. (1993) 1 SCC 645; T.M.A. Pai Foundation & Ors. vs. State of Karnataka & Ors. (2002) 8 SCC 481; Islamic Academy of Education & Anr. vs. State of Karnataka & Ors. (2003) 6 SCC 697; P.A. Inamdar & Ors. vs. State of Maharashtra & Ors. (2005) 6 SCC 537. 20 basic structure as a limit on the constituent power of the Parliament to amend the Indian Constitution. In 1952, in Sankari Prasad's case, a Constitution Bench held that any act passed by the Parliament under its amending power under Article 368 would be valid even if it abridged any of the Fundamental Rights contained in Part III of the Constitution. Again in 1964, another Constitution Bench in Sajjan Singh's case supported the views expressed in Sankari Prasad. These two cases were considered by an 11-Judge Bench in Golak Nath's case. The views expressed in Sankari Prasad and Sajjan Singh case were reversed. The Supreme Court held that fundamental rights are primordial rights necessary for development of human personality and these rights enable a man to chalk out his own life in the manner he likes best. The Bench expressed the view by majority judgement that fundamental rights are given a transcendental position under our Constitution and are kept beyond the reach of the Parliament. But, at the same time, Parts III and IV of the Constitution were held to constitute an integral scheme forming a self-contained code. The scheme is so elastic that all Sri Sankari Prasad Singh Deo vs. Union of India & State of Bihar, 1952 SCR 89 Sajjan Singh vs. State of Rajasthan (1965) 1 SCR 933 I.C. Golak Nath & Ors. vs. State of Punjab & Anr. (1967) 2 SCR 762, the Directive Principles can be reasonably enforced without abridging or abrogating the Fundamental Rights. Various constitutional amendments were made purporting to overcome the decision in Golak Nath's case. A larger Bench of 13 Judges in celebrated Kesavananda Bharati's case examined the correctness of Golak Nath's decision to determine whether the law relating to Parliament's power of amendment of Constitution had been rightly decided in Golak Nath's case or not. In Kesavananda Bharati's case, by majority, the Golak Nath's case was overruled. It was held that Article 368 does not enable the Parliament to amend the Constitution to alter the basic structure of framework of the Constitution. Implied limitations were read in Article 368. Various constitutional amendments were made after decision in Kesavananda Bharati case including 39th amendment, thereby introducing Article 329-A in the Constitution, which, inter alia, sought to exclude judicial scrutiny of election of certain Members of Parliament. The provision in clauses (4) and (5) of Article 329-A were struck down by a Constitution Bench in the case of Indira Nehru Gandhi 26 applying the His Holiness Kesavananda Bharati Sripadagalvaru vs. State of Kerala & Anr., (1973) 4 SCC 225 Smt. Indira Nehru Gandhi v. Shri Raj Narain & Anr., 1975 (Supp) SCC 1 basic structure theory. This was followed by proclamation of internal Emergency from June 1975 to March 1977, during which period, Articles 14, 19 and 21 stood suspended. Sweeping changes were also made in Article 368 with a view to providing that there shall be no limitation whatever on the constituent power of the Parliament to amend, by way of addition, variation or repeal, the provisions of the Constitution and also providing that no amendment of the Constitution including Part III thereof relating to Fundamental Rights shall be called in question on any ground. With the end of Emergency, Articles 14, 19 and 21 again became enforceable. The constitutional amendment to do away with the limitation and judicial scrutiny were struck down, inter alia, on the ground that the exclusion of judicial review would expand the amending power of the Parliament in contravention of the decision in Kesavananda Bharati's case. In Chander Kumar's case, a seven-Judge Bench held that the power of judicial review over legislative action vested in the High Courts under Article 226 and the Supreme Court under Article 32 is an integral and essential feature of the Constitution and is part of its basic structure. What is the extent of judicial review and the extent of power of the Parliament to grant immunity to a legislation by placing it in the Ninth Schedule is presently under consideration by a nine-Judges Bench. The power of the Parliament to expel its members in exercise of its power, privilege and immunity granted under Article 105 is also awaiting the decision of the Supreme Court. On the insulation of Police and other investigating agencies from any kind of external pressure, the Supreme Court issued various directions in Vineet Narain and Prakash Singh case. The paradigm of Indian judicial system is testimony to the manner in which judiciary can contribute in good governance. Indian jurisprudence would insist upon enforcement of various rights, even of persons suspected of involvement in grave crimes. The rights thus guaranteed include right to life and liberty; right against torture or inhuman degrading treatment; right against outrages upon personal dignity; right to due process and fair treatment before law; right against retrospecticity of penal law; right to all judicial guarantees as are Vineet Narain and Ors. vs. Union of India and Anr., (1998) 1 SCC 226 28 Prakash Singh and Ors. vs. Union of India and Ors., JT 2006 (12) SC 225. 24 indispensable to civilised people; right to effective means of defence when charged with a crime; right against self-incrimination; right against double jeopardy; right of presumption of innocence until proved guilty according to law; right to be tried speedily, in presence, by an impartial and regularly constituted Court; right of legal aid and advice; right of freedom of speech besides right to freedom of thought, conscience and religion. The approach of judiciary in India has time and again been that while it may be appropriate that the courts show due deference and margin of appreciation to the opinion formed by the executive, any State action making inroad into the personal liberties or basic human rights of an individual must invariably be subject to judicial scrutiny, which would rest on objective proof, relevant material in accordance to law and through a procedure that passes the muster of fairness and impartiality. It is indeed a matter of great satisfaction that the two other chief organs of the State in India have always respected the jurisdiction of the judiciary to subject every State action to "judicial review" and, therefore, have either abided by the decisions taken or taken requisite follow-up action in furtherance of such decisions. The judiciary has, thus, played a crucial role in development and evolution of society in general and in ensuring good governance by those holding reigns of power in particular. Perhaps, there can be no two views about the significance of the role expected of the judiciary vis-à-vis the goal and good governance in a free society

—Sandeep Kumar Sharma

❑

17

Changing Macro-Economic and Business Environment in India

Under Prime Minister Shri Narendra Modi: Need for Paradigm Shift in Work Culture and Skill Sets

Overall Vision Emanating from a Series of Path-Breaking Actions by the Current Government at the National and State Levels

During the last three years, since May 14, there have been major changes in strategic intent, policies and actual implementations in India. The spheres of activities include almost all segments—political, social, economic, national security and environment. It becomes very evident that the PM has a vision. He is crystal clear about what that vision implies. Most importantly, he is completely committed and devoted in his action plan for achieving the mission goals and objectives set froth by the strategic intent. Our focus in this article is to identify his vision from the actions that the Narendra Modi government has already initiated/completed. Let us first look at the actions that have already been taken and many of the projects that have been completed/nearing completion:

What Actions by the Prime Minister Depict this Vision

- **Impetus to low-cost housing:** Ambitious plans to build more than two crore houses (₹ 8 to 10 lakh) and making these affordable to the poor with EMI (180 months) less than ₹ 5000.

- **Distribution of LPG to the poorest of the poor:** More than 2.5 crore benefited from this. More poor women to be covered.
- **Direct to bank transfer through Jan Dhan accounts:** 29.33 crore accounts, 65532.77 crore balance in these accounts, 1.26 lakhs bank *mitras* delivering branchless services in subservice areas.
- Free insurance benefits (₹ 1 lakh) on zero balance as also ₹ 5000 overdraft facility after six months of maintaining the accounts.
- Crop insurance for the farmers.
- **Major infra development:**
    - **Sagarmala Project:** ₹ 12,00,000 crore project for transporting goods quickly and efficiently from all the ports.
    - **Bharatmala Project:** 5000 kms of road in five years from Gujarat to Mizoram as also in coastal areas of Maharashtra, West Bengal.
    - **Mumbai Trans-Harbour Link:** 22.5 kms sea bridge.
    - **Arunachal Pradesh on the Rail Map:** Longest rail bridge over river. 4.95 kms over Brahamputra linking Arunachal Pradesh to the rest of the world.
    - **Setu Bhartanam:** Reconstruction of 1500 bridges built during the British period.
    - **Rashtriya Rajmarg:** Connecting 100 of the 676 districts by 6600 kms modern roads by 2019.
    - **Inland water ways:** ₹ 4,000 crore on the Ganga and ₹ 50,000 crore for making Paradeep port.

  - **Gujrat Gorakhpur Pipeline:** 1987 kms pipeline to transport 3.75 million tonnes of LPG from Kandla to Gorakhpur via Ahmedabad, Ujjain, Bhopal, Kanpur, Allahabad, Varanasi, Lucknow, Gorakhpur
  - Chardham Project
  - Highest Bridge over Chenab
- Technology in support of farmers (soil testing, water conservation in agriculture, IT infrastructure, etc.).
- Voluntary declaration of cutting carbon footprint in the world forum. Reducing coal-based power generation and increasing solar and other renewable sources-based generation.
- Demonetisation, implementation of GST, insolvency law, encouraging digital transaction, curbing cash transaction, using Big Data analytics to nab fraudsters and tax evaders.
- Clamping-down on shell companies and cleaning up the financial mess.
- Stipend for researchers in IITs has been increased to ₹ 70,000/- per month from mere Rs 25000/- per month.

The Vision that Emanates From the Above Action Plan

Very authentic strategic intent that emanates from the ground reality highlights unmistakable components of national vision for this government:

- Development across all sections of society irrespective of cast, creed, gender, region or linguistic differences. In simple terms, major initiative to uplift the living conditions of the poor and the downtrodden.
- Growth in harmony with mother nature.

- Honesty, efficiency, beneficial to nation, transparency, outcome-oriented approach in all public and private dealings.
- Stringent measures to curb financial fraud, irregularities.

How we have emerged in the global macro, economic and financial environment during the last three years

Our tax-to-GDP ratio was very low compared to China and many of the developing countries. This has commenced improving post-GST and post-demonetisation. Not even 1 per cent of India pay taxes. Since most of the salaried employees pay taxes, the non-salaried people, which include many rich businesspersons, avoid paying taxes. The base is now increasing. More than one crore new tax payers have joined in.

Online Transactions

Our online transactions improved after demonetisation. However, developed nations such as Singapore, the US, Western European countries are far ahead of us, our global competitive index has steadily improved since Shri Narendra Modi took over as the Prime Minister. In fact, from 2009 till 2014, we were hovering at zero to negative growth in the Global Competitive Indices. After the new government took over in May 2014, India jumped up 16 places in 2015-16 followed by another 16 places in 2016-17.

Parameters	2015-16	2016-17
Overall ranking	55	39
Basic requirement	80	63
Infrastructure	81	68
Institution	60	42

Macro-economy environment	91	75
Health and primary education	84	85
Efficiency enhancers	58	46
Higher education and training	90	81
Goods and market efficiency	91	60
Labour market efficiency	103	84
Financial market development	53	38
Technological readiness	120	110
Market size	3	3
Innovation and sophistication	46	30
Business sophistication	52	38
innovation	42	29
***Source:* World Economic Forum, Global Competitive Indices**		

The New Paradigm, Work Culture and Skill Sets

Given the vision, plan of action and the likely trajectory of macro-economic and business environment, it is very evident that the old methods of functioning will have to change. Also it must change very fast. The new normal will entail transparency, integrity, honesty in paying taxes and disclosures, governance for the poor, technology upgradation, learning new skills. Incidentally, the way we have been making money will also change. The rent-seeking approach of earning based on licenses and quota will go. Productivity and quality will be demanded. The new generation of job-seekers needs to develop entrepreneurial approach. They need to work to ensure implementation of government policy for inclusive growth in the rural areas. In fact, inclusive growth is no more a slogan. It has become a reality.

Students in the schools will have to work hard to earn their promotion to the next class. In higher education, the standards of education, research and innovation will have to improve. Skills in IT, green energy, environmental sciences, agriculture and manufacturing will be needed. Meaningful and contextual research has been supported. Perfunctory and low-grade research will be discouraged. In fact, India is well on the way to becoming a developed nation in the next five years.

References

- Narendra Modi's top 10 signature infrastructure projects to power New India. financial express.com, 3 April 17
- Pradhan Mantri Awas Yojana— Housing for All (Urban) Credit Linked Subsidy Scheme. pib.nic.in/newsite/print Release.aspx
- All you want to know about Pradhan Mantri Awas Yojana. www.thehindubusinessline.com/opinions/column
- Pradhan Mantri Jan Dhan Accounts opened as on 31 May, 17. http://www.nabrad.org/auth/writeread data
- PM Modi's Ujjwala Scheme for poor women — a game-changer as India topples Japan as World's second largest importer of LPG. *Financial Express* online 24 April, 17
- India jumps 16 ranks in World Economic Forum Global Competitiveness index — thanks to PM Modi's reforms and cheap oil. Dinesh Unnikrisnan. First Post, 24 August, 2017.

—Ramesh Pathak

18
Towards a Women-Led Resurgent India

The word 'women' bears within itself the word 'men', signifying that a single being is capable of containing and completing a universe. In other words, the completion of this universe is unachievable without the complete and wholesome development of women. This ethos perhaps underpins Narendra Modiji's vision for women in a new, fearless and progressive India.

India is a land of dichotomies, which are coexisting and embracing the opportunities that a globalised world presents. This is especially witnessed in the case of our urban women versus their rural counterparts, when we consider their challenges encountered, rights enjoyed or empowerment experienced. The urban woman gets the required ecosystem to boost her education and independence and is increasingly becoming a significant provider and decision-maker in her family. At the same time, a remarkable section of rural women are still fighting social maladies such as female foeticide and struggling for their basic rights, which most of the time they are unaware of due to insufficient opportunities for or denial of education. On the other hand, certain essentially urban issues such as equality of pay, gender diversity in government and business, maternity benefits, etc. may be hard for the rural women to identify with.

Modiji's government has understood this unique dichotomy of our country's female population and the fact that policies for India's women can never be a straight jacket, otherwise we may risk the benefits not reaching the ones that actually need them. This is something that we have seen in the past administrations, where many measures have not percolated beyond the urban areas or have been misused by the privileged. In the last three years, Modiji and his team of administrators have studied the key issues, facing the Indian women and have made some grassroots level changes to impact the same.

When we think of rural women of India, they have been marginalised for ages when it comes to education, nutrition and opportunities. Modiji has a vision of a woman-led development in India and, therefore, his efforts are directed towards first and foremost changing the way Indians perceive a girl child. Through the 'Beti Bachao, Beti Padhao' initiative, Modiji has not only spread awareness about the worthiness of a girl child, but also made provisions to make her an educated and independent citizen. This thought process of perceiving the girl child as an asset to the family was further bolstered through the very popular campaign titled 'Selfie with daughter', which asked fathers to show off their pride – their daughters through a selfie. In 2017, a 'selfie with daughter' mobile app was launched to raise awareness and become a beacon of hope against sex selection and female foeticide.

Similarly, the Sukanya Samriddhi Yojana is aimed at removing the notion that a girl child is a burden. Through this initiative, a small regular deposit can be made in the name of the girl child until the 10th year of her life by her parent/guardian, which will go a long way in meeting her education and other expenses. Another initiative, titled the PM Jan Dhan Yojana, although was not originally targeted at women, has been observed to have the largest female beneficiaries. This initiative is aimed at easing the process of opening bank accounts for the poor and as per the latest reports, 70 per cent of the account-holders under this scheme have been women. This has significantly increased their financial independence and ensured them a secured future.

A large section of rural women still lack basic sanitation facilities and have to defecate in the open, thus exposing them to discrimination, discomfort, diseases as well as harassment. Therefore, under the 'Swachh Bharat Abhiyan', Modiji has addressed this issue and pledged to build significant number of toilets by 2019. In line with ensuring good health of women, the PM Ujjwala Yojana aims at providing clean cooking fuel. Five crore LPG connections will be provided in the name of women from BPL families so that they do not have to rely on traditional firewood, coal, etc., which have the risk of smoke and fire hazards.

Another novel initiative to be soon launched is aimed at increasing mobility and empowering rural women in backward blocks of the country. The PM Gramin Parivahan Yojana provides them a safe mode of transport in areas, where public transport is unavailable. Interest-free loans will be given to women SHGs to buy 10-12-seater vehicles and also impart driving training to women drivers. As a result, rural women can be mobile, can conduct their business beyond their own village, take farm produce to different local markets and reach towards the global market.

In addition to these initiatives, many others, such as PM Dhana Lakshmi Yojana (for foreign education of girls), Mahila Kisan Sashaktikaran Pariyojana (boost for females in agriculture), etc., have also been laid out.

The above-mentioned programmes have been crafted keeping primarily the rural women in mind, but the semi-urban and urban women have also enjoyed many of their benefits. However, not one to sideline the key issues faced by urban working women, Modiji has taken some noteworthy steps for them too. Today's modern woman is someone who wants to take her destiny in her own hands. To catalyse this trend, there has been a thrust on developing her entrepreneurial spirit by Modiji through the Pradhan Mantri Mudra Yojana and the Stand Up India scheme. Under these two schemes, women have been the biggest beneficiaries of small, and large-scale loans to start and manage their own business, thus empowering them like never before. Under the PMMY, in the year 2016-17, loans to the tune of ₹ 1.8 lakh were disbursed, out of which 70 per cent have been women beneficiaries. Under the Stand Up India scheme, it is mandatory for every bank branch to give a loan to a woman entrepreneur within the range of Rs 10 lakh to 1 crore.

Further, to ensure that an independent working woman is able to strike the balance between work and family, Modiji has provided a much-needed support through enhancement of the Maternity Benefits Programme. Now, a new mother will receive monetary help to the tune of ₹ 6000 to cover antenatal and postnatal expenses. Noteworthy is that this money will now be transferred directly to the account of the beneficiary, thus making the process completely hassle-free. Another huge step taken by Modiji is the increase of maternity leave from 12 to 26 weeks, which is more than what women enjoy in some of the developed countries such as the UK, Japan, South Korea, etc. This will encourage working women to start families, aid recovery of the mother post delivery, make better bonding between mother and child and enable longer breastfeeding thus, enhancing health of the baby.

In conclusion, Modiji's vision for the Indian woman goes beyond that of a welfare receiver to being a key contributor to the growing Indian economy. His policies give an impetus to the Indian woman to be independent, enterprising, healthy and secure. This thought process is also reflected in his own administrative team, which has the largest number of women cabinet ministers holding important portfolios and who are shining examples of what '*nari shakti*' can achieve, thus inspiring millions of young women to rise above the ordinary and take their destinies in their own hands. Going ahead, we hope Modiji's perspective becomes the norm for all Indians when they view women of new India.

—Surama Padhy

❒

19
Narendra Modi: Visionary Plans of Women Empowerment

A nation, whose leader believes in the parity of women, actualises empowerment of women. India's honourable Prime Minister Narendra Modi advocates, encourages and provides platforms for growth and development to women in all sectors. In the global purview of feminism and women empowerment over the decades, women in India are excelling in many fields. From the Modi government, philosophy of the path towards women empowerment, to Narendra Modi's resounding slogans, each action taken for the betterment of women is a long-term swing in changing the deep-rooted patriarchal mindset of India. Women are termed 'daughters', 'wives' and 'mothers' by Modi, keeping the light of our cultural values burning in the fast-tracked world of capitalism. Thoughts create action, this deep understanding of the human psyche is a futuristic and visionary permanent end to the cyclical pattern of women subjugation.

Recently, the Indian women's cricket team was one match away from victory, a proud Mr. Modi called them the "daughters" of our nation. He expressed pride of the many battles they won on the field and in their personal lives, and encouraged them to continue in their endeavour. He further stated that they "won the hearts of 1.25 billion Indians". These women are the epitome of the meaning 'doing a man's job', and Narendra Modi believes: "A woman, a mother holds the highest position, highest regard in our country. Women are two steps ahead of men. We need to recognise their power." Complimenting and serenading women is the tip of the iceberg, and our Premier has done much more than assuage women verbatim.

Article 15(3) of the Indian Constitution states that there should be provisions for the positive discrimination of women, the central thought held is against the post-invasion patriarchal culture of women's subjugation and the debilitating after effect of under privilege. Yet negative discrimination against women tends to don the mask of various social evils, one of them being discrimination against female divorcees. A pivotal positive discrimination brought by Prime Minister Modi is that a woman need not show her marriage or divorce certificate to make a passport, he provided a choice to name the mother or father in the passport. The Supreme Court ruled that in the absence of a father, the mother would have sole custody of the child, stating the name of the father in school certificates, birth certificates et al., will not be compulsory. The Modi government accepted this with open arms, as it is an unnecessary evil and negative reminder to a single mother and a child, which creates many hurdles. In the same way, the Modi government opposes triple *talaq* and stands by Muslim women in the fight for its abolition. The belief he follows is that women need to be respected and treated right, and their religion or background should not be an excuse for disrespect, that we as people should not be blind-sided by prejudice.

Schemes for women, who struggle to earn a daily meal, who have limited access to health care and lack knowledge about sanitation, have been smartly implemented by the Ministry of Women and Child Development (MWCD) under Modi's rule. One such example is the Maternity Benefits (MB) Act, which caters to women in the organised sector, and which provides a total of ₹ 6,000 before, during and after the live delivery of her first child. Yet the method to avail the said amount is by systematic registration and regular health care check-ups by the mother, this strategy provides a two-pronged solution. First, the mother will take care of all medical and hygiene-related issues to ensure the healthy birth of the child, and second, female foeticide could be impeded. The scheme curbs issues related to malnourishment of the infant. In the past, the primary focus was on the welfare of a child, but the welfare of a mother ensures the healthy upbringing of children. Instead of only focussing on a child after her/his birth, to ensure that the infant is nourished while in the mother's womb is a more effective strategy. As we look back at the Ministerial ruling in Gujarat, Narendra Modi ensured that two lakh pregnant mothers were provided safe delivery through sound medical procedures by providing an emergency number, as a serious concern during childbirth is mother mortality.

Starting the path of care from the conception of a child, Narendra Modi covers the care of women in all ages. His famous slogan – 'Beti Bachao, Beti Padhao', which is for the girl child, resonates from every television and can be read on billboards. It is testimony to BJP's first step in their core empowerment philosophy. Their philosophy first and foremost targets education for the girl child or 'Beti Padhao'. On International Women's Day, Narendra Modi stated that all the gifts he received were auctioned and the proceeds were collected for the education of girls. In Gujarat, 1.5

crore children were protected through the Child Health and Protection Scheme, which follows the second core philosophy 'knowledge about health and nutrition' or 'Beti Bachao'. Keeping in mind the high female foeticide rate in India and law banning the same, Modi reiterated: "Girls are aborted inside a mother's womb. We should not differentiate between sons and daughters".

While combating social evils of the past, Mr. Modi has created platforms to create digital empowerment. We are well aware of the fact that Mr. Modi is a tech-savvy person. With frequent updates on Twitter, a blog post and podcasts, his vision for India is to encourage each individual to have technological know-how. Upgrading skills, the second core philosophy, enables women to procure a job and earn a livelihood. Modi's progressive attitude saw the creation of 'Skill India' vision and launched the 'National Skill Development Mission'. Maneka Gandhi started 'Mahila E-Haat' as a part of Modi's 'Stand Up India', 'Digital India' initiatives. In the Union Budget announced by Arun Jaitley, SWAYAM Platforms Foundation was laid to motivate young girls towards digital learning free of cost, which bridges the gap between knowledge and economy.

The next core philosophy is financial support, testimony of which is seen by the Pradhan Mantri Mudra Yojana (PMMY), which Modi stated "promotes entrepreneurship and turns job seekers into job creators, and 70 per cent beneficiaries were women". Financial empowerment the second last core philosophy is followed by Modi's belief that women empowerment initiatives are an 'investment'. Pradhan Mantri Jan Dhan Yojana is for people who don't have a bank account, and most of the people who availed the services are women. Also Pradhan Mantri Awas Yojana

Gramin has increased allocation of investment which will increase financial security of women as houses in this scheme are primarily in the name of women.

"I don't agree with westerners' view that in India, women are good as housewives. It's our role as a part of this society to promote and give power to women," says Modi. There are some obvious differences between a man and a woman, a man might be more able to exude brute force in completing a task that requires a great amount of physical stamina. Yet during the 2015 Republic Day Parade, where Barack Obama was the chief guest, each of the three Services giving the guard of honour was commanded by a woman. No small feat as it requires a great amount of physical strength, these women broke the shackles of biological stereotype. On the other hand, through evolutionary psychology, women have garnered the strength of multi-tasking. Multi-tasking is a specialty in the managerial world, on which numerous studies have proven its feasibility. This ability could be a factor contributing to a higher success ratio despite fewer opportunities in comparison to men. According to Modi, Indian women are the best on the earth in handling numerous tasks at a time, as they have been multi-tasking for ages and their efforts have contributed a lot in the development of our nation.

Modi has struck at the very core of patriarchy. As a visionary, he has understood and implemented a concept that brings true empowerment of women in terms of thinking. As he has correctly stated: "I want to ask parents, when daughters turn 11 or 14, they keep a tab on their movements. Parents must take the responsibility to ensure that their sons don't go the wrong direction." Once this rigid thought process is changed, much can be achieved in terms of overall progressive development of women. His clever and futuristic development-centered schemes, appropriation of funding, and 'investments' into women empowerment will continue for a long time. It is certain that even after his reign ends as the Prime Minister, women will continue to reap the benefits of his hard work and the vision of women equality can be achieved.

—Lalita Nijhawan

❐

20
How Jihad Descended on the Paradise

Introduction

Kashmir is not just a political problem but, primarily, a holy war between Islam and infidelity. The armed struggle waged in Kashmir is not a war of national liberation but a jihad between Islam, on one hand, and the forces of *kufr* or disbelief on the other. The main objective is to liberate Kashmir from Indian control and merge it with Pakistan to establish an Islamic state in the region. As religious radicalisation is growing its influence in Kashmir, the majority of the Muslim youth is increasingly inclining towards extremist political, social and religious ideas repudiating and challenging the status quo. The present struggle is to terrorise the local population into submission to their reprehensible programme of creating a Wahhabi society in the state, and anyone, who puts a hurdle in their mission, gets annihilated. Rabidly fanatical clerics are indoctrinating the youth with Wahhabi ideology, whereby they reject the old Kashmiri tradition of people visiting and paying obeisance at the shrines of popular *sufis* and *rishis*, terming it a violation of the teachings of Islam. Post-1989, the jihadi orientation of these groups towards India heralded militancy in the Valley. Therefore, there is nothing indigenous about the Kashmir militancy. It has a geopolitical context rather than any internal facets. The idea is to establish *Shariah*, the code on which Islamic laws are based, not only in India but in the entire world.

The dispute over Kashmir has been the root cause of three of the four wars India and Pakistan have fought since gaining their Independence in August 1947. The origin of the conflict lies in the Partition of the Indian subcontinent and each nation's struggle for identity. Since Kashmir's population was seventy per cent Muslim, Pakistan believed it was rightfully a part of the state that was founded as the homeland for South Asia's Muslims. India, on the other hand, claimed to be a secular democracy and sought control over Kashmir to prove its secular credentials. Because India's leaders had fought vehemently against the idea of two nations in South Asia, Pakistan's leaders believed India's purpose in Kashmir was to disprove the two-nation theory, while simultaneously weakening Pakistan, so that it would collapse and return into the fold. Kashmir's implications for the ideological foundations of each state have made both sides unwilling to compromise. During the last three decades, the gap between them only seemed to widen as India battled insurgency in Kashmir that it asserts originates from, and is directed by, Pakistan.

Interference of Global Powers in Kashmir

Sheikh Abdullah, who opposed the two-nation theory of Muslim League, had rightly predicted that if residents of Jammu & Kashmir would seek independence, the region would become an arena of international intrigues. Britain and America tried for half a century to have either direct or indirect control over this area of the globe. The two countries wanted to checkmate the expansion of the communist ideology of the Soviet Union. The Soviet system has got consigned to history. America is now becoming inclusive and trying to use its resources for the United States while reducing its earlier plan of active interest in world affairs.

New powers are now expressing their desire to influence the governance system of Jammu and Kashmir. China says it is a stakeholder in the state's administration as its road from China to Pak Port Gwadar passes through its Pak-occupied Kashmir (PoK), in which Beijing has invested around $62 billion, despite India's concerns, with an eventual aim to interfere in Kashmir dispute under the guise of protecting its investments. India worries that China was internationally meddling in India-Pakistan disputes by utilising the China Pakistan Economic Corridor (CPEC), which runs through Pakistan-occupied Kashmir to grant legitimacy to Islamabad's control over the disputed region.

Saudi Arabia feels there is a good opportunity in Kashmir of spreading and strengthening of the Salafi System of Islam, as opposed to the preachings of Muslim *sufis* of tolerance against or for different faiths. The Islamic State of Iraq and Syria (ISIS) treats the Saudi thinking a soft version of the religion. It seeks Caliphate power in Pakistan, Afghanistan, India and Bangladesh.

Pakistan believes it should try to get the State of Jammu and Kashmir seceded from India and made a part of Pakistan. Pakistan's aggressive posturing could be on the nudging of Beijing that has heightened its stakes in PoK with the ambitious China-Pak Economic Corridor. Pakistan is also unhappy over the paradigm shift of India's policy towards Balochistan. Both Pakistan and Saudi Arabia day and night are broadcasting propaganda via 50 TV channels and other social media modes to glamourise electronic jihad, militancy and an ideological war through radicalisation of young Kashmiri minds. These two countries are pumping huge funds into the coffers of the separatist leaders to be spent on the poor youngsters of the Valley, who are assigned work aimed at destabilising the normal administration in the Valley.

Pak Obsession with Kashmir

Pakistan has been a doomed State since its very beginning. It was an artificial idea and 70 years after its creation, it finally seems to be falling to pieces. The "K" in Pakistan stands for Kashmir, but they failed to secure the Valley in 1947-48. They failed to get the Rann of Kutch by force in 1965, Siachen in 1984 and Kargil in 1999. To make matters worse, they lost East Pakistan in 1971. Pakistan has been one long saga of losses and heartbreaks. Pakistan is a "radical state", which is trying to take revenge of 1971 war when Bangladesh was liberated from Pakistan by India. Whatever is happening today in Kashmir is because of the losses suffered by Pakistan during wars with India. "What Pakistan could not achieve through the wars of 1947-48, 1965, 1971 and 1999 had to be achieved through an amalgam of subterfuge, subversion, force and religious fundamentalism" – writes Mr. Jagmohan, an ex-Governor of Jammu and Kashmir and author in his famous book "*My Frozen Turbulences in Kashmir*".

Kashmir was the only Muslim-majority state in India where Muslims influenced by Dara Shikoh's legacy not only happily co-existed with Hindus, but also adopted Sufism and looked for spiritual inspiration from other diverse sources. Pakistan, after facing a humiliating defeat in the 1971 Indo-Pak war when Bangladesh was born, again started laying her cunning eyes at Kashmir. Under its long-term strategy conceived in the year 1972, Pakistan, with the financial support from oil-producing Islamic countries, started "Wahhabi project" of radicalising of Kashmiris. The political leadership in Kashmir, knowingly or unknowingly, ignored this new nefarious role of Pakistan, which is unfolding, now. Kashmir is perhaps the oldest jihadi project in the world, predating all others in our neighbourhood and West Asia. It has gathered strength due to the sheer incompetence and cynical corruption of the ruling elite in Kashmir.

The Islamic revolution in Iran in 1979, followed by jihad in Afghanistan (1979-89) against the Soviet occupation, turned Pakistan as a launching pad of global jihadi movement. Large sums of money began pouring into Pakistan from USA and Saudi Arabia besides other oil-producing Islamic countries. Having captured power through a military coup in 1977, General Zia-ul-Haq made cosmetic changes in the existing Sharia law of Pakistan by introducing more stringent provisions to win the hearts of Pakistanis in the name of Islamisation, for which he won the wide support of Islamic parties like Jamaat-i-Islami Pakistan etc., who later were drawn into jihad and sponsored their own militant outfits. Linked to the Islamisation project, Pakistani political and non-political leaders urged Gen. Zia to pursue vigorously the Kashmir policy. As a result thereof, hundreds of Islamic seminaries or *madrasas* mushroomed all over the Kashmir Valley and Jamaat-i-Islami Jammu and Kashmir, which had remained a marginal political force in Kashmir till 1980, got revival due to kickstart money pumped from Pakistan and Saudi Arabia. So, the process of radicalisation of Kashmiri Muslim youth in the Valley was set into motion in the year 1980.

Pak ISI's Insurgency in Kashmir under "Operation Topac"

Zia-ul-Haq's obsession with Kashmir was very well known as he went on record shouting slogans "*Kashmir Banega Pakistan*" (Kashmir will become a part of Pakistan) almost in every rally organised in Pakistan. He, therefore, planned a move to prolong his rule by involving the majority community of Kashmiri Muslims without repeating the mistakes committed in 1965 when missions like the "Gibraltar" and the "Grand Slam" failed miserably due to lukewarm support from the local Kashmiri Muslims. In May 1984, Amanullah Khan, the then Chairman of Jammu and Kashmir Liberation Front (JKLF), was contacted by Lt. Gen. Akhtar Abdul Rehman, a very close confidante and advisor of President Zia, the then head of Pakistan's Inter-Services Intelligence (ISI) and the star of Pakistan's campaign against Soviets in Afghanistan, to enlist the support of JKLF in initiating insurgency in Indian Administered Jammu and Kashmir. The blueprint of meticulous political planning conceived in 1984 was unveiled in the year 1987.

Pakistan had pre-planned an operation, referred to by several names, viz. "Operation Topac", "Kashmir Plan" or "Zia Plan" for initiating terrorism and unleashing a proxy war in the State of Jammu and Kashmir with an objective of making it a part of Pakistan. "Operation Topac", a brain-child of President Zia-ul-Haq of Pakistan, had a three-phase action plan from covert support to armed insurgency in Indian-Administered Jammu and Kashmir. Under the first phase, youth from Jammu and Kashmir were to cross the de facto border (Line of Control—LoC) to seek weapon training at various training camps in Pakistan-Administered Jammu and Kashmir. During the second phase, called 'Operation Stage', the Pak-trained youth were expected to indulge in large-scale subversive activities like bomb blasts and shoot-outs creating an atmosphere of terror and demoralising the administration. The third phase, which was supposed to be the final stage of the operation, was to liberate the Muslim-majority Kashmir Valley and establish an independent Islamic state, which, at a later date, will be merged with Pakistan.

There are documentary evidences involving Pakistani-based sources, corroborating their complicity in the violence in the Kashmir Valley. JKLF, supported by the Pakistani army, established training camps in Pakistan-Administered Jammu and Kashmir with plans of weapons training for the youth from the Kashmir Valley. Heini G. Kiessling, in his book "*The ISI of Pakistan*", says: "From 1988, the ISI began to organise training camps for young militants from the Valley. At the beginning, their partner was the Jammu and Kashmir Liberation Front (JKLF), who was responsible for recruiting the fighters, while the ISI delivered training and equipment. Funding came from the Gulf region and the drug trade, and donations were collected in the mosques of Pakistan, the US and Western Europe. All this ensured the requirement and training of new young volunteers and the deployment of battle-hardened mujahideen from Afghanistan. The recruits came mainly from Punjab and NWFP, but young Muslims were also enlisted from abroad. The training camps for the volunteers from Jammu and Kashmir were located in Azad Kashmir, also called Pakistan-occupied Kashmir, an area close to the LoC and the training camps for Pakistanis and foreigners were set up in Punjab and NWFP."

Flashpoint of Insurgency in Kashmir

In 1986, G.M. Shah's government was dismissed after communal riots in South Kashmir, and a new National

Conference government was sworn in with Dr. Farooq Abdullah as the Chief Minister, after Rajiv-Farooq accord, which left the people of Kashmir Valley somewhat disillusioned and confused. They once again thought that their trust had been betrayed, which was followed by communal riots in the following year, led to the birth of a new political party, Muslim Muttahida Mahaz (Muslim United Front/MUF), a group of eleven-party alliance including Jamaat-e-Islami Jammu & Kashmir. It was formally launched to safeguard the interest of Muslims and vitalise their identity and aspirations. MUF acquired motivation from various fundamentalist groups, their focus being Islamic solidarity and restoration of religious and political rights. The traditional *sufi* culture was repugnant to its doctrine and its affiliates too began Islamising Kashmir politics. In 1987, MUF fought the elections on the identity of Muslim brotherhood, Kashmiri identity and the ideology of an Islamic state. Some observers suggest that the election was massively rigged by the Rajiv-Farooq alliance and Muslim United Front believed it received maximum votes and support compared to the National Conference that was declared the winner of the elections. The election results met with an upsurge of rage and opposition, with mass demonstration held against the Indian state for subverting the democratic process, which again resulted in strikes and incidences of violence. Then, in 1988, after arrival of Pak-trained militants in Kashmir, an armed struggle for liberation of Kashmir from Indian rule was launched.

Ethnic Cleansing

Terrorism, in the guise of Islamic jihad, made its entry in the state in the second half of 1989. By January 1990, the terrorists acting on the instructions of their Pakistani masters decided to go for ethnic cleansing of Kashmiri Pandits as the first step towards setting-up of *Nizam-e-Mustafa* (Rule of Mustafa or Muhammad) in the state. Provocative calls were being made from mosques to target Hindu men and women. These mosques were used to broadcast jihadi sermons and revolutionary songs interspersed with blood curdling shouts and shrieks to terrorise Kashmiri Pandits to flee from Kashmir. Some of the slogans used were:

Selective Kashmiri Pandits were subjected to all kinds of persecution that included brutal killings of men and rape of women followed by arson, loot and torching of their houses. The purpose of attacks was to free this soil from the minority community and also to occupy their properties and assets. The persecution became so intense that "Kashmiri Pandits" were left with no other choice than to move out of the state and this exodus led 4.50 lakh Kashmiri Pandits to become refugees in their own country, which is considered to be a sovereign, socialist, secular and democratic nation.

Both Central and state governments have failed squarely to protect the Kashmiri Pandits against Islamic terrorism. The state of Jammu and Kashmir being the only Muslim-majority state in the whole of India, the protection of minorities and their living peacefully in their homeland is crucial for India to remain as a secular democratic state. Ethnic cleansing of Kashmiri Pandits from the Kashmir valley is the failure of the Indian state to uphold its commitments to the people of India as enshrined in the Indian constitution which provides right to live with dignity and honour to every citizen irrespective of caste, creed, colour, race or religion.

Pakistan Tries to Internationalise the Kashmir Issue

Pakistan knows it fully well that Kashmir can be instigated and mishandled and then tell the world that Kashmiris are suppressed and oppressed by the security forces. Terrorists are using more and more civilians to conduct such type of activities that result in unrest in the Kashmir Valley. They torch school buildings in the hope that school-going children will be forced to say goodbye to the government schools and head towards Jamaat-e-Islami seminaries or *madrasas*, where they undergo intensive brainwashing. Intransigent political leadership in Kashmir under the Wahhabi influence is also behaving irresponsibly and, thus, adds fuel to the fire and worsens the situation.

Pseudo-seculars, liberals and leftists in India too are acting as apologists for Islamic terror. Knowing fully about the Islamic terrorism in Kashmir, they will cry wolf at non-existent threats from "saffron terror" or "Hindu terror" in India to hide the real problem of Islamic fundamentalism and rather exploit the sentiments of Kashmiris in the name of fight for justice or equality. An effort is underway in India to link Hindu groups with Taliban in Afghanistan. There is an even more sinister effort to paint Hindu Indian society as intolerant and anti-Muslim and out to deny minority rights. In international media, India is painted as aggressive Hindutva, rising Hindu intolerance in an effort to smear Indian society, to wash off the sins of Islamic radical preachers and extremists and whitewash the depredations of Islamic terrorists across the border. Pakistan army continues to abet infiltrations and cause trans-Line of Control firings to keep the country off balance and draw international mediation into the so-called dispute of Kashmir.

Solution to the Kashmir Conundrum

The jihadi militancy in the Kashmir Valley must be viewed from the prism of geopolitics, i.e., the global jihadi discourse, territorial ambition of Pakistan, and strategic imperatives of powers like China. It can, thus, be averred that jihadi militancy in Kashmir is mainly spurred by a thriving local economy subsidised by India and the Gulf countries, mainly Saudi Arabia. The Saudi brand of Islam, i.e., Wahhabism, has spread in the Valley purely on the strength of money. It is this brand of Islam that has proliferated and is providing a rich harvest of jihadis. Thus, the jihad in Kashmir cannot survive without logistical, financial and material support from Pakistan, China and Saudi Arabia.

It is, therefore, high time for India to take an offensive approach rather than being defensive in its strategy. The policy blowing hot and blowing cold doesn't help but sends mixed signals. Without framing the broad contours of Kashmir-centric policy, Kashmir problem cannot be resolved merely by embracing Kashmiris. India has to fight global jihad on its own and other powers will align and realign in this war depending on their respective strategic interests, which are anything but permanent.

The government must act with all urgency and resources at its command to address the twin cancer of radical Islamisation and mal-governance in the Valley. It must be understood that the alienation of the Valley is the culmination of the sordid saga of arrest and dismissal of CMs on dubious grounds, rigged elections, mal-governance, rampant corruption, lack of employment, steep decline in tourism, excessive use of force by security agencies and, of course, the role of Pakistan in providing funds and arms to militants to indulge in subversive activities in the Kashmir Valley. Successive governments of different political affiliations, both in New Delhi and Srinagar, have contributed to the mess we are in. We need to find out why most people in the Valley don't feel connected with the rest of the country.

There should be a concerted attempt to win over the hearts and minds of the Kashmiri youth, who have been radicalised over the years, if not decades.

India should upgrade its surveillance and intelligence gathering information to apprehend infiltrators at the porous entry points. By banning cross-border travel and trade, *hawala* routes used to fund terrorist activities and radicalisation in Kashmir should be effectively plugged. Salafi mosques and *madrasas* mushroomed over the years in the Valley to radicalise youth should be shut down and non-Kashmiri *mullahas*, *muftis*, *imams* and *khidmatgars* be asked to leave the Valley. Political and non-political leaders who support terrorism and don't accept India's Constitution must be put behind the bar indefinitely. The Government of India should launch mega skill development programmes to create employment opportunities for the unemployed youth besides involving industry captains to set up their establishments in Kashmir.

Exploit Internal Problems of Pakistan

Pakistan is an artificially created entity on a fictitious notion of religious nationalism. As a result, it has many fault lines along ethnic, cultural, linguistic, ideological and tribal lines. It is high time for India to have a comprehensive approach towards Pakistan and must leverage its economic and diplomatic powers, while using the military means. India should act in a mature manner so that Pakistan realises its folly and pays heavy price for abetting and perpetuating terrorism in Kashmir.

India must set up a separate cell at intelligence and diplomatic level with expertise on the area to exploit the visible fault lines existing in Pakistan. For example, atrocities committed by Pakistani security forces in Balochistan and

Pakistan-occupied Kashmir, Sindh exploitation, Punjabi dominance, Shia-Sunni divide, internal threat from Tehrik-e-Taliban Pakistan (TTP) and complete mismatch of Sunni religious extremists such as Lashkar-e-Jhangvi, Sipah-e-Sahaba, Taliban, Jaish-al-Adl, Al Qaida, Markaz, soft and pro-Pak Islamists like Jamaat-e-Islami, nationalist freedom fighters and the ISIS-affiliated groups.

India should also leverage its strong diplomatic clout with the US, Turkey, Saudi Arabia and other Gulf countries to choke or restrict the free flow of weapons, financial aids and charity funds coming to Pakistan, which are being used to nurture extremism and fund terrorist operations.

Conclusion

Zulfikar Ali Bhutto's declaration of a 1,000-year war with India over Kashmir or Muhammed Sayeed's dream of "*Ghazwa-e-Hind*" (Islamic barbaric war of conquering India) or Gen. Zia-ul-Haq's dream to liberate and amalgamate Kashmir with Pakistan under "Operation Topac" as well as global issues like the rise of Islamic State (ISIS), all impact the Kashmir issue. Foreign powers with vested interests will prefer to meddle in the affairs of Jammu and Kashmir. Thus, the bloodbath in Kashmir will continue to remain unabated and the ambience will become like that of Syria, Iraq or Afghanistan.

Peace will return to Kashmir only when Kashmiris realise this, else they will be part of the 1,000-year war that Bhutto had promised and wait for those many years for the chimera of independence. Kashmiri intellectuals ought to give it a thought. It is high time for media, civil society, political leadership in Delhi and Srinagar to engage and educate the youth of the Valley not to worship radicalised militants as heroes. A de-radicalisation process on war-footing should be initiated in the Kashmir Valley to save youth from getting swayed by religious fundamentalism, which deprives them of education, employment and economic opportunities.

—C.L. Shah

❐

21
Role of Ideology in Politics

The Bharatiya Janata Party, after decades of struggle, is in power at the Centre and in many states. After three decades, the BJP can boast of having ended the coalition era, the Congress is at its lowest-ever political prominence and the BJP is today ruling over two-thirds of India's population.

For the first time, the President, the Vice President and the Prime Minister have the BJP background. The BJP is in a position to impact national life in a big way. Since 2014, Indian politics has witnessed a tectonic shift from the Congress brand of green to the BJP's saffron. Here the role of the BJP's ideology in national life and policies is of utmost relevance.

It is important also because in the fast-changing political situation after the BJP emerged as the central ideological pole in the country, a peculiar kind of tendency to oppose the BJP by certain parties even sacrificing their own core ideology has come to be practised. This is seen in the Parliament. In the recent assembly polls in Kerala, the Congress joined hands with Marxists, though they are the main rivals, only to defeat BJP in constituencies where it had good chance. The same happened in West Bengal to defeat BJP and Trinamool Congress, though both are ideologically poles apart. The grand alliance was in Bihar where the sworn enemies Lalu and Nitish joined hands with the sole purpose of defeating the BJP.

The jihadi ISIS violence in various parts of the world is an occasion for a comprehensive assessment of political ideology. Equally important are the happenings in Europe, where the Brexit vote has come to threaten European Unity, which has strengthened the idea of nation states and weakened globalisation drive started after the fall of Soviet Union in 1989. To understand the subject, one needs to turn to the basic question – what is ideology?

The Oxford Dictionary meaning of ideology is a system of ideas or principles forming the basis of economic or political theory. The set of beliefs held by a particular group is also called ideology. And what is politics? It is defined as activities relating to government or public affairs of a country. That means we are discussing the guiding principles of our daily political behaviour. There are people in politics, who believe that there is no need of ideology to succeed in politics. There are others, for whom ideology is only a façade. There are some for whom ideology is everything. Where does BJP stand? What is its ideology? How relevant is it in today's context when the world is undergoing a great churning with the clear failure of Communism and the established inadequacies of globalisation and the intense desire to redefine the architecture of world economic order?

Francis Fukuyama, one of the leading political thinkers of today after the fall of Communism, wrote about the End of History. What he meant was the emerging homogeneity in political discourse after the end of cold war and the unipolarity of world power axis with the US dominating world. In his recent book, *Political Order Political Decay*,

Fukuyama has turned his earlier theory on its head and accepts the world has become multipolar, there are many stakeholders, many success stories, emerging world powers, democracies and dictatorships, collapsing regimes and fascinating democratic experiments. How do societies develop strong, impersonal and accountable political institutions? From French Revolution to Arab Spring to deep dysfunctions of contemporary American politics and Asian successes, Fukuyama credits India as a successful democracy. The rising global middle class, entrenched political paralysis of the West and civil disorder are some of the major concerns he highlights and believes that societies decay because of corruption.

Look at this in the context of the big success India has achieved in fighting corruption under Narendra Modi. And the nation successfully overcame the political and economic policy paralysis inherited from the UPA. A number of studies in recent times have indicated a decline in the West and the fact that India is a global bright spot. We often claim that this century belongs to us. Any ideology has to be analysed in this global perspective. What is unique about the BJP ideology that has stood the test of time? From just two seats in 1980 to 274 seats in 2014, what is the inspiration that sustained it all these years? The most unique aspect of this political thought is that for us, it is not a goal in itself. Atalji often used to say, "*Rajniti hamare liye ek sadhan hai, sadhyaa nahi.*" Not an end in itself. When the BJP was formed in 1980, Advaniji used to say the aim was to emerge as a stable ideological pole in Indian polity. Back then, to become the ruling party was only a distant dream. In 1989, when V.P. Singh formed the government, the BJP was the second pillar along with the Left holding it afloat. Now where is the Left? Insignificant and in the lap of the Congress.

From the supporting role, by 1998 under Atalji, BJP was running the government at the head of the NDA. The BJP grew convincing the Indian voter – we are sincere, we are different and we have a goal to fulfill. Our ultimate goal and ideology is in a single word '*param vaibhav*' of our motherland. What are the aspects of this '*param vaibhav*?' Is an ideology needed to achieve this goal? Is it practical in electoral politics? Will there be compromises? Is it possible without compromise? Some cite the example of PDP-BJP pact in Jammu and Kashmir to buttress this aspect.

Ideology has to be understood in the global and national context. It has a historic perspective. One cannot import or transplant ideologies. One cannot even borrow or hybrid ideologies. The failure of Communists in India and the Swatantra Party in the seventies are best examples of this. Any ideology to succeed has to have the fragrance of the native soil. It has to grow out of the collective cultural synthesis of the nation.

The benchmark of the western ideological thought is the French Revolution (1789), which firmly established the idea of democracy, equality, fraternity and liberty. It was inspired by Plato, Aristotle writings and Rousseu, Voltaire and Montesquieu. All the contemporary and latter revolutions in the West were also inspired by the same thought. The American revolution of 1783 was inspired by the same values as that of the French Revolution. Likewise, the Russian revolution of 1917, though inspired by Marx and Lenin, also had the echo of the French Revolution. All of them placed Christian values at their core. Like Arab Spring, all the turbulences in West Asia are influenced by Islamic thoughts.

Indian political ideology is shaped by the freedom movement. The values espoused in the freedom movement continue to inspire our politics even today. Like in Europe and the US, where the political struggles were inspired by Christian values, the Indian freedom movement was inspired by the Hindu spiritual thoughts of the Gita. A large number of studies have established how Tilak, Gandhi, Aurobindo, Madan Mohan Malaviya, Netaji and other leading lights of the freedom struggle were inspired by the Gita and Swami Vivekananda. There was also a spiritual side to this national movement.

The life of Tilak, Gandhi and other leaders of early Congress was spiritual. India is the only country that upholds dharma at the core of its political thought. This has grown over thousands of years in the teachings of Yoga Vashist, Sukra Niti, Vidur Niti, Gita and Yudhisthir Niti all in the Mahabharata and Arthashastra of Chanakya and Kalidasa in modern times. It is this collective wisdom which Deendayalji codified in the *Ekatma Manav Darshan* which conceived Antyodaya as the BJP's economic goal.

This is fundamentally different from Western thought. The West thinks of the maximum good of the maximum number. In India, we aspire for the emancipation of the last man in the queue. It is in this background we have to see contemporary politics and ideology in that context.

"We will not compromise on our ideology" – this is a qualifying statement with every party. But much has changed after globalisation, the fall of communism across the globe and the end of Congress party dominance in Indian polity. In the nineties, the CPI (M) leader Shri E.M.S. Namboodiripad discovered political untouchability in the name of secularism as his new credo. This was convenient to court the decimating Congress and to keep the emerging BJP on the sidelines.

Keeping BJP out is a ploy that works even today. The UPA popularised and promoted secularism as minorityism as its new existential ethics. Vajpayee often described the BJP's secularism as positive. He proved the most successful mastermind of coalition politics, sewing up as many as 22 parties to run the NDA government for six years. Such integration of the body politic through critical 'interest blocs' into major economic interests, as they say in the US, cannot be a long-term strategy. In a way, the relevance that the Left gained after the 2004 general election was mainly because of the Congress strategic folly. And it was short-lived. Even in Kerala this year, CPM won because of Congress failure.

It was Mark Hanna in the last century in the US who propounded politics without ideology. According to Peter F. Drucker, he deflected American politics away from ideology. Hanna laid the intellectual foundation to create the organisation needed to convert his 'political concepts into political performance'. He said it was not ideology but performance that mattered. Now Trump is working on similar premises. Hanna had recreated the Republican Party.

Respectable politics is ideological politics. Political scientists insist that respectable politics must deal with issues rather than with performance. "But whatever has worked in American politics for almost a century has been based on Mark Hanna's economic interests and their political integration. They immediately gave victory and power," wrote famous political philosopher, Peter Drucker.

By the turn of the 21st century, this trend got reversed and both in Europe and the US, as Drucker emphasised, philosophical synthesis, common culture and nationalism began to dominate political discourse and ideology became fashionable. The Brexit aftermath, as cited earlier, reinforced this.

The parties that look at politics from the spectrum of power have very little use for ideology. This is true of most regional parties. So, they can make and break alliances opportunistically. In 1996, Congress and Communists together installed Deve Gowda first and then I.K. Gujral to keep the BJP out. No ideology was involved here. There is always a debate in certain quarters that political integration through economic promise of prosperity, as against political ideology, can work better. Perhaps we have seen the apogee of this idea in the UPA-1 when Left was in the company of Congress. But the nuclear deal split them. Now they are again together to stop BJP. These are what are known as opportunistic adjustments. The communists standing with their ideological label have almost ceased to matter in most societies, while we have witnessed world over leaders claiming political successes through anti-ideological interest bloc integration. These leaders did not pay the slightest attention to the ideological manifestoes of their own parties. Unity based on common economic interests works in the short run. But the empowering of these groups changes the format of the political mosaic faster than one would expect. This creates the search for a more enduring adhesive. What works in the long run to give substance and mass involvement to political action is culture, as the more recent trends indicate.

The Brexit, for instance, highlighted again the role of ideology in canvassing for votes. Nationalism along with culture is another plank getting renewed currency in the West. This is the reverse of what is happening in India. In parties such as Congress, RJD, Samajwadi Party, or even regional formations such as DMK, Trinamool, etc., the ideology is the position the leader takes. Be it Sonia Gandhi or Lalu Yadav, the policy is what the leader at a particular point of time finds convenient and politically rewarding.

Only the BJP, as of now, can be qualified as ideology-driven political formation. Some leaders believe that ideology is dispensable and that it has nothing to do in practical politics. In cadre-based parties, normally ideologies take precedence over political convenience. And the decision-making is through collective inner-party deliberations.

In this context, what Dattopant Thengadi, the late RSS thinker, used to say is relevant. He used to categorise politicians in three segments. One is pure and simple idealist. He, such a pure and simple idealist, has practically no interest in politics. For him, power had no charm and he works in society unmindful of consequences because of his faith in the ultimate victory. There is a second category who are pure and simple politicians. This segment we see in plenty today. They are also not worried about ideology because they are in power for selfish reasons. They will do anything for power as we witnessed last week in Arunachal and Uttarakhand. They are everywhere. A third lot, according to Thengadiji, is essentially a politician, incidentally an idealist. For such politicians, ideology is a matter of popularity, fashionable, perhaps politically rewarding too. So, like a headgear, they wear ideology whenever it suits them. These people are also least bothered about ideology.

The only one set of politicians, the fourth category, who are essentially idealist and incidentally a politician – they are nation-builders – ideology is important. They have their base rules. They won't easily compromise. They hold their values high. They are in politics to promote their ideology. They are not ruffled by successes and failures. It is with this mettle BJP workers are made. So, we bounced back like Phoenix from the ashes from two to 274. Ideology is for this category of politicians.

Some political practitioners say that for the party to grow, it has to move out of its traditional constituency. This feeling is backed by an analysis that the very purpose of the party is to grab power. In this pursuit, ideology is a hindrance.

The BJP is not like the Congress. The Congress abandoned democracy in 1975 to stay in power and imposed Emergency. Over the years, it abandoned the values that inspired the fight for freedom. It forgot swadeshi and Gandhiji and mortgaged the party to a family. This, friends, is crass opportunism. A political party grows by creating a constituency of its own. It has to establish its raison d'etre, it has to have a committed electoral base, and on top of that, attract the floating vote in order to win an election.

The BJP has been able to win such a big victory because of the strength and credibility of its ideology. The ideology could be convincingly sold to the electorate because of the huge credibility Narendra Modi enjoyed. We have fundamentally changed the grammar of politics. The BJP campaign so far has been about branding our core values of democracy, cultural nationalism, equity, unity and "*sabka saath, sabka vikas*". I will briefly list the big impact we made in the political discourse in the country.

During the peak of the Anna movement in 2011, politicians were lampooned as a bunch of arrogant, corrupt and sartorial elite who cornered all pelf and privileges for their flashy lifestyle. Narendra Modiji changed all that. He set rigorous high standards for himself. The craze for entitlements found no place in Modiji's scheme. For him, being in public life is a mission. This restored people's faith in the leadership.

Modiji followed up words with matching action. It was his performance in Gujarat that built his credibility and won him the Lok Sabha mandate. His innovative approach has forced conventional politics stand on its head. Modiji changed the idiom of the discourse in such a way that conventional politicians looked perplexed. They looked out of sync with their hackneyed ideas of caste, clan, language and chauvinism. That is why, the caste politics of the INLD failed to enthuse the voter in Haryana. Modiji factored in the demographic change and cosmopolitanism to redefine and refine the ways politics is practised. Thus, he changed at least seven political habits so far considered passé in the electoral dynamics.

Modiji's charismatic appeal revived the carnival of mass rallies in poll campaign. Rebuilding India as a modern superpower was his theme. The message of '*Ek Bharat, shreshth Bharat*' established an instant connect with the aspirational youngsters looking for opportunities. Faced with this message, the opposition harangue anchored on communal and caste card fell flat. For long, the Indian politics suffered from absence of political gravitas. He established a political stake for the common man and the youth active on the social media by connecting to them directly. This actually democratised our democracy like never before.

Modiji came as an antidote to the middle-class refrain of "nothing can change, nothing will move in India". But people got interested in politics, there was hope that progress can come through democratic means. "All are thieves" refrain has given way to a restored credibility for the political class. That's why, those who claimed they had never turned up at a polling booth came in large numbers to endorse the Modi brand. This was possible because of the moral edge the BJP presented. Ideology is what makes a party, a government or a leader different from the rest.

When the BJP emphasises its commitment to ideology, it is implicitly posing a virtue and alerting its cadre to the dangers of deviation. The cultural nationalism the BJP represents involves absorbing the essence of national life, social institutions and collective memory and harnessing it to the project for national reconstruction. There should be a common minimum ideology for all parties to agree. On national integrity, everybody is one. Likewise, there is consensus on curbing corruption. On the economic agenda, all except perhaps the Left, there is commonality. This is the way to nation building.

Simply put, commitment to the nation is ideology. Ideology is to politics is what religion is to society, said veteran socialist leader George Fernandes. Ideologies must be inspirational, educational, motivational and sentimental, he added. It should have a sound underpinning of morality and ethics, he said. Whether political parties adopt capitalism, communism, socialism or any other 'ism', basically all deal with the issue of how best to cater to the aspirations of people how to conduct a society so that it removes disparity. If polity is an aggregate of actions of political parties, ideology is the equity of a party. The massive mandate the BJP got in the 2014 election is India's endorsement of the BJP ideology and our commitment to that ideology.

The emerging world order beckons us to adhere them earnestly.

—Dr. R. Balashankar

❐

22

Life Insurance Progress, Competition and Road Ahead

Insurance is a mega sector in India, with largest number of life insurance policies in the world. It is growing at a CAGR of 7.5 per cent and presently (FY 2016) is the order of USD 27.5 billion. Globally, the share of life insurance business in total premium was 55.6 per cent. The share of life insurance business in India was at 79 per cent while that of non-life insurance business was at 21 per cent. India's share in global life insurance market was 2.24 per cent during 2015, whereas it was 2.08 per cent in 2014. The share of Indian non-life insurance premium in global non-life insurance premium was at 0.75 per cent.

Insurance penetration of India, i.e., premium collected by Indian insurers as percentage of GDP has reported consistent increase from 2.71 per cent in 2001 to 5.2 per cent in 2009. Since then, the level of penetration was decli6ning. In the year 2015, it was 3.44 per cent compared to 3.3 per cent in the year 2014. Per capita premium underwritten, i.e., Insurance density in India during 2015-16 was US$54.7.

A well-developed and evolved insurance sector is much needed for economic development as it provides long-term funds for infrastructure development and also strengthens the nation's risk-bearing capacity. India being a developing country, the importance of life insurance in the national economy is paramount.

Insurance in India has gone through two radical transformations. Before 1956, insurance was private, with minimum government intervention. Oriental Life Insurance Company was the first life insurance company on the Indian soil started by Europeans in Calcutta in the year 1818. Bombay Mutual Life Assurance was the first Indian life insurance in the year 1870, and it covered Indian lives at normal rates.

In 1956, life insurance was nationalised and a monopoly was created. The Life Insurance Corporation of India (LIC) came into existence on 1st September, 1956. 154 Indian insurance companies, 16 non-Indian companies and 75 provident funds were operating in India at the time of nationalisation. LIC continues to be the dominant life insurer even in the liberalised scenario and moving fast on a new growth trajectory, surpassing its own past records. In 1972, general insurance was also nationalised.

As a part of the general opening of the economy after 1992, government appointed a committee which recommended that in the Insurance sector, private companies should be allowed to operate. On 7th December, 1999, the government passed the Insurance Regulatory and Development Authority IRDA Act. Starting in early 2000, the started granting charters to private life and general insurance companies. However, foreign ownership was restricted to 26 percent, which was later enhanced to 49 percent. Also, IRDA was renamed as IRDAI.

As on date, 24 life insurance companies and 31 non-life insurance companies are in the fray. Total life insurance industry premium income in 215-16 was worth ₹ 3,66,943 crores. New policies issued by life insurance industry during the year 2015-16 were worth 267.38 lakhs. Total capital of life insurance companies as at 31.03.2016 was worth 26691.41 crores. Life insurance industry settled 8.54 lakh claims on individual policies and total benefits paid were worth ₹ 2,01,766.10 crores. In life insurance, LIC is the only state-owned player continuing its market leadership with more than 70 per cent market share.

Nearly 70 per cent of Indian population, especially rural, is without life insurance cover, while health insurance and non-life insurance continues to be below international standards. This 70 per cent population contains huge insurable population, which is still out of reach of insurers. They face weak social security and lack of pension. This presents a huge opportunity for insurers to cover the untapped population. Also, the growing number of wealthier as well as aging Indian middle class is set to offer a strong business potential. Growing awareness of need for protection and retirement planning will support the growth of Indian life insurance market. Life insurance is a big saving vehicle in this uncertain economic environment. In this world of individualism, where joint family is losing grounds, a provision for the maintenance of the family is very essential and no wise man goes without having some life insurance. In case the bread-winner meets untimely death, his family is saved from devastation, misery and chaos. With over 40 crores of India's population belonging to the youth, as the number of standard lives is at its peak, it is the best time to sell life insurance.

The government has taken various steps to increase the insurance coverage especially to the rural and urban poor people, living below the poverty line and marginally above the poverty line at subsidised rates under Social Security Group Schemes through Aam Aadmi Bima Yojana (AABY) operated by LIC. A free add-on scholarship benefit is available for the children of the members who are covered under AABY and for targeting comprehensive financial solution has introduced in August 2014 a scheme by way of Pradhan Mantri Jan Dhan Yojana (PMJDY). Similarly, recently, a pension scheme for senior citizens, Pradhan Mantri Vaya Vandan Yojana has been launched.

India's insurable population is anticipated to touch 750 million in 2020, with life expectancy reaching 74 years. India's insurance market offers a host of opportunities across business lines, namely micro insurance, health insurance, pension business, crop insurance, motor insurance, direct insurance, etc.

In order to facilitate penetration of insurance to the lower segments of population, IRDAI had formulated the micro-insurance regulations to enable micro-insurance to be an integral part of the country's wider insurance system.

For health insurance, awareness has to be spread. Considering the lack of social security schemes, increasing cost of medical care and hospitalisation, etc., there is a vast scope for health insurance.

There is huge potential for pension market due to non-existence of any social security schemes by the government, large workforce in unorganised sector and increase in life expectancy.

To cover the untapped insurance market, specialised niche products for HNIs are to be introduced. Similarly, E-services providing more online products is necessary.

There are immense opportunities in the Indian insurance market, mainly due to rapidly growing economy, fast development of rural India, the government thrust on financial inclusion, increasing insurance awareness, etc.

Life insurance market with huge potential is also challenging for the players. They have to not only increase the reach of life insurance, but also understand the new generation's buying preferences and patterns. Regulations at the same time are more exhaustive and customer-oriented. To make life insurance more attractive, industry has to bring in innovative products and accordingly prepare their intermediaries to face the challenges.

Looking at the huge potential, life insurance industry is poised for good growth, provided the marketing of life insurance products has to face and fulfil the challenges thrown to them and it will be "survival of the fittest and fastest" for all the players.

—Kamal Kishore Singhal

❐

23
Unshackling the Indian Economy

New Government

When Narendra Modi (Modiji) became the Prime Minister of India on May 26, 2014, it became evident that his thoughts and actions were focussed on progressing India through a systematic and planned unshackling of the Indian economy in a way never seen before. He had been witness to the slow pace India had been moving at, and the many bureaucratic hurdles in the way of progress, with an environment steeped in corruption and a government moving in tandem at an extremely slow pace. There were several hurdles that needed to be crossed.

Back to the Roots

Modiji and his team reasoned that India needed strong medicine to make it go back to its original and Indian roots of professionalism, accountability, transparency and honesty. The Prime Minister's office, key ministries and government departments worked in tandem and started to make the vision come true. The common man started seeing the action on ground, and a real change from the normal.

Technology-friendly Leader

It is such a joy to see a Prime Minister who is so aware of technology and its power. Modiji seems to enjoy the usage of the technological medium and actively participates in it. His electoral team has utilised the power of social media like no other Indian election campaign, building the campaign from strength to strength based on a deep understanding of demographics and utilisation of the online medium effectively. This has also given the government the opportunity to redefine the framework and rules for e-commerce in an industry-friendly way, because the understanding of the medium is key.

Strong Diplomacy

India's biggest strength since Modiji government has been the strong diplomacy. He is perhaps the best ambassador the country could have asked for. Witness his interactions with two US Presidents across the spectrum, who differ on policies completely. But perhaps both the US Presidents would agree that Modiji is a friend! Travelling and promoting India and business is one of Modiji's greatest strengths – his charm has won the world over.

Accountability at Government Offices

One of the key moves was an exercise in accountability at the central government offices. Every central government employee is now required to come in on time, do a biometric sign-in, and the attendance is being monitored by managers. Work needs to be done professionally, and the government employees have started becoming the key enablers. This was clearly a game changer, since accountability in government offices is showing the path to accountability to others. Clean governance has suddenly become the default buzzword, with Ministers who were pushing for what can be described as Swachh governance: taking feedback, listening, understanding, and then implementing the policy for growth. It seems the Parliament also has taken a cue and become more action-oriented. Several critical and long-standing bills were passed, and it started enabling effective legislation and governance in tune with the needs of the country.

Swachh Bharat

Swachh Bharat contributed to cleanliness, and in many ways, accountability and self-discipline through highly publicised effort to enable cleanliness including asking major film personalities to help in advertising efforts, the use of toilets instead of open defecation, giving incentives to build toilets, and involving all Indians regardless of gender, caste and creed in a national movement to eliminate throwing of waste in the wrong place. Elimating waste is also about enabling cleanliness of body, mind and soul – a traditional Indian philosophy.

e-tendering

With a non-uniform process for tendering at the centre, the tendering method was suspect and supportive of corruption. The central government introduced a new process for e-tendering, called GOI – Central Public Procurement Portal, allowing for download of a tender schedule, and then submitting the bid through the portal. The method enables a uniform tender process, and roots out corruption, making the process more accountable and visible from a central source.

NITI Aayog

Planning Commission, a heavyweight in governance, was disbanded, and a NITI Aayog was incepted – a leaner body which will enable the infrastructure and entrepreneurship needed for a New India, including the now famous 'Make in India' and 'Start up India' programmes, to mention a few. Modiji and his team were well versed with technology and its usage, and started building these initiatives with relevant technology into the DNA of India. NITI Aayog has also gone about systematically enhancing private participation in selected PSUs, with a realisation that the government cannot run everything. The government must enable business in the country through sensible policy actions.

Make in India

The initiatives have started a revolution, which will help Indian entrepreneurs and businessmen alike believe in themselves, and start creating/incepting businesses that add tangible value. 'Make in India' actually strikes at the root of business in India, because we cannot survive just buying and consuming products built by other countries. We must strive to make on our own high-quality products, akin to Gandhiji's *charkha*. I guess it is not a coincidence that Modiji and Gandhiji come from the same part of India – Gujarat. When we make our own, it is possible to be self-sufficient, and be distant from currency shocks, building viable local alternatives.

Capital Market

Perhaps no part of the Indian economy has seen as many reforms as the capital market. SEBI was set up by a previous government primarily to deal with the crisis and effects of scams, including the Harshad Mehta scam. But SEBI had never been as busy as it has been recently. Armed with new teeth, post the new company laws and with more wide-ranging powers, SEBI is in the process of announcing several guidelines that strengthen the framework for the stock market including the rules and framework for all participants in the securities market. SEBI has new powers that allow it to punish violators of security market laws instead of the now traditional small fines handed out in the past – making SEBI more effective and abler to make companies comply.

Data Linking and Compliance

The government has made it compulsory to link PAN and Aadhaar for filing of tax returns, and may in the near future start linking data from its various agencies to get a stronger understanding of individuals through inter-linkages. Having national numbers that are linked will give the government strong capabilities to recognise offenders/evaders in the populace, and take necessary actions when required. Key enablers such as CAs, CSs, CWAs have been strongly advised to be compliant, and to ask clients to be honest so that there can be effective tax compliance.

Roads

Enhancing transportation is one of the pillars of the Modi government strategy, and of the many sectors that are part of this sector, the new policies in the aviation and roads and highways sector do stand out. They say that the roads built America, and these words ring true in India too. When the Narendra Modi government took over in May 2014, the construction rate stood at 11.67 km/day. Under the new regime, it grew to 12 km/day in 2014-15, 16.6 km/day in 2015-16, and became 22.5 km/day in 2016-2017. While the previous government awarded work for 15,380 km of highways in its last three years, the awards under the new government shot up to 34,349 km for the 2014-17 period. The BJP government has also taken several steps to reverse the drying up of investments in the sector by easing existing rules to bring investments into new projects, and made the approval process simpler and faster.

UDAN

In March 2017, India's aviation ministry allowed the issue of seats in flights at as little as ₹ 2,500 to connect big cities and small town India, authorising five airlines to operate on the regional routes. UDAN offers inexpensive connectivity, enabling the middle class in small town India to take their first flights, and in the medium-to long-term spurs economic demand and the build-up of business in the small town cities due to stronger connectivity. UDAN allows 31 small cities to get connected, which previously had no flights at all.

Electricity

India's rank increased to 26 in 2017, from 99 in 2015 on the World Bank's ease of getting electricity index. There has been a 60GW addition in conventional power capacity over the past three years. Transmission is being transformed through a 40 per cent increase in transformation capacity. Under the UJALA scheme, over 23 crore LED bulbs were distributed, leading to consumers saving about ₹ 12,000 crores. 13,511 out of 18,452 villages that were in darkness during the last 70 years have been illuminated. The thrust on solar energy is going to yield very tangible results.

Oil Decontrol

A long-standing demand of the fuels (petrol, diesel) industry has been a complete decontrol, so that pricing can be done in a market-determined way. India has moved to daily pricing of petrol and diesel, which is paving the way for private investments in the sector. The pricing will now be market-determined, and not government discretionary.

LPG Subsidy

One of the pillars of Modiji's policy has been the LPG subsidy optional withdrawal programme. This programme reached out to those in the higher income groups and urged them to give up their LPG subsidy so that the benefits could be given to the poorer sections of the society. The programme has achieved immense success, highlighting the strong public support for the BJP government.

Automatic Approvals

In May 2017, the BJP government facilitated ease of doing business by abolishing the Foreign Investment Promotion Board (FIPB), which used to vet foreign investment proposals. Over the past three years, around 91-95 per cent of the Foreign Direct Investment (FDI) had come through an automatic approval route. Only 11 sectors would need prior government approvals for FDI.

MCA

Ministry of Corporate Affairs (MCA) is making significant changes to spur ease of doing business through lower turnaround times for name reservation (reduced to 0.54 days in May 2017); incorporation (at 0.78 days in May 2017). To enhance speed, MCA has clubbed five procedures relating to starting of businesses, deleted five rules relating to name reservation of companies and automated 26 rules, which were previously checked manually by the officers.

Resolving Debt Issues

Recent steps by the government indicate that it is moving swiftly to correct the debt issues at banks. The government has identified the top debtors, moved their cases to the appropriate legal/resolution forums with priority (including creating a cleaner structure for insolvency and debt), is receiving the requisite approvals, and quickened the process of selling and/or restructuring assets of the companies. Banks have been asked to create stronger frameworks for sensible lending so that debt issues do not recur.

Sucking Cash Out of the System

The November 2016 demonetisation process had its share of supporters and critics alike, but one of the key aspects delivered by demonetisation was awareness that India can change. The common man put his weight behind Modiji and whole-heartedly supported demonetisation, through thick and thin, including growing lines at banks, and disruption of work. There is a stronger recognition now that India can work, even without cash, and achieve results too, which has given a huge boost to the digital economy. Cash is no more king, and businessmen are learning to work in a cashless way. The GST framework is also enabling and putting pressure on businesses to work in a systematic way without loopholes, and contributing to the elimination of cash from the system.

Fastest GDP Growth in the World

Narendra Modi's government has built up a strong foundation for Indian economic success over the past three years. India's GDP is still the fastest growing GDP in the world, at a growth of around 7.1 per cent (2016). With more than 50 per cent of its population below age 25, and more than 65 per cent of the population below age 35, India is ready to harness opportunities and emerge as a true superpower.

My Suggestions for Future Growth Focus

Access to the Essentials

The future can roughly be translated into a vision to provide access to essentials to the populace. The essentials have changed, so we no more think of just food, clothing and shelter. The future should be about food, clothing, shelter and connectivity (through telecommunication and ease of transportation).

Food

Food should be of a good wholesome quality, and should be delivered fresh to the table. For this, we would need a cold chain, which helps preserve the freshness of the food, and a strong delivery network to help get it to the customer. Farmers should have consolidated land-holdings, so that their produce can be profitable and use modern equipment. At the same time, the farmer should be aware of the benefits of organic food, and how to grow it, get the best variety of seeds, proper irrigation through available water supply. This will help the farmer focus on making the best agricultural produce in the world. Through river inter-linking and intelligent management of water, the farmer will not be dependent on the monsoons. The farmer can be enabled with a support helpline through an app or phone line and advanced information technology tools. The farmer can then ask experts questions on seeds, timing of planting, sowing, best place to sell, and fertilisers. The farmer's products could then be sold through an e-portal marketplace for the sale of farm produce.

Clothing

The textile sector in India is in dire need of modernisation, and the government must help by providing the most modern equipment possible. India is fortunate that it has several traditional niche segments in textiles, where the art and *karigari* are such that these are not replicable anywhere in the world. Indian textiles can give competition a run for their money if the right machinery is installed, and the requisite support provided. The government needs to incentivise 'Make in India' in the textile industry – we cannot continue just buying cloth from other countries – Swadeshi is the best, but it needs to be quality- and price-competitive.

Housing

The Indian populace is readily embracing the government's concept of housing for all. Special schemes are being rolled out to enable low-cost housing so that this vision becomes a reality. The housing sector has been going through a bad phase for the past few years, and is in dire need of special incentives to revive the sector. These incentives should be based on actual progress made by the builder (in an honest way) towards the housing for all. Builders following RERA regulations and delivering on time should be rewarded by the government so that an example is set. There should be strong penalties for builders who do not comply.

Telecom

India's telecom subscriber base, mobile and landline combined grew to 1.18 billion mark at the end of February 2017, and has become a critical enabling sector of the economy. The younger generation in India uses telecom services as a primary means of expression, communication and education. The government must partner with major telecom players (government and private) to enable high-quality internet coverage across the country at very fast speeds, at a low price.

Conclusion

The measures outlined above are not all-encompassing. They outline just some of the guideposts that should be utilised to make the Indian economy successful. But utilising the methods outlined above are likely to cause an unshackling of the economy, making it rise higher and higher, to reach its ultimate potential of being a high performance knowledge economy and a leader in the world.

—Vivek Bhojwani

❐

24
India's Rising Economy : Its Challenges, Opportunities and Impact

India is the world's fourth-largest economy. It produced $9.4 trillion in goods and services in 2017. But it has a long way to go to beat the top three: China ($23.1 trillion), the European Union ($19.9 trillion) and the United States ($17.4 trillion).

India has had rapid growth despite the Great Recession. It grew 6.7 per cent in 2017, 7.1 per cent in 2016, and 8.0 per cent in 2015. From 2008 through 2014, it grew between 5 per cent and 11 per cent.

That phenomenal growth rate has reduced poverty by 10 per cent in the last decade.

On May 16, 2014, India elected Narendra Modi as Prime Minister. By doing so, it rejected 60 years of leadership by the party started by Mahatma Gandhi. Mr. Modi promised to reduce bureaucracy and regulation, greenlight infrastructure projects and simplify the tax code.

What Type of Economy is India?

India has a mixed economy. Half of India's workers rely on agriculture, the signature of a traditional economy. One-third of its workers are employed by the services industry, which contributes two-thirds of India's output. The productivity of this segment is made possible by India's shift towards a market economy. Since 1990s, India has deregulated several industries, privatised many state-owned enterprises and opened doors to foreign direct investment.

India's Strengths and Opportunities

India is an attractive country for outsourcing and a cheap source of imports. That's because its economy has these comparative advantages:

1. The cost of living is lower than that in the United States. Its GDP per capita is half that of other poor countries like Iraq or Ukraine. This is an advantage because Indian workers don't need as much in wages, since everything costs less.
2. India has many well-educated technology workers.
3. English is one of India's official languages. Many Indians speak it. This, combined with the high level of education, attracts U.S. technology and call centres to India. For example, an Indian call centre employee only costs $12 per hour. That's almost half the American counterpart of $20 an hour. As a result, more than 250,000 call centre jobs were outsourced to India and the Philippines between 2001 and 2003 (*Source*: Technology Manufacturing Corp.).

In March 2016, Mr. Modi dedicated $1.5 billion in funding and tax breaks to boost high-tech startups. The programme will streamline patent applications and investments. That should double India's new startups to 11,500 in the next five years (Source: "India Bets Big on Startup Companies," *Global Finance,* March 2016).

There is certainly no formula to become a successful entrepreneur. Some may succeed and make good profits, others sink along the way. Which are the most lucrative sectors for entrepreneurs? Here's a list of 20 good opportunities entrepreneurs can look at.

1. Tourism

Tourism is a booming industry in India. With the number of domestic and international tourists rising every year, this is one hot sector entrepreneurs must focus on. India with its diverse culture and rich heritage has a lot to offer to foreign tourists. Beaches, hill stations, heritage sites, wildlife and rural life, India has everything tourists are looking for.

2. Automobile

India is now a hot spot for automobiles and auto components. A cost-effective hub for auto components sourcing for global auto-makers, the automotive sector is the potential sector for entrepreneurs.

3. Textiles

India is famous for its textiles. Each state has its unique style in terms of apparels. India can grow as a preferred location for manufacturing textiles taking into account the huge demand for garments. Places like Tirupur and Ludhiana are now export hubs for textiles. A better understanding of the markets and customers' needs can boost growth in this sector.

4. Social Ventures

Many entrepreneurs are taking up social entrepreneurship. Helping the less privileged get into employment and make a viable business is quite a challenge. There are many who have succeeded in setting up social ventures. With a growing young population in rural areas, who have the drive and enthusiasm to work, entrepreneurs can focus on this segment.

5. Software

India's software and services exports are likely to rise with export revenue growth projected at 13 to 15 per cent to hit about $57 billion by March 2011.

With one of the largest pools of software engineers, Indian entrepreneurs can set higher targets in hardware and software development.

The information technology-enabled services have contributed substantially to the economy. With more companies outsourcing contracts to India, business-to-business solutions and services would be required. Entrepreneurs can cash in on the rise in demand for these services with innovative and cost-effective solutions.

6. Engineering Goods

India continues to be one of the fastest growing cxporters of engineering goods, growing at a rate of 30.1 percent. The government has set a target of $110 billion by 2014 for total engineering exports. Entrepreneurs must capitalise on the booming demand for products from the engineering industry.

7. Franchising

India is well connected with the world. Hence, franchising with leading brands who want to spread across the country could also offer ample opportunities for young entrepreneurs. With many small towns developing at a fast pace in India, the franchising model is bound to succeed.

8. Education and Training

There is a good demand for education and online tutorial services. With good facilities at competitive rates, India can attract more students from abroad. Unique teaching methods, educational portals and tools can be used effectively to make the sector useful and interesting.

9. Food Processing

India's mainstay is agriculture. Entrepreneurs can explore many options in the food grain cultivation and marketing segments. Inefficient management, lack of infrastructure, proper storage facilities lead to huge losses of food grains and fresh produce in India.

Entrepreneurs can add value with proper management and marketing initiatives. The processed food market opens a great potential for entrepreneurs — be it fast food, packaged food or organic food. Fresh fruits and vegetables too have a good demand abroad. A good network of food processing units can help potential exporters build a good business.

10. Corporate Demands

There will be a good demand for formal attire with more companies opening their offices in India. People who can meet this demand in a cost-effective way can make a good business. With corporate gifting getting very popular, this is also a unique business to explore.

11. Ayurveda and Traditional Medicine

India is well known for its herbal and ayurvedic products. With increasing awareness about the ill-effects of allopathic medicines, there will be a huge demand for cosmetics, natural medicines and remedies.

12. Organic Farming

Organic farming has been in India for a long time. The importance of organic farming will grow at a fast pace, especially with many foreigners preferring only organic products. Entrepreneurs can focus on business opportunities in this sector. There are many small-time farmers who have adopted organic farming but the demand is still unmet, offering many opportunities for those who can promote organic farming on a large scale.

13. Media

The media industry has huge opportunities to offer young entrepreneurs. With the huge growth of this segment, any business in this field will help entrepreneurs reap huge benefits. Television, advertising, print and digital media have seen a boom in business.

Digitisation, regionalisation, competition, innovation, process, marketing and distribution will drive the growth of India's media and entertainment sector, according to FICCI.

14. Packaging

With China invading the markets with cheap plastic goods and packaging materials, there is a good opportunity to develop good packaging materials to meet domestic and foreign demand. There is a huge demand in various sectors, such as agriculture, automotive, consumer goods, healthcare infrastructure and packaging sectors for plastics.

15. Floriculture

India's floriculture segment is small and unorganised. There is a lot to be done in this lucrative sector. The global trade in floriculture products is worth $9.4 billion. With an 8 per cent growth, it is expected to grow to $16 billion by 2010. India's share in world trade is just 0.18 percent.

This is a huge market to be tapped considering the rising demand for fresh flowers. More awareness and better farming and infrastructure can boost exports.

16. Toys

Another evergreen industry is toy manufacturing. India has potential to manufacture cost-effective and safe toys for the world. With Chinese toys being pulled up for toxins, the market for safe and good-quality toys beckons Indian entrepreneurs.

17. Healthcare Sector

India's healthcare sector is dismal. The private sector can play a vital role in developing this sector. With medical tourism also gaining momentum, the sector can attract foreigners who are looking for cost-effective treatment in countries like India.

18. Biotechnology

After the software sector, biotechnology opens a huge potential. Entrepreneurs can look at a plethora of options with the application of biotechnology in agriculture, horticulture, sericulture, poultry, dairy and production of fruits and vegetables.

19. Energy Solutions

In a power-starved nation, the need to develop cost-effective and power-saving devices is gaining more significance. There is a huge demand for low-cost sustainable energy-saving devices as well.

The government has already unveiled the National Solar Mission, which has set a target of 20,000 MW of solar-generating capacity by the end of the 13th Five-Year Plan.

Former Prime Minister Manmohan Singh had urged the industry to see the huge business opportunity and set up 'Solar Valleys' on the lines of the Silicon Valleys. These solar valleys can become hubs for solar science, solar engineering and solar research, fabrication and manufacturing. So, there is a big opportunity for entrepreneurs in this sector as well.

20. Recycling Business

E-waste will rise to alarming proportions in the developing world within a decade, with computer waste in India alone to grow by 500 per cent from 2007 levels by 2020, according to a UN study. This sector opens a viable business opportunity for entrepreneurs in terms of e-waste management and disposal.

Modi's 10 Step Plans

India's former President, Pranab Mukherjee outlined 10 steps the Modi government plans to take:

1. **Food Inflation:** Increase the supply of food to lower costs. Prepare to help farmers during a possible subnormal monsoon season.
2. **Economy:** Usher the economy into a high growth path. Rein in inflation. Reignite the investment cycle. Restore the confidence of the domestic as well as international community.
3. **Jobs:** Strategically promote labour-intensive manufacturing. Promote tourism and farming.
4. **Taxes:** Retrospective tax laws, introduced in 2012-13, have been described as the single biggest impediment to foreign investment in India. The Modi government will embark on rationalisation and simplification of the tax regime to make it non-adversarial and conducive to investment, enterprise and growth. The government will make every effort to introduce a Goods and Services Tax while addressing the concerns of states.
5. **Reforms:** Reform regulations to encourage investments, especially in sectors that create jobs.
6. **Agriculture:** Increase investment in agri-infrastructure. Address issues pertaining to pricing and procurement of agricultural produce, crop insurance and post-harvest management. Incentivise the setting up of food processing industries.
7. **Reviving Manufacturing:** Set up world-class investment and industrial regions, particularly along

the dedicated freight corridors and industrial corridors. Create a single-window system of clearances at both the centre and the states through a hub-spoke model.

8. **Infrastructure:** A new 10-year plan will modernise railways, including the Diamond Quadrilateral high-speed train project. Execute the national highways programme. Build more low-cost airports in smaller towns. Develop inland and coastal waterways as major transport routes.
9. **Energy Security:** Augment electricity-generation capacity through both conventional and non-conventional sources. Reform the coal sector to attract private investment.
10. **Urbanisation:** Build 100 cities focussed on specialised domains and equipped with world-class amenities. By the time the nation reaches the 75th anniversary of its independence, every family will have a good house (known as a *pucca* house) with running water, plumbing, 24/7 electricity supply. (Source: Interview with Ramesh Kumar Nanjundaiya, CEO of Triniti Solutions.)

—G.L. Aggarwal

❐

25

How Non-Governmental Organisations (NGOs) can be an Effective Tool for Socio-Political Change

Despite governmental controls, NGOs still present a plethora of opportunities for political organisations and corporations to make a difference in a strategic way that supports their overall goals. (Refer to *1 for a brief primer on how to set up an NGO in India).

NGOs were an idea that came up in 1945 under Article 71 of the United Nations Charter. NGOs are private sector, voluntary (usually non-profit and non-sectarian) organisations that participate in cooperation projects, education, training, humanitarian, progressive or even watchdog activities.

Political organisations do not qualify as NGOs, though political parties can also work through NGOs that are set up by allied personnel. Some NGOs can also be not-for-profit corporations.

NGOs in India

In 2014, the CBI estimated that there were over 20 lakh NGOs in India, that is, one NGO for every 600 Indians. Kerala led the states with 3.69 lakh NGOs or one NGO for every

93 Keralaites. Even allowing for a substantial portion of inactive or defunct NGOs, the numbers are phenomenal. Interestingly, there was at that time only one policeman for every 943 Indians.

Funding NGOs in India

NGOs have typically relied on public and corporate donations.

Corporate Responsibility Funding

In 2013, the corporate responsibility provisions of the Indian Companies Act came into force requiring companies with any one of the following provisions to set up a Corporate Responsibility Program:

- Annual revenues of ₹ 1000 crores or more,
- Assets of ₹ 500 crores or more,
- Net profits of ₹ 5 crores or more.

Companies that qualified under one or more of the above criteria were required to spend two per cent of their average profits for the year on Corporate Social Responsibility Programmes that were to be supervised by a committee constituted for the purpose.

New Funding Tools for NGO

Crowd-funding sites like Indiegogo.com are sources of funding for both for profits and not for profits. Funders are typically offered a reward for giving.

Governmental Controls on Foreign Funding of NGOs

The Foreign Contribution Regulation Act of 2010 (FCRA) has requirements for registration and re-registration of NGOs who wish to receive funding from abroad. In 2016, 11,319 NGOs, who did not renew their registration, lost their ability to receive funds. A further 25 lost their licenses based on "field reports" by regulatory authorities who are not required to cite the grounds on which their report was based. Groups like Amnesty International, Greenpeace and the Lawyers Collective, who have been critical of the government, have been targeted.

(Refer to *2 for the provisions of the FCRA Act of 2010)

"In order to be registered under the FCRA, an NGO must be in existence for at least three years and must have undertaken reasonable activity in its field, for which the foreign contribution is proposed to be utilised. Further, it must have spent at least INR 1,000,000 over three years preceding the date of its application on its activities. The registration certificate is valid for a period of five years and must be thereafter renewed in the prescribed manner."

Socio-Political Benefits of Involving NGOs

NGOs are the most effective means for engaging and empowering politically significant groups like women, which are relatively inaccessible by conventional political methods. This is particularly relevant in politically opinionated states like Kerala. Any organisation seeking to propagate new political ideas is well advised to focus on the populations that do not have entrenched political opinions. In Kerala, for example, this would indicate women as being more amenable to new political ideas.

NGOs that emphasise empowerment through training, empowerment and micro-finance programmes are suitable ways to engage female populations and, thereby, introduce them to political workers who run NGO programmes.

Programmes Benefitting Scheduled Caste Groups

Overall, it must be noted that India is a complex nation of 121 crore individuals, with some 20 per cent of the population belonging to disadvantaged groups like the scheduled caste community. This is another politically significant group. There is regrettably a strong correlation between the scheduled caste community and poverty. NGOs can work effectively in these clearly defined communities. For example, Punjab has the highest scheduled caste population in India (30 percent). Over thirty-nine per cent of this group, for example, still live in slums.

Types of NGOs

There are a wide variety of tools that planners can employ. NGOs can be classified based on their orientation or level of cooperation. Some of the famous terms used for NGOs are mentioned below:

BINGO – It is a short term used for business-friendly international NGO.

CITS – It is a type of NGO that is basically devoted in helping the scientific community by motivating the young talent towards R&D.

CSO – It is short term for civil society organisation.

DONGO – It refers to the Donor Organised NGO.

ENGO – It is an abbreviated form of environmental NGO.

GONGO – It refers to the government-operated NGO.

INGO – It is an abbreviated form of international NGO like Oxfam.

QUANGO – It refers to the quasi-autonomous NGO like an ISO non-governmental organisations such as the International Organization for Standardisation (ISO).

TANGO – It refers to the technical assistance NGO.

GSO – It stands for the Grassroots Support Organisation.

MANGO – It refers to the market advocacy NGO.

CHARDS – It is a short form for Community Health and Rural Development Society.

According to the World Bank, NGOs can be classified into Operational and Advocacy NGOs. The purpose of an operational NGO is to design and implement development-related projects. The purpose of an advocacy NGO is to promote a specific cause. It makes efforts to raise awareness through activities such as lobbying, press work and activist events.

India has a plethora of problems that NGOs can help address. Their scope of NGOs can be national or even community-based. Socio-political and corporate organisations with honest and helpful intentions can still do a lot of good despite growing attention from governments wary of criticism and interference. A multi-pronged funding strategy, transparent financial reporting, good governance and a little tact will help Indian NGOs function effectively as they help solve the myriad problems faced by India.

—Girish Chaudhry

❒

26
Role and Need of North-East Region in National Development

North-East India, commonly known as the "Seven Sisters", is comprised of seven states. They are Arunachal Pradesh, Assam, Manipur, Meghalaya Mizoram, Nagaland and Tripura. Each state has its distinct languages, cultures, faith and traditions. It is most ethnically and linguistically diverse region in Asia. The region is a true frontier having 2000 km of border with Bhutan, China, Myanmar and Bangladesh and is connected to the rest of India by a narrow 22-km-wide corridor of land known as The Siliguri Corridor or Chicken's Neck. It is important to understand that Mughals could not conquer the North-East states, rather they were defeated 17 times by the Ahoms. Similarly, the British could colonise the region much after they conquered the rest of India. The British initially considered it an extension of Bengal and only created the Province of Assam in 1874.

The festivals and celebrations in the North-East states are a colourful reflection of the people and their lives. Throughout the year, different people celebrate festivals with a lot of fanfare in different ways, most of whom centreing around their modes of living and livelihood. The region can be rightly called a traveller's paradise, with picturesque hills and green meadows, which shelters thousands of species of flora and fauna. In addition, the states provide scope for angling, boating, rafting, trekking and hiking. Besides, there are a number of wildlife sanctuaries and national parks, where there are rare animals, birds and plants, which will surely provide fascinating insight to the visitors.

The region is endowed with bountiful of natural resources, viz., highly fertile soil, perennial mighty rivers, mineral deposits, such as oil and gas, coal, limestone, etc., huge hydropower prospective, agro-horticultural resources, dense forest. The literacy rate of the region is much higher than the all-India figure. It has 8 per cent of India's land area and 3.7 per cent of its population and, thus, enjoys a distinct demographic edge over the rest of the country. Yet, regardless of the abundance of both human and natural resources, the region has lagged behind many Indian states on key development indicators.

The region till Independence was at the forefront of development. The Partition in 1947 played a detrimental role in transforming the economic scenario of the region. The immediate impact of the Partition was that the North-East was cut off from the rest of India. With East Bengal becoming part of Pakistan, the traditional trade and communication with the North-East were almost snapped. Further, the frontier routes with Myanmar and China also died down and, as a result, the region became landlocked. The successive governments at the Centre paid very little attention towards the economic development of the region. As a result, there was negligible industrialisation.

Further, post-Partition, Assam witnessed a large-scale population explosion due to illegal immigration from East Pakistan (now Bangladesh) over several decades. This illegal immigration has altered the demographic condition of the state and caused a grave threat not only to the identity of the Assamese people but also to India's security. It reduced the Assamese people to a minority in their own state as happened in Tripura and Sikkim. It is a pity that still immigration continues to be treated as a political issue despite threat to people's land and identity and political parties exploit it for their own objectives. Barring BJP and its ally AGP, all other political parties are using immigrants as vote bank.

There are many factors that caused insurgency in the North-East region. They are lack of economic opportunity, rising unemployment, illegal immigration causing identity crisis, exploitation and poor governance. The unemployed youth ultimately took a wrong path and became rebellion and/or insurgents. It is pertinent to add here that on large-scale illegal migration from East Pakistan (now Bangladesh), the then Governor of Assam, Lt. Gen. (Retd.) S.K. Sinha, PVSM, submitted a special report to the President of India in 1988. In his report, the late Sinha Sir had not only penned on the seriousness of this issue, but also recommended a host of measures.

During the NDA-I regime, for the first time, the North-East received the much-needed attention. The Ministry of Development of North-eastern Region was set up in 2001 to specially oversee socio-economic development in the region. To accelerate economy and security, cooperation with South-East Asia became one of the main agenda of India's 'Look East' Policy. Apart from the obvious economic convenience, India also wants to send a clear message to China— it wants to be a key regional power and will achieve this by fostering closer ties with South-East Asian nations to counter China's increasing dominance in the region.

It is pertinent to note that India's land connection with South-East Asia is through its North-East region, which the Centre has for long neglected primarily due to the region's relatively weak representation in parliament. Without a reasonable level of economic development and stability in India's North-East states, as well as better infrastructure on its borders, India's 'Look East' Policy cannot become a reality. The present BJP government has realised that ties with Myanmar — as well as Bangladesh — are largely dependent upon the infrastructure in India's states in the North-East, including Manipur, Mizoram, Arunachal Pradesh and Tripura.

A successful 'Look East' Policy will only be possible if the Centre invests not just economically but also politically in the North-East region. A comprehensive policy should be formulated to increase connectivity with Myanmar, Thailand, Cambodia, Vietnam, etc. through India's North-East states. India needs a stronger policy—one that focusses on greater and comprehensive development of the North-East States by allowing them to be key stakeholders in all stages of the decision-making process. In doing so, states will feel integrated with the rest of the country and benefit from better relations with its South-East Asian neighbours.

China is well ahead of India on this front. Many of China's border provinces now act as smooth conduits linking China with its neighbouring countries. Development in the Chinese province of Yunnan, which shares border with Myanmar, is an example of China's move towards establishing better ties with its neighbours, via its border regions. India must do the same if it wants to bolster its standing as a regional power. India should take a number of steps to achieve this.

First, the primary focus should be on the region's economic development. Prioritising a few projects in the

North-East is not enough — the central government should also boost the local economy of these states by encouraging industrial growth and creating a strong service sector by promoting tourism in the region. Also there is a great opportunity in the I.T. sector owing to higher literacy in the region and, more particularly, majority of populace are fluent in English.

It is a good thing that Hon'ble Prime Minister Shri Narendra Modi has a sincere desire for the development of the North-East states. He wants to take forward the vision of former Prime Minister Shri Atal Bihari Vajpayee for the North-Eastern region. Modiji's first foreign visit as the Prime Minister to Bhutan is a very positive beginning. The visit to a large extent has been able to shed off the popular belief, particularly among the smaller neighbours that India is only interested in Pakistan and hardly makes any effort in reaching out to its eastern neighbours. After Shri Modi became Prime Minister, he has been categorical about pronouncing his foreign policy priorities with its neighbourhood, more precisely India's eastern/south-eastern neighbours.

Fortunately, the present government is focussing on removing the connectivity handicap of the region and has been formulating a comprehensive policy to transform the geographical location to an advantage for the region. Proposal for India and Bhutan to form a holistic approach for tourism and develop a circuit combining India's North-Eastern states and Bhutan is a welcome step of the present dispensation. Similarly, efforts are on with Bangladesh for increasing connectivity with the country and also the issue of transit, which will help the region reduce its landlocked status, as this will open not only access to the sea but also better communication with greater part of India, boosting trade and economic development. The Modi government is not only proposing new measures and initiatives for improvement of trade and connectivity but also simultaneously is completing the already proposed projects that would benefit the region. Opportunities are waiting for the region, one hopes both the Centre and the state governments will endeavour to fulfil the promises they made to the people of the region and bring cheers to their life.

—C.A. Pawan Kumar Sharma

❐

27
Indian Youth – Towards Excellence

Sigmund Freud said: "If youth knew, if age could."

The wisdom of age, and the power of youth are both invaluable. When we are young, with a great capacity to do, we lack wisdom that comes with age and experience, and are prone to act without thinking about consequences. When we are old and have experience, we may want to redo many things in the light of our wisdom, but lack the energy of youth to act. There are so many secrets that become clear to us only with age and experience. If youth only knew these secrets, and if age did not diminish our capacity to do things, then the world would be a different place.

We would not waste our youth and would remain young forever by doing what we did, in our youth, even when we grew old. But youth never knew until age caught up, and old age brought with it the realisation that one could no longer do what one did when young. Youth and experience are the best blend for progress and the Indian demography promises us this dividend. Let's see how we could make the most of this opportunity.

The youth of India are poised to become its biggest strength over the coming decades. The demography of India, unlike many western countries, consists of 27.5 per cent of its population between the ages of 15 and 29 years.

If 27.5 per cent of the population are youth, it is vital that they participate in the development of the country at all levels. Only the participation of youth can ensure the fulfilment of India's vision and mission of becoming the foremost democracy in the world. The active participation of youth in politics, democracy, accountability and governance will help create a strong and able India, with its future leaders guiding us towards our goals of better governance, stable welfare and a developed nation.

Without the participation of youth, we stand at the crossroads of anarchy and helplessness, with 27.5 per cent of its most valuable resource disengaged from active participation in the march towards our goals and missions. An engaged youth, and citizenry would help us build accountability and ensure better governance, and can also facilitate the implementation of schemes. The youth could be leveraged as a resource to monitor and aid the implementation and promote accountability of welfare schemes and development projects across the country.

Youth in the age group of 15-29 years comprise 27.5 per cent of the population. By 2025, India is expected to become the 4th largest economy in the world, next only to the US, China and Japan and contribute about 5.5 per cent-6 per cent to the world GDP. While the US, China and Japan face the risk of an ageing workforce, India is expected to have a very favourable demographic profile. The population of India is expected to exceed 1.3 billion by 2020 with a median age of 28, which is considerably less than the expected median ages of China and Japan. The working population of India is expected to increase to 592 million by 2020, next only to

China (776 million), pointing to the fact that youth would play an increasingly important role in all walks of life, especially the economic development of the country. This 'demographic dividend' offers a great opportunity to India.

In this article, I want to highlight three important aspects of life that the youth must master in order to progress in this journey towards excellence. "*Satyam, Shivam, Sundaram*"; "*Brahma, Vishnu, Mahesh*" – our universe is full of trinities and the following trinity is my prescription and message for Indian youth to help them march towards excellence.

1. **Build Strong Personalities:** Strong personalities create strong nations. The strong and charismatic personality of our Prime Minister, Shri Narendra Bhai Damodar Das Modi, has taken the whole world by storm. For decades, India had been seeking a leader like Shri Narendra Modi and having found him, we are extremely proud of his words and deeds. When Modiji speaks, the whole world listens. He has given India the much-needed voice and stature that had been missing for the past couple of decades. Such is his personality that even his opponents try hard as they may get no weak spots to point fingers at him. Our youth could do with such role models. Our history is replete with great personalities, on whom our youth could build their personalities, but it helps in having present-day leaders who can act as true role models, and icons for our youth.

   To transform into strong personalities, our youth must:

   a. **Come Out of Comfort Zone:** When you decide to leave your comfort zone, you begin your journey towards excellence. This is the first step. The journey towards excellence and personality building starts with this step. If you are not willing to leave your comfort zone, then you would never achieve the greatness you are meant to achieve. Moving out of your comfort zone means that you have to start struggling – even to be accepted as an equal human being – by your peers and world at large. If the struggle makes you go back to your comfort zone, then the battle is lost, it is over. If you decide that quitting is not an option, you come out of your cocoon and life forces you to learn to deal with a lot of things that eventually change you as a person. I would like to share a small poem I wrote to inspire my readers to leave their comfort zones and progress towards a new dawn.

इक नई सुबह

इक नई सुबह की ओर चलें
हर नई रात से टकराएँ,
छँटे अँधियारे इस जीवन के
खुशियों के बादल मँडराएँ।

इक नई सुबह की ओर चलें
कुछ प्रेम सभी पर बरसाएँ,
दु:ख घटे सभी के जीवन से
कुछ ऐसा हम-तुम कर जाएँ।

इक नई सुबह की ओर चलें
और दूर हो सबकी निराशाएँ,
हर ओर खुशी का आलम हो
हर दिल में नई हो आशाएँ।
इक नई सुबह की ओर चलें

उस ओर चलें चलते जाएँ,
हर कदम पे सच्चे दोस्त मिलें
और सफर खुशी से कट जाए।

❋ ❋ ❋

b. **Increase Knowledge and Awareness:** These are the days of the knowledge economy and it is the information age. The internet is a rich source of information but a great distraction too. Getting all your knowledge from the internet may be counter-productive. All information on the net may not be true or authentic. Newspapers and books still remain the most authentic sources of information. Please increase your awareness through reading, not just through the internet. Be careful of the knowledge you get on the internet. It is another form of slavery to the west. I would like to share a small poem that I wrote, just when the internet came to India, warning us about the bad effects of the net:

इंटरनेट

वो देखो आया इंटरनेट
ये तो था पहले से ही सेट
इसने बातों ही बातों में
हमें बाँध दिया है रातों में।

बच्चे-बूढ़े नानी-दादी
सब हो गए अब इसके आदी,
सब कहते हैं कुछ खेल करो
और जल्दी से इ-मेल करो।

हम फिर गुलाम हो गए बंधु
इंटरनेट-केबुल टी.वी. के,
इसने हमको झकझोरा है
जो किया अभी वो थोड़ा है।

भारत नहीं आएँगे अंग्रेज
वो देंगे इंटरनेट को भेज,
इंटरनेट हमें नचाएगा
जो चाहेगा करवाएगा।

You are not exposed to a lot of things in your village or town. By listening to news, reading a newspaper, going through books, your awareness would increase. When I moved to a big city, my awareness about many things increased – some by design (reading newspaper, listening to news) and some by just being there in a set-up that had more to offer. As I became more aware, my outlook towards life matured, my behaviour changed and I became a better informed person. All of you, our young men and women, must work towards becoming more aware citizens of the world. Knowledge and awareness lead to confidence.

c. **Manage Time:** As you get involved in more and more activities, you will have less and less time for leisure and recreation. You have to learn to manage your time better in order to do justice to all important tasks. Your sleeping hours too may get reduced. As you learn to utilise your time better, your performance would improve and you would gain further confidence in your abilities.

Shared below is a small poem on time:

वक्त

जो वक्त से पहले चलते हैं
वो वक्त से पहले ढलते हैं,
उनके लगवाए अंकुर भी
एक वक्त के बाद ही फलते हैं।

जिनके भी साथ में वक्त चला
उनका तो हर एक काम फला,
जो वक्त के साथ न चल पाए
पिछड़े हुए लोग वो कहलाए।

हम किसको कहते वक्त भला
और कौन है इसके साथ चला,
ये वक्त नहीं चलते-फिरते
हम दीये की भाँति जलते हैं।

हमको करने हैं काम बहुत
और थोड़ा दीये में तेल मिला,
और बाग में जाकर देखो तो
हर रोज नया एक फूल खिला।

2. **Be Socially Responsible:** The society we live in is our responsibility. The way most citizens think and act decides what kind of a society we become. For the Swachh Bharat Abhiyan, our Prime Minister, Shri Narendra Modi has left no stone unturned, but India is still far from clean because our mindset and paradigms need to change for a permanent change in behaviour. Social responsibility also means working and participating in government schemes for the

good of all – including ourselves. Let us see how we may build a more responsible and responsive society.

a. **"Be the Change, then See the Change":** Be the change, then see the change is my formula for any change that one speaks about. This is the most difficult thing to achieve because we resist change the most. It is said – old habits die hard. So, if we want to see a change, we should first be ready to be the change. You cannot expect everyone, and everything else to change – except you. If you find it very difficult to change, then imagine the same for everyone else. Change bad habits, change wrong mindsets, but keep your core pure. Keep your values intact. Keep your traditions safe. Keep the child within you alive. A small poem on this theme written when I was in high school:

बड़प्पन का एहसास

बचपन में मैं सोचा करता था
कैसा होता है बड़प्पन का एहसास,
अकसर यही विचार
मँडराया करता था मेरे आसपास।

कुछ बड़ा हुआ हूँ मैं अब
पर अब भी यह जिज्ञासा —
कैसा होता है बड़प्पन का एहसास
यथावत् है।

एक दिन मैं सचमुच
बड़ा हो जाऊँगा,
पर क्या तब भी इतना
बेबाक रह पाऊँगा ?

और क्या
उम्र में बूढ़ा हो जाना
सचमुच
परिपक्व होना है ?

✻ ✻ ✻

b. Value Values: As we progress, we leave behind our home, hearth, people and move on in life. Never leave behind your values. Values alone make a society. Our beliefs, paradigms and behaviour are based on our values. The moment we let go our values, we start declining. A small poem I wrote, years ago, when I found western values and culture taking over our lives:

कैसा आया वक्त निराला

कैसा आया वक्त निराला
हरेक के हाथ में है एक प्याला
आपस में मिलते नर-नारी
मिल के बन जाते व्यभिचारी।

मिलना-जुलना क्लब में होता
हाय-हेलो से स्वागत,
पी के मदिरा मूड बनाते
और जुए से किस्मत।
मूल्यों का अब हुआ पलायन
भ्रष्ट हुआ जग सारा,
क्षणिक सुखों के कोलाहल ने
लूटा चैन हमारा।

कहाँ गए सिद्धांत हमारे
कहाँ है सभ्य समाज,
कल कैसा है किसने जाना
बिगड़ गया जब आज।

You can never hope for a good tomorrow if your values are flawed today. A decline in values leads to overall deterioration in society. Today, we have so many crimes against women. This is a result of declining values and commodification of women in the eyes of such persons. These are also fuelled by the western mindset and events. A small poem showing how some of our ladies become slaves of the western beauty industry:

भारतीय सौंदर्य की...

भारतीय सौंदर्य की
खूब मची है धूम,
विश्व सुंदरी ताज पहन
रही है जग में घूम।
रीता, ऐश्वर्या, सुष्मिता,
डायना, युक्ता, लारा,
इनके देशी सौंदर्य से
सारा जग हारा।
भारत के कभी पहचान थे-
गौतम, गांधी, टैगोर,
पर अब तो चमकते चेहरे ही
आते हैं नजर सब ओर।

नारी की बाँकी चितवन का
सब करते अवलोकन,
और देते नंबर आँककर
जो मोहे सबका मन।

हम भी सौंदर्य के प्रेमी हैं
हम भी हैं भारतवासी,
पर क्यों बनती हैं बेटियाँ
सौंदर्य दलालों की दासी।

Let us not become slaves of a western mindset. Our Prime Minister, Shri Narendra Modi made the whole world do Yoga on World Yoga Day. He has encouraged so many organisations to spread Indianness across the world. Can we not become a part of this great initiative? Can we not hold on to our values? Can we not value our age-old values? Can we not rebuild our nation into the golden bird that it was once upon a time?

3. **Care for the Environment:** Our environment sustains us. If we do not conserve our environment, we will cease to exist. The rate of decline in the environment is slow. So, no one is bothered because we know what we do to the environment may not necessarily affect us. It would affect future generations, but since we would be gone by then, why should we care? A few aspects of our environment that need to be cared for are dealt with below.

   a. **Water:** After air, water is the most important ingredient that sustains life. The next wars would be fought over water. We already have, pending in courts, long-standing water disputes between states of India. A small poem to highlight this important facet:

पानी

यह सुन के होगी हैरानी
न मिलेगा पीने को पानी,
नदियों का जल तो दूषित है
और वातावरण प्रदूषित है।

जितने जंगल काटे जाते
क्या उतने पेड़ लगा पाते?
कुएँ भी कब तक देंगे जल
नीचे जाता है जल का तल।

सागर का जल तो खारा है
क्या वो जल तुम्हें गवारा है?
न होंगे जंगल-जंगलात
तो कैसे होगी बरसात?

जब दिन आएँगे पानी बिन
जीवन हमसे जाएगा छिन,
पानी को बचा के खर्च करो
या एक दिन बिन पानी के मरो।

b. **Flora & Fauna:** If we continue to neglect our flora and fauna, we look at a future where a lot of our earth sustaining plants, and animals would become extinct. Human life is also threatened if our flora and fauna are threatened. It is like cutting the branch you are sitting on. A small poem to drive home this point:

प्रकृति विनाश

हम बच्चों ने क्या बिगाड़ा है
क्यों वनों को तुमने उजाड़ा है ?
जंतु ने क्या लिया तुम्हारा है
जो इस बेरहमी से मारा है।

क्या तुमको इतना भी न पता
पेड़ों में भी तो जीवन है,
इन जीवों को इतना न सता
इनका घर भी तो यही वन है।

प्रकृति को हम कहते जननी
पर नोच-नोच ले जाते हैं,
जब कोई करे ऐसी करनी
बादल विनाश के आते हैं।

प्रकृति विनाश मत होने दो
अब बंद करो ये पागलपन,
क्या होगा धन और वैभव का
न रहेगा जब ये तन और मन।

Unless we create a socially responsible, environmentally sensitive, and value-driven society, we risk losing our demographic dividend. Our youth must bring back our old value systems, best practices, and marry them with present-day needs, in order to make India great again. Our youth towards excellence would ensure the supremacy of the world's largest democracy in a world starved of good leadership. India must

lead the world, as it did in the not-so-distant past. India must regain its old days of glory and it would never be possible without the strength of our youth, and wisdom of our senior citizens – "If Youth Knew, If Age Could."
A prayer to end this article:

जग का पालनहारा

कौन है जग का पालनहारा ?
किसने किया यह जग उजियारा ?
यहाँ नहीं है, वहाँ नहीं है
देखो तो वह कहाँ नहीं है,
तुममें, मुझमें, इसमें, उसमें
उसके बिन यह जहाँ नहीं है,

शीश नमन करते उसको हम
ज्ञान की ज्योति जगाओ भगवन्,
दूर करो जग के अँधियारे
धार तेज है दूर किनारे।

गुरु की शिक्षा
प्रेम की दीक्षा,
हो सारे जग का कल्याण
भगवन् दूर करो अज्ञान,
भगवन् दूर करो अज्ञान!

—Atul Sharma

28

Impact of NPAs on Banking Sector of Indian Economy

Indian economy is staring at slowdown due to crisis of confidence amongst all the banks and financial institutions vis-à-vis the entrepreneurs who borrow money from them to part finance their ventures. In the recent past, a spate of loans has become bad and doubtful from lenders' point of view, due to which banks have lost a lot of money and are scared to lend except to already well-established business units. However, in order to achieve growth in the economy to the maximum possible level for a developing economy like India, it is necessary that the private sector has enough funds at their disposal including the borrowed funds to invest in the economy. As the things stand today, most of the public-sector banks are besieged with a large number of bad loans disbursed in the past, which are not likely to be returned back to these banks; in some cases, not even to the extent of 10 per cent of the loans disbursed. Such bad loans are sort of non-performing assets which are abbreviated as NPAs in popular terminology. In this light, reviving public-sector banks and financial institutions and infusing confidence in them to lend to the entrepreneurs has become an absolute necessity.

NPA's Definition by Reserve Bank of India (RBI)

An asset, including a leased asset, becomes non-performing when it ceases to generate income for the bank/ financial institution.

NPA is a loan or an advance where

- interest and/or installment of principal remains overdue for a period of more than 90 days in respect of a term loan.
- the account remains 'out of order' in respect of an Overdraft/Cash Credit (OD/CC) by whatever reason including due to LC development and/or bank guarantee invocation for a period of 90 days or more.
- the bill remains overdue for a period of more than 90 days in the case of bills purchased and discounted.
- the installment of principal or interest thereon remains overdue for two crop seasons for short-duration crops.
- the installment of principal or interest thereon remains overdue for one crop season for long-duration crops.
- the amount of liquidity facility remains outstanding for more than 90 days, in respect of a securitisation transaction undertaken in terms of guidelines on securitisation, dated February 1, 2006.
- in respect of derivative transactions, the overdue receivables representing positive mark-to-market value of a derivative contract, if these remain unpaid for a period of 90 days from the specified due date for payment.

Non-performing assets, which are notoriously called NPAs by the banking sector, have become a pain for both public, and private sector banks in India.

How Grim is the Situation?

- More than ₹ 8 lakh crores worth of loans are classified as non-performing loans in India. This is a huge amount.
- The figure roughly translates to near 10 per cent of all loans given.
- This means that about 10 per cent of loans are never paid back, resulting in substantial loss of money to the banks.
- When restructured assets and potential NPAs are added, the total stressed assets would be 15-20 per cent of total loans.
- NPA crisis in India is set to worsen.
- Restructuring norms are being misused.
- This bad performance is not a good sign and can result in crashing of banks as happened in the sub-prime crisis of 2008 in the United States of America.
- For the 10 worst PSBs, gross NPAs averaged 16.4 per cent of gross advances as in December 2016, from 22.4 per cent for the Indian Overseas Bank to 14.1 per cent for the Central Bank of India – in effect, each having thoroughly destroyed its balance sheet.
- The system does not seem to have enough capital to take care of its bad loans.

What Led to this Situation?

- In an exuberant milieu that started with the UPA-1 government and continued until three years after the global financial crisis of 2008, large corporations conceived major project proposals in capital-intensive sectors, such as power, ports, airports, housing, reality and highway construction.

- Banks were only too keen to lend, often without sufficient evaluation of risks and returns. A large number of loans were given due to pressure from corrupt elements amongst political class in the UPA government.
- Things started worsening with the policy paralysis brought about by regular happening of scams in general and the spectrum and coal-mining scandals in particular.
- Soon, most projects were getting stuck, especially in power, steel, aviation and highways, and banks found their loans going doubtful or stressed.
- Initially, the extent of non-performing loan assets (NPAs) was hidden by "ever-greening" effected through restructuring of loans and giving further loans to defaulters so as to regularise the defaulted account.
- They were inevitably exposed with the advent of NDA regime as the RBI tightened the norms.

How are Businesses Getting Affected?

- The entrepreneurs who have cheated or taken the banks for a ride (and there are thousands and thousands of them) and have got their names imprinted in CIBIL data maintained by RBI website are as such permanently debarred from approaching again to any institutional lenders with the result that less and less experienced and business-minded entrepreneurs are left to merit availment of loans from banks and become capable to set up new units or indulge in expansions, thus resulting in negative business growth to some extent.

- Even some of the genuine businessmen are not getting funds from banks, firstly the bankers are not trusting them easily, secondly, bank officials are scared of taking personal accountability, fearing criminal action against them just in cases where loans recommended/sanctioned by them become bad and CBI gets into action for such 'wrong doings' on part of such officials.
- Due to spurt in bad loans, the bankers are unable to reduce interest rates to cover up for losses caused by defaulted and written off loans and, as such, Indian products are becoming uncompetitive in international markets and are unable to compete against cheaper imports.

How have the Public Sector Banks Behaved in such Circumstances?

With large losses on account of heavy provisioning and bad loans eroding their balance sheets, the PSBs have literally curtailed loans and advances. Obviously, this may result in reduced or even negative growth in GDP in spite of the best-intended efforts of the government of the day.

Were the Banks Alone at Fault? If not, Who else and What Other Factors too are Responsible?

- There is a myth that the main reason for rise in NPA in public-sector banks was priority sector lending (PSL). However, according to the findings of Standing Committee on Finance, NPAs in the corporate sector are far higher than those in the priority or agriculture sector. However, even the PSL sector has contributed substantially to the NPAs. As per the latest estimates by the SBI, education loans too contribute substantially to its NPAs.

- Wrongful diversion of funds to unrelated businesses and real assets acquisition.
- Lapses on part of bank officials to properly and regularly conduct due diligence, risk analysis, proper appraisal of project reports, proper verification of drawing power (DP) statements, failure to carry out objective inspections of the units funded by the banks with most of the inspection visits of bank officials getting reduced to be mere picnic visits to such units that are followed by borrowers giving gifts to the bank officials, thus resulting in dilution of whatever adverse reporting the bank officials were intending to make.
- Business losses due to changes in business/regulatory environment.
- Lack of morale amongst borrowers, particularly after government schemes, which had written off loans in the past.
- Global, regional or national financial crisis results in erosion of margins and profits of companies, therefore, stressing their balance sheet, which finally results into non-servicing of interest and loan payments. For example, the 2008 global financial crisis.
- The general slowdown of entire economy, for example, after 2011, there was a slowdown in the Indian economy, which resulted in the faster growth of NPAs.
- The slowdown in a specific industrial segment, therefore, companies in that area bear the heat and some may become NPAs.
- Unplanned expansion of corporate houses during boom period and loan taken at low rates later being serviced at high rates, therefore, resulting into NPAs.

- Due to mismanagement of funds by the borrowers, for example, indulging in excess borrowing and diverting excessive funds so borrowed in acquiring non-earning reality assets, which were purchased with an eye on earning from appreciation which went on unabated during 2004-12, but have started by and large to have a freefall in certain types of real assets especially in industrial properties, shops, etc. in malls.
- Due to misgovernance and policy paralysis, which hampers the timeline and speed of projects, therefore, loans become NPAs. For example, in infrastructure sector.
- Severe competition in any particular market segment. For example, telecom sector in India.
- Delay in land acquisition and getting clearance from various governmental authorities due to social, political, cultural and environmental reasons.
- A bad lending practice, which is a non-transparent way of giving loans.
- In some cases, mainly in agriculture sector even due to natural reasons, such as floods, droughts, disease outbreak, earthquakes, tsunami, etc.
- Cheap imports due to dumping lead to business loss of domestic companies. For example, steel sector in India.

Other Factors

- Banks did not conduct adequate contingency planning, especially for mitigating project risk. They did not factor eventualities like failure of gas projects to ensure supply of gas or failure of land acquisition process for highways.

- Restructuring of loan facility was extended to companies that were facing larger problems of over-leverage and inadequate profitability. This problem was more in the public-sector banks.
- Companies with dwindling debt repayment capacity were raising more and more debt from the system through falsely showing rosy picture of their past and recent past performance in their balance sheets. Some of these companies even provided for higher taxation provision on inflated profits, whereas, in actuality, they were suffering losses.

What is the Impact of NPAs?

- Lenders suffer lowering of profit margins and some have even lost more than their share capital and reserves and surplus of the past.
- Stress in banking sector causes less money available to fund other projects, therefore, negative impact on the larger national economy.
- Higher interest rates by the banks to maintain the profit margin.
- Redirecting funds from the good projects to the bad ones.
- As investments got stuck, it may result in unemployment.
- In the case of public-sector banks, the bad health of banks means a bad return for a shareholder, which means that the government of India gets less money as a dividend. Therefore, it may impact easy deployment of money for social and infrastructure development and result in social and political cost.
- Investors do not get rightful returns.

- Balance sheet syndrome of Indian characteristics that is both the banks and the corporate sector have stressed balance sheet and causes halting of the investment-led development process.
- NPAs-related cases add more pressure to already pending cases with the judiciary.
- The nation gets a bad name in the global market, the banks' credit rating goes down and borrowing from overseas lenders becomes costlier.

Steps Taken by RBI and Government in the Last Few Years to Curb NPA

- The government has launched 'Mission Indradhanush' to make the working of public-sector bank more transparent and professional in order to curb the menace of NPA in future.
- The government has introduced bankruptcy code.
- RBI introduced number of measures in the last few years, which include tightening the Corporate Debt Restructuring (CDR) mechanism, setting up a Joint Lenders' Forum, prodding banks to disclose the real picture of bad loans, asking them to increase provisioning for stressed assets, introducing a 5:25 scheme, where loans are to be amortised over 25 years with refinancing option after every five years, and empowering them to take majority control in defaulting companies under the Strategic Debt Restructuring (SDR) scheme.
- NPA story is not new in India and there have been several steps taken by the GoI on legal, financial, policy-level reforms. In the year 1991, Narasimham Committee recommended many reforms to tackle NPAs. Some of these were implemented.

The Debt Recovery Tribunals (DRTs) – 1993

To decrease the time required for settling cases. They are governed by the provisions of the Recovery of Debt Due to Banks and Financial Institutions Act, 1993. However, their number is not sufficient. Therefore, they also suffer from time lag and cases are pending for more than two-three years in many areas.

Credit Information Bureau – 2000

A good information system is required to prevent loan falling into bad hands and, therefore, prevention of NPAs. It helps banks by maintaining and sharing data of individual defaulters and willful defaulters.

Lok Adalats – 2001

They are helpful in tackling and recovery of small loans. However, they are limited up to five lakh rupee loans only by the RBI guidelines issued in 2001. They are positive in the sense that they avoid more cases into the legal system.

Compromise Settlement – 2001

- It provides a simple mechanism for recovery of NPA for the advances below ₹ 10 crores.
- It covers lawsuits with courts and DRTs (Debt Recovery Tribunals). However, willful default and fraud cases are excluded.

SARFAESI Act – 2002

- The Securitisation and Reconstruction of Financial Assets and Enforcement of Security Interest (SARFAESI) Act, 2002 – The Act permits banks/ financial institutions to recover their NPAs without the involvement of the court, through acquiring and disposing of the secured assets in NPA accounts with an outstanding amount of ₹ 1 lakh and above.

- The banks have to first issue a notice. Then, on the borrower's failure to repay, they can:
    - Take ownership of security.
    - Control over the management of the borrowing concern.
    - Appoint a person to manage the concern.
- Further, this Act has been amended last year to make its enforcement faster.

ARCs (Asset Reconstruction Companies)

- The RBI gave license to 14 new ARCs recently after the amendment of the SARFAESI Act of 2002.
- These companies are created to unlock value from stressed loans. Before this law came into force, lenders could enforce their security interests only through courts, which was a time-consuming process.
- An ARC acquires bad loans from banks and financial institutions, usually at a discount, and works to recover them through a variety of measures, including sale of assets or a turnaround steered by professional management. Relieved of their NPA burden, the banks can focus on their core activity of lending.

Corporate Debt Restructuring – 2005

It is for reducing the burden of the debts on the company by decreasing the rates paid and increasing the time the company has to pay the obligation back.

5:25 Rule – 2014

- Also known as Flexible Structuring of Long-Term Project Loans to Infrastructure and Core Industries.
- It was proposed to maintain the cash flow of such companies since the project timeline is long and they do not get the money back into their books for a long

time. Therefore, the requirement of loans at every five-seven years and, thus, refinancing for long-term projects.

Joint Lenders Forum – 2014

It was created by the inclusion of all PSBs, whose loans had become stressed. It is present so as to avoid loan to same individual or company from different banks. It is formulated to prevent the instances where one person takes a loan from one bank to give a loan of the other bank.

Long-term Measures

- Improving credit risk management – This includes credit appraisal, credit monitoring and efficient system of fixing accountability and analysing trends in group leverage, to which the borrowing firm belongs.
- Sources/structure of equity capital – Banks need to see that promoter's contribution is funded through equity and not debt.
- Banks should conduct necessary sensitivity analysis and contingency planning while appraising the projects and it should build adequate safeguards against such external factors.
- Strengthen credit monitoring – Develop an early warning mechanism and comprehensive MIS (Management Information System) can play an important role in it. MIS must enable timely detection of problem accounts, flag early signs of delinquencies and facilitate timely information to the management on these aspects.
- Enforce accountability – Till now, lower-ring officials considered accountable even though loaning decisions are taken at higher levels. Thus, sanction official should also share the burden of responsibility.

- Restructured accounts should be treated as non-performing and technical write offs where banks remove NPAs from their balance sheets permanently should be dispensed with.
- Address corporate governance issues in PSBs. These include explicit fit and proper criteria for appointment of top executives and instituting system of an open market wide search for chairman.

—Rajesh Khattar

❐

29

The Insolvency and Bankruptcy Code, 2016 (IBC), Another Revolutionary Step by the Government of India

The stressed assets, in the Indian banking industry, have peaked up, due to the lack of concrete and effective steps by the previous Government. We had multiple rules and regulations and multiple adjudicating authorities to tackle the recovery measures. But, none of the measures had a force to yield the desired results.

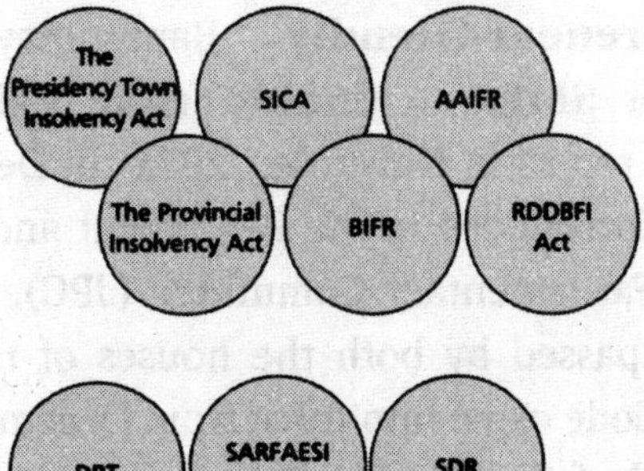

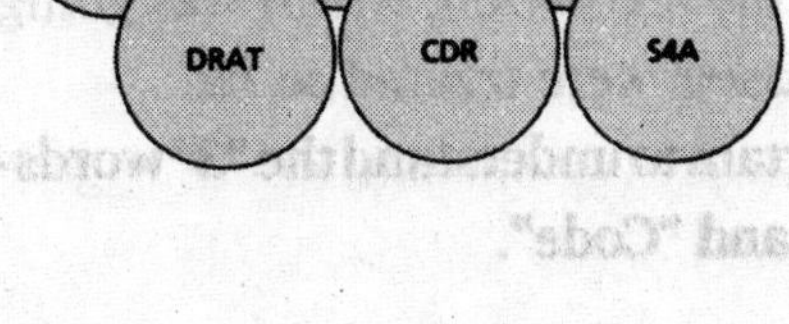

A need was felt to have the law to **consolidate** and amend the laws relating to

- ✓ reorganisation and insolvency resolution
- ✓ corporate persons, partnership firms and individuals
- ✓ in a **time-bound manner**
- ✓ for the **maximisation of value of assets** of such persons
- ✓ to promote entrepreneurship, availability of credit and balance the interests of all the stakeholders
- ✓ including alteration in the **order of priority of payment of Government dues**.

The Government, under the leadership of Hon'ble Prime Minister Narendrabhai Modi, was determined to crack this disease faced by the banking sector, in particular, public sector banks. The Government was determined to enact the legislation and made it operational in the shortest possible time frame. With this objective, the Bankruptcy Law Reforms Committee (BLRC) was formed in August 2014 under the chairmanship of Dr. T.K. Viswanathan. In the Budget speech for the FY 2014-15, the Finance Minister announced that an **Entrepreneur-friendly** Bankruptcy framework developed for **SMEs** to **enable easy exit**. The BLRC submitted its report in November 2015. In December 2015, the IBC was introduced in the Parliament and was referred to the Joint Parliamentary Committee (JPC). In May 2016, the Bill was passed by both the houses of the Parliament and the IBC Code came into force from December 2016. The decisive mind of the present Government made it possible to implement the legislation, which was going to change the way the bad assets were treated so far.

It is important to understand the "3" words – "Insolvency", "Bankruptcy" and "Code".

Insolvency

"Insolvency" is the inability of an entity – a person, family, or company – to pay its lenders back on time. In general, this occurs when the entity's cash inflow is lesser than its cash outflow or the incomes are too low to pay off the debts or assets are less than one's liabilities.

Bankruptcy

"Bankruptcy" is a legal declaration of one's inability to pay off debts.

Code

"Code" is a systematic and comprehensive compilation of laws, rules or regulations that are consolidated and classified according to a particular subject matter.

The IBC attempts to address the lacuna under the current system. Under the Sick Industrial Companies Act (SICA), the criterion was the erosion of the net worth of an entity. Under the IBC, the criterion has been shifted to the inability of a debtor to pay off its creditors, irrespective of its net-worth. It is a bold attempt to consolidate multiplicity of laws and to provide a definite time-bound process for the remedial measures.

Applicability of the Code

The IBC is applicable to:

- ✓ All Companies, whether Private Limited or Public Limited
- ✓ Limited Liability Partnership Firms
- ✓ Partnership Firms
- ✓ Individuals

The IBC is not applicable to Financial Service Providers, like Banks and Insurance Companies.

Qualification & Eligibility to become an IP:

1. Passing the "National Insolvency Examination" and
2. 10 years of professional experience as a Chartered Accountant OR a Cost Accountant OR a Company Secretary OR an Advocate OR 15 years of experience in Management after Graduation.
3. Should be a person resident in India.
4. Should not have been convicted for an offense punishable with imprisonment for a term exceeding 6 months, within a period of 5 years or imprisonment for a period of 7 years or more anytime.
5. Should not be an undischarged insolvent.
6. Should not be in employment.

There are 3 IPAs registered with an IBBI:

- ❖ Insolvency Professional Agency of Institute of Cost Accountants of India
- ❖ Indian Institute of Insolvency Professionals of ICAI
- ❖ ICSI Insolvency Professional Agency.

It is open for the professional to register with any of the IPAs. Once the registration certificate is issued by IBBI, the person can act as an Insolvency Professional.

An Insolvency Professional can also form Insolvency Professional Entity, wherein majority of members should be IP.

Role of Insolvency Professional

The Bankruptcy Law Reforms Committee, in para 4.4 of its report, narrated the role of insolvency professionals as under:

"Insolvency professionals play a vital role in the insolvency and bankruptcy resolution process as envisaged by the Committee and as detailed in chapters 5 and 6. As mentioned in these chapters, insolvency and bankruptcy resolution under the Code will proceed in two phases, for registered entities as well as for individuals. The first phase of the insolvency and bankruptcy process is the period of insolvency resolution during which insolvency is assessed and a solution is reached within a stipulated time period. In case a solution is not reached within the specified time limit, the second phase of the process begins, wherein the entity is declared bankrupt. At this point, a registered entity enters into liquidation, whereas an individual enters into bankruptcy resolution. This entire insolvency and bankruptcy process is managed by a regulated and licensed professional, namely the Insolvency Professional or an IP, appointed by the adjudicator. In an insolvency and bankruptcy resolution process driven by the law, there are judicial decisions being taken by the adjudicator. But, there are also checks and accounting as well as conduct of due process that are carried out by the IPs. Insolvency professionals form a crucial pillar upon which rests the effective, timely functioning as well as credibility of the entire edifice of the Insolvency & Bankruptcy Resolution Process.

An IP may hold any of the following roles under the Code:

1. Resolution professional (RP) to resolve insolvency for a firm or an individual;
2. Bankruptcy trustee in an individual bankruptcy process;
3. Liquidator in a firm liquidation process.

In administering the resolution outcomes, the role of the IP encompasses a wide range of functions, which include adhering to the procedure of the law, as well as accounting and finance-related functions. The latter include the identification of the assets and liabilities of the defaulting debtor, its management during the insolvency proceedings if it is an enterprise, preparation of the resolution proposal, implementation of the solution for individual resolution, the construction, negotiation and mediation of deals as well as distribution of the realisation proceeds under bankruptcy resolution. In performing these tasks, an IP acts as an agent of the adjudicator. In a way, the adjudicator depends on the specialised skills and expertise of the IPs to carry out these tasks in an efficient and professional manner. The role of the IPs is, thus, vital to the efficient operation of the insolvency and bankruptcy resolution process. A well-functioning system of resolution driven by IPs enables the adjudicator to delegate more and more powers and duties to the professionals. This creates the positive externality of better utilisation of judicial time. The worse the performance of IPs, the more the adjudicator may need to personally supervise the process, which, in turn, my cause inordinate delays. Consumers in a well-functioning market for IPs are likely to have greater trust in the overall insolvency resolution system. On the other hand, poor-quality services, and recurring instances of malpractice and fraud erode consumer trust."

Role of Insolvency Professionals as "Resolution Professional"

Under the earlier mechanism of SICA, the theme was that of 'debtor-in-possession'. This implied that the debtor continues to remain in possession of the management of the entity during the entire process of the resolution. First time, the theme has been shifted from the "Debtor-in-possession" to the "Creditor-in-possession". This implies that the entire management of the affairs of the Corporate Debtor will shift from the Debtor to the Creditors through the Resolution Professional. The powers of the Board of Directors of the corporate debtor stands suspended and the same will be exercised by the Resolution Professional.

Once the Corporate Insolvency Resolution Process (CIRP) is initiated, the Insolvency Professional is appointed as "Interim Resolution Professional" for a period of 30 days. In the first meeting of the "Committee of Creditors (COC)" that takes place within 30 days, the members of the COC either confirm the appointment of "Interim Resolution Professional" as "Resolution Professional" (RP) or appoint a new RP.

Eligibility Criteria for Resolution Professional

The RP must be independent to a Corporate Debtor –

- ✓ Should be eligible to be appointed as an independent director on the board of the corporate debtor under Section 149 of the Companies Act, 2013.
- ✓ Should not be a related party of the corporate debtor or
- ✓ Should not be an employee or proprietor or a partner of firm of CA, CS or CMA.
- ✓ Should not be an employee or proprietor or a partner of a legal or a consulting firm that has or had any transaction amounting to 10% or more of the gross turnover of such firm, in the last 3 FY.
- ✓ No disciplinary proceedings should be pending against proposed RP.

Actions to be Taken by Interim Resolution Professional (IRP)

1. Public announcement within 3 days
    - ✓ In one English newspaper with wide circulation
    - ✓ In one Regional Language newspaper with wide circulation

- ✓ On the website of Corporate Debtor
- ✓ On the website of IBBI

2. Collect all information relating to the corporate debtor, including information relating to
   - ✓ business operations for the previous two years;
   - ✓ financial and operational payments for the previous two years;
   - ✓ List of assets and liabilities as on the initiation date
3. Receive and collate all the claims submitted by creditors.
4. Verify every claim within 7 days from the last date of receipt of claims.
5. Constitute a committee of creditors.
6. Monitor the assets of the corporate debtor and manage its operations until a resolution professional is appointed by the committee of creditors.
7. Take control and custody of all the assets of the corporate debtor.
8. Manage the operations as a going concern.
9. Within 30 days, file a report before NCLT for constitution of committee of creditors (COC).
10. Within next 7 days, call the first meeting of COC.

Actions to be taken by a Resolution Professional (RP)

1. Take custody and control of all the assets and records
2. Represent and act on behalf of the corporate debtor
3. Raise interim finances subject to the approval of the COC
4. Appoint accountants, legal or other professionals
5. Maintain an updated list of claims
6. Convene and attend all meetings of the COC
7. Prepare the Information Memorandum

8. Invite prospective resolution applicants to submit a resolution plan
9. Present all resolution plans at the meetings of the COC
10. Submit the approved resolution plan to NCLT

Role of an Insolvency Professional as a Liquidator

- Insolvency Resolution process period is 180 days and can be extended by a maximum period of 90 days with the approval of NCLT.
- Liquidation process is commenced:
  - if no resolution plan is received by the NCLT before the expiry of Insolvency Resolution Process period.
  - if the resolution plan is rejected by NCLT.
  - if the Resolution Professional, unless replaced by the NCLT, will be appointed as the liquidator.

Duties of an IP as a Liquidator

- Take control and custody of all the assets and properties and protect and preserve the same.
- Verify the claims of all the creditors.
- Institute or defend any legal case.
- Sell assets and properties.
- Maintain all the relevant records.
- Distribute the sales proceeds as per waterfall arrangement prescribed under the law.

The beginning of the insolvency regime is a part of the initiative taken by the Government of India in improving the rating of "ease of doing the business". The IBC, being an emerging law in our country, there is no precedent with regard to insolvency laws in India. The concept of 'creditor in possession' has scared the defaulting promoters of the corporates, as they lose their control over their entity. Since the inception of the law, the number of cases is admitted each day. The "12" big NPA cases were referred to NCLT and are yielding the solutions which no one thought was possible to achieve. For the first time, we have seen the law which has put a hammer on the defaulting promoters. The Government is also very pro-active and is carrying our suitable amendments in the Code to make it more effective and to seal any of the practical difficulties faced during its implementation. With such kind of reforms taken by the Government under the dynamic leadership of Hon'ble Prime Minister, Shri Narendrabhai Modi, our country has seen the improvement in the ranking of "ease of doing business".

—C.A. Dakshesh Choksi

❐

30
Rural Skill Development – An Overview in Indian Context

A useful conceptual approach to make sense of rural skill development is to think of it in terms of a skill supply and demand system. Within each sector, industry and workplace – whether these are classified as formal or informal – the types and levels of skills demanded and supplied vary.

Rural skills are traditionally associated with workplace and occupational profiles in natural resource-dependent sectors, especially modern and traditional farming systems (or primary agriculture).

Participation in and uptake of standard and vocational skills development programmes is an important element and indicator of skill demand. This relates to the needs felt among workers to undertake job skill training in an effort to upgrade their current and future performance in a specified occupation. In other words, to climb the occupation ladder, workers demand skill training.

In this regard, it is crucial to isolate the factors that encourage or discourage participation among individuals in skill development initiatives on offer. Put differently, it enables the identification of the determinants of demand for skill development. What types or kinds of interventions are necessary to encourage individual workers to demand further skill training? How must these training programmes be tailored to effectively meet the demands of participants and industries?

In this context, there is a need to distinguish between the training of rural people (who largely tend to migrate to urban areas with acquired skills) and the training in or provision of skills to rural people for rural development. A proper support system is required for the various cooperatives that exist in rural and urban areas and to provide them with customised programmes and skills. Many issues are involved in implementing the Skills Development Programme in Rural Areas, a few of them are reviewed here.

First, there appears to be a dearth of research on rural skill supply and demand. There is not a large body of literature that focusses on the supply of and demand for skills in rural area per se. Agriculture is perhaps the most researched sector in the rural areas. Agricultural studies have tended to focus on agricultural extension, technology adoption and the skills required. However, even in these studies, there is very limited focus on the supply and demand for these skills. A more robust analysis of skill supply and demand in rural areas and specifically for rural development is required.

Historically, the focus has been on. the supply of agricultural skills, a focus which still prevails to some extent, while the increasing demand by many of the rural population has been for skills that increase mobility and the chances of seeking employment outside of the rural areas.

Agriculture, for example, is modernising fast and this is evident from its increasing reliance on modern systems of technology development and transfers and innovations. Although traditional agriculture continues to be the mainstay in rural employment, rising shares of non-farm rural employment are rapidly expanding and resulting in a wide variety of occupations (self-employed farmers, artisanal manufacturers, tourism, etc.) and skill levels. Most 'rural research' that focusses on skills, training and education tends to link these to agricultural and farming technical requirements.

Commercially oriented small-scale farmers, engaging or intending to engage in national and global commodity chains will require new technologies and management skills to increase their overall productivity and competitiveness. To use new technologies, these farmers will need to be better resourced (in terms of education, skills and finances). Other rural residents who consider agriculture as a livelihood safety net will require cost-effective appropriate technologies and skills that improve efficiency and protect the natural resources (e.g., agroecological farming skills).We should also consider the case of skill demand along the agricultural value chain, agroprocessing tends to be more skill-intensive than primary agriculture and it is expected that agroprocessors will demand relatively more skilled workers. Structural change and changing production methods in farming resulted in declines in the demand for unskilled labour.

Second, other industries exist in rural areas such as mining and minerals, forestry (sawmills), crafts, tourism and hospitality, clothing and textiles, and retail, but the supply and demand for associated skills remain unclear. The geographic location and intensity of these industries is diversely spread across the various rural areas. However, like agriculture, their secondary downstream value-adding activities may well be located in urban and peri-urban areas. Furthermore, as with agriculture, these industries are represented at various scales and with diverse degrees of sustainability and levels of formalisation, demanding access to a variety of skills. Skill demand is basically a function of the economic performance and technological requirements of firms, industries or economic sectors. Tertiary and service industries usually demand a larger proportion of high-skilled professionals than primary sectors (like farming, mining and fishing). The demand for skill, therefore, varies across the value chain.

For example, construction contractors tended to come from outside the rural areas and, in some cases, used external labour. This might mean that certain construction-related skills at various levels are in short supply, the irregular demand is not sufficient to warrant that rural people with these skills remain in the rural areas, or rural people are unaware of or unable to respond to opportunities (i.e., tenders) for providing services as they do not have there requisite skills to complete the technical and detailed service provider application documents.

A new approach is required to analyse other economic sectors within rural areas to find out where the skill demand lies or possibly which elements might be more suited to rural locations. If they are currently urban-based suppliers to rural firms, primarily the interest would be in upstream and downstream needs and skills required, and where these are best located. ICT is one example. Technicians and support services are required in rural areas (although demand may be less than in urban areas), but other ICT components such as infrastructure, hardware and software design, development and supply could be urban, rural or peri-urban based. Analysis of suitability of location is required. For retail supermarkets, distribution is centralised and primarily urban based, although fresh produce is primarily sourced from the rural areas. This centralisation of distribution may effectively increase the price of fresh food in rural areas due to transport costs. Assessments across the value chains of various sectors will also assist in establishing the role played by employers and employees in the informal sector and the skills they require.

Third, obtaining access to post-school education in rural areas is problematic for a number of reasons including the following: insufficient finances, access to institutions is constrained by the distances that have to be covered, education and training at many of these rural institutions is of a low quality, and the low quality of schooling in rural areas also prevents access to these institutions and can result in poor academic performance and increasing number of dropouts. The supply side of the skills system includes formal educational institutions – such as schools and various providers of higher education. A relatively smaller proportion of universities and colleges might be located in rural areas, implying an unequal spatial spread of skill supply institutions in favour of localities with better socio-economic infrastructure, and so on. Vocational and on-the-job training schemes add to skill supply but such skill development interventions are often informal and, therefore, harder to monitor and assess especially in rural localities.

Fourth, while the state would like to encourage rural people to adopt skills that enable them to carry out and support rural development, this idea is challenged by the fact that many want to leave the rural areas and also by the lack of clear understanding of what is rural development and how it can be achieved. Community Development Workers (CDWs) at village level are considered crucial to this job creation. Their role is to train and mentor identified community members to ensure the latter's gainful entrance into the economy. Changing rural-urban migration dynamics and rising levels in agricultural productivity, for example, continue to restructure the skill profiles in rural areas. Rural learners may well still want skills that enable them to relocate outside of the rural areas.

Fifth, while skill bias technical change reflects industry demands for skilled workers, whether it is resource-based or in services, the determinants of individual demand for and participation in vocational training interventions also require attention, given government's commitment to better rural service delivery. Investment in rural infrastructure has received more attention than skill development, but rural infrastructure does not automatically translate into rural skill development.

Rural skill demand critically depends on the skill bias of industries and economic sectors concentrated in these localities. In addition to macro-demand for skills from industries and sectors, it is important also to focus on individual demand for skills training or willingness to enrol skill development programmes. Determinants of individual uptake of vocational training schemes are particularly important for the design of effective state-funded skill development interventions.

Research is required to reach agreement on how best to conceptualise rural development and the roles of different sectors. Part of this work would entail the identification of the crucial drivers in different sectors in the various regions and provinces and an analysis of the skills required over the medium term. What other sectors, besides agriculture, contribute to rural development, how best can they do this and what skills are required? Rightly argued that a coherent and longer term government strategy is required to increase job opportunities in low-skilled activities and to reduce the vulnerability of low-skilled workers to low wages, insecure employment, poor conditions and, ultimately, unemployment.

—C.A. Lalit Mahajan

❐

31

Skill Development Mission – An Overview in Indian Context

The vision of our Hon'ble Prime Minister Shri Narendra Modi in Skill India Mission is to make a bridge between the skill supply and demand system which is the main feature of Skill Development. Within each sector, industry and workplace – whether these are classified as formal or informal – the types and levels of skills demand and supply vary.

India is blessed with a vast young manpower which resides in rural areas in different states. The motive of the Government of India is to bring a tapestry of change by inviting and attracting Multinational Companies in India by equipping the young rural manpower with requisite skills through various programmes implemented through various Ministries under Central and State Governments which is not only focussed for youths but also categorised into:

(a) Women empowerment

(b) Tribal Empowerment

(c) Minority Empowerment

Various Ministries and Schemes like:

- **Ministry of Social Justice and Empowerment,** Govt. of India, funded : Swastha Programme & Mukhya Mantri Nari Shakti Yojna for Women

- **Ministry of Minority Affairs,** Govt. of India funded Nai Manzil and Sheekho aur Kamao Programme, Khwaja Garib Nawaj, MANAS for Minority Youths
- **Integrated Livelihood Skill Programme** by National Urban Livelihood Mission, Govt. of India
- **Ministry of Rural Development,** Govt. of India funded Deendayal Upadhyaya Gramin Kaushal Yojna (For Rural Youths), ROSHNI, SAGARMALA (for Coastal youths funded by Ministry of Shipping) and HIMAYAT (for J&K Youths) **to name a few programmes.**

Rural skills were traditionally associated with workplace and occupational profiles in natural resource-dependent sectors, especially modern and traditional farming systems (or primary agriculture). The Government is also concentrating on the aspect to train the Rural youths for Agriculture domain also, **IFAD and World Bank** is committed to meet the target to control the migration of Rural Youths from the hilly and coastal areas also.

Participation in and uptake of standard and vocational skills development programmes is an important element and indicator of skill demand. This relates to the needs felt among workers to undertake job skill training in an effort to upgrade their current and future performance in a specified occupation. In other words, to climb the occupation ladder, workers demand skill training.

The mandate of the Government is to join all youths of the Nation (indifferent to their Creed, Culture and Geographical presence may it be from Kashmir to Tamil Nadu and from Arunachal Pradesh to Gujarat) to join together to make the dream of Make in India a grand success. The Government apart from skilling through various programme has also introduced D-VOC and B-VOC programme through AICTE so that the industrial workers can also upgrade their knowledge for vertical movement in their pace of expertise, in order to combine the strength of the Skill India Mission, the Govt. has also started certifying the candidates through Recognition of Prior Learning (RPL) who are already engaged in various professions without proper academics but play a vital role in making the Smart Cities and other construction projects like National Highways, Prime Minister Awas Yojana, etc.

In this regard, it is crucial to isolate the factors that encourage or discourage participation among individuals in skill development initiatives on offer. Put differently, it enables the identification of the determinants of demand for skill development. What types or kinds of interventions are necessary to encourage individual workers to demand further skill training? How must these training programmes be tailored to effectively meet the demands of participants and industries? To meet this requirement, **National Skill Development Corporation (NSDC)** is set up under Ministry of Skill Development and Entrepreneurship (MSDE) Government of India to streamline a set of modules which should be NSQF (National Skill Qualification Framework) complaint, Sector Skill Councils of various domains have been established and Government of India from August 2018 have made a Single Window Programme for all the Skill Development Projects through Certification of the candidates only through Sector Skill Councils for the Modules which are NSQF complaint.

To identify the Skill Gap, MSME has prepared the Skill Gap Analysis of all the states and the opportunity of gainful employment in all domains district-wise which helps out the

Government department to specify the target of Skilling in Block level in various states of India.

The Government through **Request For Proposal (RFPs)** invites applications from Program Implementing Agencies (PIAs) and after proper scrutiny of each proposal, **Proposal Appraisal Committee** (headed by Additional Chief Secretary of the State) finalise the list of PIAs who are capable of implementing the project, in order to secure the output, ***Performance Bank Guarantee, Cash flow statement based on Project Perspective Work Schedule (PPWS) as well as free fund flow (certified by Chartered Accountant) statement of the PIA is also obtained before the implementation of the Project.***

The finances and Utility Certificates submitted by the PIA is closely monitored through periodic audits done by the finance head of the concerned Government department, for that purpose every PIA is required to appoint Periodic Auditor as well as third party auditor is also required to be appointed for the reports on the implementation of the project which consists of Mobilisation through Information-Education-Communication (IEC) of the candidates, Delivery of the Training, Placement of the candidates (70% of the approved target) and Post Placement Support (50% retention of the candidates till 12 months).

The Ministries have set up Program Management Unit (PMU) where third-party experts like KPMG, Accenture, Nascom, NIRD, E&Y, to name a few, are appointed for Quality Control of the implementation of the Skill Development Projects.

In various speeches of our Hon'ble Prime Minister during his visits in various countries, he had always quoted that Indian Youths equipped with skilling in various domains will not only give a substantial strength to the Nation but also will fulfill the demand of the world.

Skill India Mandate simply may be defined as:

"Skill for all, Insurance of future to all and productivity of the entire nation by joining them in the mainstream of the Society for all."

—Dr. Jaideep Dasgupta

—Chandrashekhar Rai

❑

32
Real Estate Background and Land Acquisition

The real estate sector is one of the most globally recognised sectors. In India, real estate is the second largest employer after agriculture and is slated to grow at 30 per cent over the next decade. The real estate sector comprises four sub-sectors – housing, retail, hospitality and commercial. The growth of this sector is well complemented by the growth of the corporate environment and the demand for office space as well as urban and semi-urban accommodations. The construction industry ranks third among the 14 major sectors in terms of direct and indirect and induced effects in all sectors of the economy.

It is also expected that this sector will attract more non-resident Indian (NRI) investments in both the short-term and the long-term.

The Indian real estate market is expected to touch US$ 180 billion by 2020. The housing sector alone contributes 5-6 per cent to the country's Gross Domestic Product (GDP).

For the past few years, the prices of real estate has been stable or downwards in a few cases. This is basically because of the sudden growth of the real estate sector before the prices went down. Such a scenario is basically a correction scenario, which is likely to complete its cycle. However, where the developer has been facing severe problems due to lack of growth of prices of houses, the buyer, on the other hand, has an opportunity to purchase such houses today at a lower rate. This is also good for the economy as inflation in real estate is not productive for the economy. The gap in the demand and supply of real estate is due to the increased supply of the higher and middle income segments. However, there is still a wide gap in LIG and EWS houses, some approx. 20 million. On the other side, new land acquisition law has become effective due to this. Land acquisition has become difficult and genuine development work of infrastructure is also hampered. Unfortunately, it is a general perception that whenever any land is acquired, it is mostly against the farmer's will. On the other side, farmers themselves want their land to be acquired because they get good compensation as compared to earning from agriculture. Another perception that is still being continued by the people, who support farmers for their rights, is that they have to oppose land acquisition to favour the farmer's will. They are not worried about the actual problems of the farmer as to why the farmer is not getting the actual price of his crop, why his crop has not been insured. Why his loan has not been paid on time, etc. By opposing land acquisition, we actually favour big farmers or land mafia instead of understanding the problems of marginal farmers.

One of the practices that is still followed, which needs to be changed, is the method of providing compensation for compulsory land acquisition. In today's practice, government provides a monetary compensation in consideration of compulsory land acquisition. This practice is traditional and benefits only the land owner, to whom monetary amount is paid, yet there is no direct benefit to the farmers of the surrounding lands. This also creates more corruption and nexus between land mafia and acquisition authorities/ officers. The compensation that is offered by the government for land acquisition is generally two to four times the circle rate depending upon whether it is rural or urban land. Besides, the government provides several other benefits, despite good compensation, we generally see lot of agitation & resistance from the land owners, whose land is being acquired. At this point, the other opposition parties come in support of the farmer/land owner and ask for higher compensation. Many times, it also happens that the land mafia people, who were already aware of the proposed acquisition, acquire the land from the poor farmers at a much cheaper rate. So, the demand for the higher compensation from the government actually comes from these new land owners. In that case, whatever benefit comes from the government for the land acquisition goes to these new owners instead of the poor farmers, who owned the land initially. With the process, there is direct benefit of only a very few people, whose lands are being acquired. We would like to suggest a model, wherein the land owners of the surrounding area can benefit and the process of acquisiton can become smooth and litigation-free.

To justify and speed up the process of land acquisition, the government may, in the form of consideration, offer either monetary compensation as per Land Acquisition Act or provide land, which would be equal to certain multiplier, say double the area of the present land currently owned by the farmer. This land could be preferably purchased by the government/acquisition authority from the surrounding farmers through tenders.

We propose that where the land to be acquired is not specified, the acquisition could be made through direct negotiation or by inviting tenders with minimum support acquisiton price. In cases, where specific land is to be acquired, the following process can be followed:

By offering exchange of land in the nearby area equivalent to a pre-decided multiplier, say double or 2.5 times.

OR

By offering cash compensation equivalent to cost of the above-mentioned land to be exchanged.

The cost of the exchanged land would be determined by inviting tenders from the nearby farmers with minimum support acquisition price.

By the above practice, no development work would be hampered and fair compensation would be provided to the farmers, whose land has been acquired. The other surrounding farmers will also prosper as they'll also get the opportunity to sell their land.

Afforadable Housing

Affordability, especially in the Indian real estate sector, can mean a wide range of things. Specifically, the term holds different meanings for different categories of demographics. Further, there are also several socio-economic variables governing a city or location to consider. Generally, 'affordable housing' refers to residences that have been especially designed for the economically weaker section (EWS) and Lower Income Group (LIG), who are looking for the same comfort and security of a self-owned property/home that the more fortunate middle class enjoys.

In the earlier years of real estate development in India, the EWS and LIG categories did not get much attention to their needs. However, with changes in administration and especially with the current government coming to power, a significant amount of changes have taken place in this respect. These two sections make up the thickest segment of the demography for India, and form the base of the country's economy. It has been overdue that their requirements are looked into. Due to lack of availability of real affordable housing, people tend to move towards unauthorised colonies for their requirement. As a result, following implications occur:

1. Financial burden on healthcare facilities.
2. Financial burden on development authorities to develop the basic amenities.
3. Degradation of environment, visual pollution and overcrowding of town and cities.
4. Revenue losses for the government.
5. Increase in crimes and lack of proper law and order.
6. Additional financial burden on municipal corporations to maintain the basic amenities.

Overall, the buyer still lives in an unhygienic environment even after paying a heavy price for the houses.

Possible solutions for such a problem can be:

- Ease in government regulations and by-laws.
- At present, the upper cap in the affordable housing segment is provided at one level for all kinds of houses. Maximum sales price for different categories of houses in different towns should be listed, instead of keeping general cap on affordable housing without considering the locality of houses.
- PMAY also provides loan subsidy. Also known as credit-linked subsidy, it is very useful, yet the benefit could not be availed by EWS. New models are being proposed to enable EWS to get home loans with either the builder or the government giving the guarantee to the bank.

- Giving land to developers at a subsidised rate for building affordable houses and other houses, and, therefore, reducing the cost of affordable houses through cross-subsidisation.
- Reducing the sale price of affordable houses through different models.

Conclusion

Responding to an increasingly well-informed consumer base and, bearing in mind the aspect of globalisation and with the new Real Estate Regulation Act commenced from 1st May, 2017, Indian real estate developers have shifted gears and accepted fresh challenges. The most marked change has been the shift from family-owned businesses to that of professionally managed ones. Real estate developers, in meeting the growing need for managing multiple projects across cities, are also investing in centralised processes to source material and organise manpower and hiring qualified professionals in areas such as project management, architecture and engineering. RERA is very effective for regulating the real estate market, which was going unregulated till 2017, but it is more effective for new projects. In case of existing projects under default, through RERA, it is difficult to identify between willful defaulters and genuine business defaulters. For the existing projects, RERA will be more effective with restructuring of the existing real estate companies through a separate professionally specialised restructuring authority.

—Kamal Kant Jain

❑

33
Corporate Governance Framework in India – Aiming at Value beyond Compliance

Whether introduction of regulatory changes will lead to improved corporate governance and sustainable value creation? This is a question that needs to be asked. It is worth noting that following the Enron and WorldCom debacles at the turn of this century, regulatory changes came about (e.g., the Sarbanes Oxley Act, referred to as SOX).

Ever since the governance failure unearthed at Satyam Computer Services Limited, the concerns about good Corporate Governance have increased phenomenally.

The Indian framework on Corporate Governance has been vastly in sync with the international standards. Broadly, the Indian framework on Corporate Governance can be described as follows:

1. The Companies Act, 2013 has provisions concerning Independent Directors, Board Constitution, General meetings, Board meetings, Board processes, Related Party Transactions, Audit Committees, etc.

2. SEBI (Securities and Exchange Board of India) Guidelines ensure the protection of investors and have mandated the companies to adhere to the best practices mentioned in the guidelines.

3. Accounting Standards issued by the ICAI (Institute of Chartered Accountants of India) wherein the ICAI is an autonomous body and issues accounting standards. The disclosure of financial statements is also made mandatory by the ICAI backed by the Companies Act, 2013, Sec. 129.

4. Standard Listing Agreement of Stock Exchanges applies to the companies whose shares are listed on various stock exchanges.

5. Secretarial Standards Issued by the ICSI (Institute of Company Secretaries of India) issues standards on 'Meetings of the Board of Directors', General Meetings', etc. The Companies Act, 2013 empowers this autonomous body to provide standards which every company is required to adhere to.

The new norms after the Companies Act, 2013 came into the picture are very balanced and innovative. They have helped reform the growth of Indian companies as per the international standards.

Too much of regulations and making them more prescriptive gives rise to the risk that companies approach corporate governance as an exercise in regulatory compliance. While regulations can at best be a good starting point, it is equally important to have national-level institutions that research and disseminate good governance practices across the corporate landscape. Thereafter, it is up to every company to imbibe these governance principles and practices into their ecosystem that will best meet its challenges.

Corporate Governance practices in India are still evolving. It is a process of engaging shareholders and the management effectively to enhance the organisation's value. It involves participation of various stakeholders and management, communication, exchanging and validating ideas, and lots of debates and discussions. Hence, Corporate Governance is essentially a function of the mindset and culture prevalent in the organisation's operating environment. Corporate Governance cannot be looked at in isolation; it is heavily influenced by the overall governance ecosystem. Recent scandals in corporate India have raised questions not only about the practices adopted by the companies to solicit business but also about the standards of accountability in public administration including within the government machinery and institutions. These larger governance issues will need to be addressed alongside governance issues within corporates.

Corporate Governance in India faces its own set of challenge. Select ones are mentioned as below:

1. There is a gap between corporate governance standards in the public sector and the private sector. PSUs are subjected to varying levels of government interference in their routine functioning, undermining their autonomy.

2. Although India has numerous regulations, their enforcement is quite weak. Numerous government departments, multiple layers of bureaucracy and complex power-sharing equations among them stifle stringent enforcement of regulations. Private enforcement, i.e., enforcement by shareholders and market intermediaries is weak too. There needs to be an objective debate in corporate India about what is required to be done to make independent directors more effective. In the past, there has been a tendency to blame independent directors for governance issues. It is important to address the challenges such as true independence, developing the institution and

pool of personnel with diverse skill sets who can provide exemplary board service and improve corporate functioning and taking concrete measures to improve their functioning through a combination of orientation, training, clear roles and adequate remuneration.

3. There is substantial room for improvement in enhancing accountability. Within many board rooms in India, the topic of CEO succession is not often discussed. CEO succession planning calls for wider debate and rigorous processes than the ones currently followed, especially in owner-managed businesses. Also, boards need to be held more accountable for their decisions and actions.

4. Investor activism in India is relatively muted. As experience has shown, greater investor scrutiny could bring about substantial improvement in corporate governance. This is an important area where India needs to catch up with the developed world fast.

To overcome these challenges, there needs to be clear separation of ownership, control, and management functions. Successful owner-managed companies are those that balance the entrepreneurial approach with the right blend of professionalism and empower professional managers to act decisively. Holistically looking, good governance entails ~ succession planning in the family, effective board to add value, clearly defined roles for board and management, constructive board meetings, robust strategic planning, focus on risk management, robust monitoring of business performance, management assurance – management controls, internal audit and external audit.

Good Corporate Governance essentially flows from the top and trickles down to the lowest levels in an organisation, thereby deeply integrating with its routine functioning.

A company that has good corporate governance has a much higher level of confidence amongst the shareholders associated with that company. Active and independent directors contribute towards a positive outlook of the company in the financial market, positively influencing share prices. Corporate Governance is one of the important criteria for foreign institutional investors to decide on which company to invest in. The corporate practices in India emphasise the functions of audit and finances that have legal, moral and ethical implications for the business and its impact on the shareholders.

Corporate Governance safeguards not only the management, but the interests of the stakeholders as well and fosters the economic progress of India in the roaring economies of the world.

—C.A. Sidheshwar Bhalla

❐

34
New India – Dreams of Senior citizens

Senior citizens have built this shining India and will play a crucial role to build New India. As we know, ageing is a process which starts from the day of conceiving to till death. The old age is a part of it. Old age comprises "the latter part of life or the period of life after youth, a middle age usually with reference to deterioration".

When old age begins cannot be universally defined because it shifts according to the context. Throughout the world, human beings are living longer than ever before. It is thus natural that national health systems should review their approach to the ever-increasing population of older people from time to time. Due to advancement of medical science, a better standard of life and overall development in the country, not only is the number of old people growing rapidly, but their life expectancy is also gaining new heights every year.

The United Nations has agreed that 60+ years may be usually denoted as old age. This is the first attempt at an international definition of old age. Most developed western countries set the age of 60 to 65 for retirement and old-age social programmes eligibility. However, various countries and societies reckon the onset of old age as anywhere from the mid-40s to the 70s. Furthermore, the fact that life expectancy beyond 80 has become widespread has shifted definitions of old age. The maximum human life span is estimated to be 121 years (Arking 1998). The life spans of tortoises and lake trouts are both unknown, but are estimated to be more than 150 years.

In India, the elderly population (60 years and above) is around 104 million as per Census 2011 and is projected to increase to 144 million by 20121 and 173 million by 2016. Beyond numbers, the elderly have specific needs and are entitled to a life of dignity. Majority of the elderly live in rural areas and among women, nearly half are widowed. There is a growing trend of elderly either living alone or living with their spouses only. In view of the changing Indian family systems, the social isolation among the elderly and their proper care requires particular attention while planning for ever-increasing number of elderly population.

Most of the elderly are engaged in the informal sector. Given the physical, social, economic and emotional vulnerability of this cohort, there is a need for the society and governments to take a more proactive role in the care and development of the elderly.

Well-being and care of elderly has varied gamut of issues and requires equal and active participation of the concerned ministries. The National Policy on Older Persons, 1999, the Maintenance and Welfare of Parents and Senior Citizens Act, 2007 and the Old Age Pension Scheme are some of the measures taken by the government. The Ministry of Social Justice and Empowerment has adopted an Integrated Programme for the Older Persons (IPOP), Ministry of Health & Family Welfare has established "National Programme for Healthcare for the Elderly".

Some more initiatives that are currently being supported financially by the government include those implemented through Panchayati Raj institutions, self-help groups, day care centres, programmes for the widowed elderly, Diva day care centres for patients with Alzheimer's disease and dementia, mobile medical units and physiotherapy clinics.

There is a need to design policies and programmes based on current evidences and future trends, promoting inter-generational bondage and fostering innovations, such as establishment of day care centres, community networks, creating a cadre of care-givers and home care services and improving effectiveness of the existing programmes and schemes for the well-being of the elderly. Thus, only we make New India more prosperous and developed.

In our country, we not only have regards for elders, but worship them like they are living gods. However, there are exceptions to these thoughts also. Some youngsters are influenced by the western culture and are not taking care of their parents. They are enjoying their life outside India with their spouses and children and forget about their parents. This is a very shameful and disgusting act. The parents who brought you up take you to this level in society. To forget them is not desired and expected from a person of the India origin. The Government of India, particularly government under the tenure of PM Narendra Bhai Modi, has launched various schemes to take care of such deprived parents and also to help assist old-age people and senior citizens.

The following are the schemes launched by the Government of India under the Prime Ministership of Narendra Bhai Modi:

1. Pradhan Mantri Vaya Vandana Yojana: This scheme was launched in May 2017 to provide social security during old age. The pension amount has been doubled to ₹ 10,000 per month. As of March 2018, a total number of 2.23 lakh senior citizens were getting regular pension under this scheme. As on 30th November, 2017, a total of number of 1,83,842 persons are being benefited under PMVVY.

2. Rashtriya Vayoshri Yojana (RVY): Under this scheme, aids and assistive living devices are provided to senior citizens belonging to BPL category, who suffer from age-related disabilities, such as low vision, hearing impairment, loss of teeth and locomotor disabilities and much more. The scheme will be implemented in 260 districts and benefit 5,20,000 beneficiaries up to 2019-20.

3. Integrated Programme for Older Persons (IPOP): Under this scheme grants are given for running and maintenance of old-age homes, day care centres, mobile medicare units, multi-facility care centres for older widows, etc. In the year 2016-17, a total of 396 old-age homes were granted under this scheme. The total grant amount was ₹ 36.99 crores, covering a total of 40,200 beneficiaries.

4. Varishtha Pension Bima Yojana (VPBY): This is a social security scheme for senior citizens intended to give an assured minimum pension on a guaranteed minimum return on the subscription amount. As on 31 March 2017, a total of 2,74,885 beneficiaries and 3,11,981 beneficiaries are being benefited under VPBY 2003 and VPBY 2014, respectively.

5. National Programme for the Health Care of Elderly (NPHCE): The major objective under this scheme is towards district-level activities of the NPHCE are to provide dedicated health facilities in district hospitals, community health centres (CHC), primary health centres (PHC) and sub-centres (SC) through State Health Society. The healthcare facilities, being provided under this programme, are either free or highly subsidised.

There is still a lot of scope in socialising and helping the senior citizens in India. We hope that Modi's NEW INDIA concept shall take care of this aspect in the near future.

—Muni Shankar Pandey

❒

35

SOCIORICH : Do Good – Have Good – Be Good SOCIORICH: A New Social Currency

In today's time, social media has become more of a hype and used by almost everyone but there exists no platform which inspires you to do good deeds. Keeping this in mind and to separate hype from reality, Socio team has introduced the concept of social currency for the first time with a vision to promote parity amongst all living beings.

Presently, there is a unit only to measure the economic activities and that is money. No unit is available to measure other important aspects of human life such as love and affection, spiritual growth, social contributions, compassion, etc. We draw power through money and in the process of earning money, we sometimes cause harm to the society.

SocioRich is the first social media platform that will motivate you to do good deeds to earn social currency. Through SocioRich, one can post his or someone else's good deeds, on which other peers shall give you Equacredit, a digital social currency provided to all the users equally by the portal. This currency when donated to other users on the platform would become the SocioCredit of the earners.

These earned SocioCredits will become your non-transferable social currency which will indicate your social status. These SocioCredits can help you get priority in jobs, educational admissions, elections campaigns and many other aspects of day-to-day life. SocioRich will become a parameter to judge your selfless social contribution towards society.

Apart from this, companies, NGO's and social activists can also use this portal to share their current or future social activities including their CSR activities. This would help in spreading awareness about their social causes and CSR programs and, thus, the common man would benefit more from them.

World is full of generous people. People who love to help and care. But unlike economic transactions, there isn't any way to measure help and care.

Today, modern technology allows people to connect directly.

Voice, video, pictures and emails can easily be shared between people.

So, why not rewards for their kindness gets paid digitally? Something that can be measured like money and elate their social status too?

SocioRich a digital social currency, earned for your hard work and kindness.

So, how does it work?

SocioRich is based on good deeds.

Anyone who signs up gets a certain amount of social currency called Equa Credits for a specific period of time.

Now for every generous act posted anyone can donate a small amount from their social currency to the creator of that post. This will add up in their initial social currency reserve. The more good deeds they do, the more they receive and simultaneously their reputation improves.

Since is a non-transferable currency, it will become your asset for lifetime.

You can't buy it, you can't sell it, you can only earn it through your kindness.

A good social status will open a lot of opportunities for any individual. It will give recognition in college admission, jobs, loans, subsidies, judicial cases, election campaign and many more areas of your day-to-day life.

Socio-Rich – "The Bank of Good Deeds"

It is a platform for you, run by you, for the benefit of you. It is a web portal designed to recognise and incentivise good deeds for even the smallest act of kindness you indulge yourself into. It not only recognises or inspires people to do a kind act, but also creates awareness on how to be a good human being and extend an helping hand to the people in need.

Apart from motivating people to do good acts, SocioRich is a platform to connect social activists, NGOs and CSR companies to share and promote good deeds.

This drive is not for the real money but for the social cause which will inculcate a sense of doing good for the world and will help to increase the social status and creditworthiness of that person manifold by motivating them to add scores to their list.

A good deed is helping someone without looking for a reward or a pat on the back. However, Socio-Rich gives you the reward by providing you with the social currency called 'SocioCredit' and benefits for the future as well. Whatever good actions you will be doing will be authenticated and ratified by the other people through verification, which makes the verifier also responsible that the act was vouched by him. Nothing will go in vain as they will help you to get admission in an educational institute, good jobs, CSR credibility for organisations and NGOs, election campaign standing and much more. We are looking for a good deed which is not a duty but a privilege to others. Let's solemnly pledge to make our deeds count as no beauty shines better than a good heart.

This is a New Concept To Make New India.

Let us Work For Rebuilding New India – Vishwa Guru India

—C.A. Sunil Vashisht

□

Pillars of Strength

1. *C.A. Varun Vashisht, F.C.A., ACS, LLB, DISA (ICAI)*
2. *Dr. Girish Ahuja, M.Com., Ph.D., FCA, Chartered Accountant*
3. *C.A. Sunil Vashisht, B.Com, F.C.A., Social & Political Analyst*
4. *Shri Anup Sinha, Senior Journalist*
5. *Dr. D.K Upadhyaya, Ph.D in Literature & President Awardee*
6. *Shri Basant Seth, Ex-CIC, Ex-MD Syndicate Bank, Presently, Director SBI*
7. *Shri P.N. Vijay, Economist & Investment Banker, Political & Social Analyst*
8. *Dr. Rajeev Lochan Bishnoi, F.C.A., Ex. Director, Bank of India*
9. *C.A. Jayank Gokhale, F.C.A., Academician*
10. *Prof. G. Ramesh, Professor, IIM Bangalore*
11. *Smt. Vandana Kumari Jena, Ex-IAS Officer, Ex-Secretary, Government of India*
12. *C.A. Ashok Batra, F.C.A., Expert in Indirect Taxation*
13. *Shri Ajay Banerjee, Ex-GM, Bank of Maharashtra*
14. *Dr. Rashmi Tripathi, Chief Economist & AGM, Syndicate Bank*
15. *Brig. Dr. Ashok Pathak, Retd. Brigadier Indian Army*
16. *Sh. Sandeep Kumar Sharma, LLM & Consultant in Ministry of Law & Justice*

17. *Shri Ramesh Pathak, B.Com, I.C.W.A. & Financial Advisor*
18. *Smt. Surama Padhy, Political & Social Analyst*
19. *Smt. Lalita Nijhawan, Business Women & Social Activist*
20. *C.A. C.L. Shah, F.C.A., F.C.S., I.C.W.A. & Financial Analyst*
21. *Dr. R. Balashankar, Political & Social Analyst*
22. *C.A. Kamal Kishore Singhal, F.C.A., Ex-ED, LIC of India*
23. *Shri Vivek Bhojwani, M.B.A. & Economic Researcher*
24. *C.A. G.L. Aggarwal, F.C.A., Social Activist*
25. *Shri Girish Chaudhry, Political & Social Analyst*
26. *C.A. P.K. Sharma, F.C.A., Ex-Director, Vijaya Bank*
27. *Shri Atul Sharma, Motivator & Corporate Trainer*
28. *C.A. Rajesh Khattar, F.C.A., Banking & Financial Consultant*
29. *C.A. Dakshesh Choksi, F.C.A., Insolvency Professional*
30. *C.A. Lalit Mahajan, F.C.A., Consultant in Skill Development*
31. *Shri Chandrashekhar Rai, Social Activist and Entrepreneur, Skill India*
32. *C.A. Kamal Kant Jain, Enterprenuer & Social Activist*
33. *C.A. Sidheshwar Bhalla, Partner, Business Advisory Services, BDO India LLP*
34. *Shri Muni Shankar Pandey, Centre for Economic Policy Research*
35. *C.A. Sunil Vashisht, B.Com, F.C.A., Social & Political Analyst*
36. *All Other Wishers*

❐

At the end, I convey my sincere regards, thanks and best wishes to may family, relatives and friends and particularly Smt. Sudershan Vashisht, Smt. Asha Vashisht (Retd. RBI Manager), Shri Ashish Sharma (M.B.A.), Smt. Swati Vashisht (F.C.A.), Smt. Roli Gaur Vashisht, Shri Yashpal Saini (F.C.A.), Shri Sharad Sharma (F.C.A.), Shri Sahil Goyal (A.C.A.), Shri Mayank Kulshreshta (F.C.A.), Shri Pradeep Sharma, Shri Vijay Kumar and all well wishers.

—C.A. Sunil Vashisht

❑❑❑